I0740557

Grace Mortimer

The Two Barbaras

A Novel

Grace Mortimer

The Two Barbaras
A Novel

ISBN/EAN: 9783337026455

Printed in Europe, USA, Canada, Australia, Japan

Cover: Foto ©Andreas Hilbeck / pixelio.de

More available books at **www.hansebooks.com**

THE TWO BARBARAS.

A Novel.

BY

GRACE MORTIMER,

AUTHOR OF

"BOSOM FOES," "PAPER WALLS," ETC., ETC.

Wilt thou learn what love is worth?
Ah! She sits above,
Sighing, "Weigh me not with earth,
Love's worth is love."
JEAN INGELOW.

NEW YORK:

G. W. Carleton & Co., Publishers.
LONDON: S. LOW & CO.
MDCCCLXXVI.

John F. Trow & Son,
Printers and Stereotypers,
205–213 *East 12th Street*,
New York.

TO

My Mother:

WHO GAVE ME ALL THE GEMS

WHICH GLIMMER UPON THE MODEST WEB HEREIN UNROLLED;

BELIEF IN TRUE LOVE;

RESPECT FOR STERLING WORTH WHEREVER FOUND;

SYMPATHY WITH THE ERRING;

AND ASSURANCE OF THEIR PARDON WHEN

REPENTANT.

New York, March, 1876.

CONTENTS.

THE TWO BARBARAS.

CHAPTER I.

FLYING down the rugged mountain-path, her cheeks flaming, her hair streaming, her great red-brown eyes flashing!

"I won't! I won't! I won't!" screamed Barbara Pomeroy, and the barren mountain-peaks echoed back her fierce cry; and the light wind caught it up and carried it across the deep, dark lake to the black row of pines and silver-leaved aspens; and the pines stood transfixed, while the aspens shivered.

A grand creature was this mountain maid; bounteous in outline, statuesque in limb; her coloring superb; her motions strong and graceful as those of any bounding deer.

1*

What if her dress was calico, neither ruffled nor trailing? her rich, exuberant beauty would have made you forget her dress, had it been the gem-bespangled, ermine-bordered robe of royalty.

She sprang upon a rustic bridge which spanned a rivulet. Above, the waters leaped in glancing cascades; here, under this rotten, vine-swathed arch, they stood still, resting them for the wild leap into the valley down there. She stood still also, looking about her vacantly.

"What am I doing here?" whispered Barbara Pomeroy, paling to the red, ripe lips. "Am I going mad? Lord, have mercy! How did I come here?"

She put her hands to her bare head; the scorching sun beat full upon it; she looked back at the winding, precipitous path she had traversed, up, up the autumn-crimsoned hillside, to the sharp white gable of a solitary house, and a choking gasp escaped her.

She went to the crazy rail and leaned far over it, till her long, black hair, and her reaching hand almost touched its shining surface.

"I'd rather die than marry Dr. Hugh Wayne *now!*" she muttered between her clenched teeth. "Wedding clothes, bridesmaids, lover's kisses—oh! oh! why can't I fling myself down there? Why don't I? I will, some day!" she hissed, her eyes gleaming.

"Barry! My dear Barry!" exclaimed a shocked voice behind her.

She started round—face, neck, even to her firm, round, uncovered arms, assuming a burning glow.

For he was that demi-god to country maidens—a soft-tongued, gallant, idle city gentleman; and he had passed a most amusing month up there among the lonely mountains, with this enchanting dryad to give him the homage which he felt was due to a man of his superior merits.

"Harrison!" faltered the girl, "where were you? I didn't see you."

"I rather agree with you there, my dear," smiled the keen man of pleasure, gloating his eyes upon her quivering, conscious face. "What a young Hecate you are! You tore down that deer-path like a veritable fury. Now, why would you rather die than marry the excellent doctor at this juncture?"

She turned, abashed, from his smiling gaze, and leaned over the rail of the old bridge once more.

He joined her, leaning there elbow to elbow, with his breath fanning the cheek of the girl, whose heart, erring as it was, as yet was unsullied as heart of cradled infant.

"Won't answer, eh?" laughed he. "Very good, you needn't trouble; perhaps I can guess more truly than you would tell me. You want to throw your-

self into this stream, and end all the marriage flutter
and lover's kisses in the maddest, saddest grave this
world can afford?"   He was serious enough now,
and gravity sat well upon him.   "Do you see those
pebbles at the bottom?"   The sun lighting up the
shingle bed through the amber water revealed them
gleaming with opalescent hues, rich deep blue, brilliant green, gold and bronze colored, like fairy gems.
"Who notices those worthless stones as they lie
there?" asked he.   "Their beauty is taken by the
country dolts who are used to them as a matter of
course.   But let a cultivated eye catch a glimpse of
their splendor; oh, then they are appreciated!   The
proudest beauty-lover in New York would call them
beautiful.   So with you, Barry."   He looked into
her eyes with a luring smile, and she, blushing and
bewitched, lowered her long lashes, trembling.
"Yes, you are too lovely to be buried forever among
the wilds of Thunder Peak," resumed he; "and
your own heart revolts at the unnatural idea.   Any
drawing-room would be honored by the presence of
such royal beauty.   Then what have you to do in a
country doctor's dingy parlor?"

A low sob escaped her—instantly suppressed, however—as her cheek burned more brightly, and her
eyes sparkled with anger.

"And I've just heard that the wedding is to be

a week sooner, because Hugh has to go to Albany on business," said she, wrathfully plucking the leaves off the old rail, and tearing them to pieces. "Why can't he see that I ain't in a hurry? Why don't he ever suspect that I care no more for him than I do for this trash?" and she sent a long honeysuckle spray spinning into the brook.

"And you don't care one particle for him?" queried her companion, beaming.

"You know I don't!" said she, flashing an arrow glance at him.

"Because you are heartless, eh?" whispered the gentleman.

"No!" said Barry, softly.

"Why, then, why?"

"I've tried to, and I can't."

"Then you like some one better?"

No answer to this.

"Do you, Barry?"

Still no answer; nothing but drooping head and burning cheeks.

"Barry, I have guessed it long ago. *You love me!*"

Ah, the passionate eloquence of the rich, bending face! the slow swell of the sumptuous bosom: the yielding, yet half-reluctant attitude — womanly— modest!

"You do! You do, my sweet girl!" breathed the luring voice in her ear, while the soft hands, diamond bedecked, of the city gentleman seized the brown ones of the country maid, pressing them with practised eloquence. "If we had only met before this foolish engagement was made, how blest for both of us! But now——" He drew her to his breast with a sigh.

She looked up, shy, yet radiant as a goddess.

"You love me, too, don't you, Harrison?" murmured she.

"As I shall never love again."

She yielded yet more to his encircling arm.

"Then don't be unhappy, for nobody on earth could be so cruel as to part two people who love each other like we do!" cried she, with a burst of joy. "Hugh is a good fellow, and will give me up, I know, when we tell him just how it is; and then mother—oh, she couldn't cross me in anything. I'm the very apple of her eye!"

Harrison Fairleigh, eldest son of the ancient Virginian family of that name, possessor of eighty thousand dollars a year, and ornament of Fifth Avenue and Harlem Road, stared at the girl in his arms in consternation, which gradually brightened into amusement.

He indemnified himself for the momentary discomfort he had suffered, in robbing her pure lips of a kiss.

"You witch, you almost make the thing seem possible!" exclaimed he. "How I envy those country clods of Thunder Peak! For if I were one of them I might hope to marry you; but now——"

"But now?" gasped Barry, opening her innocent eyes wide.

The amusement in Fairleigh's glance sent a sudden rush of flame through all her veins. She freed herself with one movement, and stood off, gazing at him wildly.

"Harrison Fairleigh," panted she, "I don't seem to get at your meaning. Will you put it in plainer words?"

"Mercy on us, what a young tigress you are!" ejaculated he, impatiently. "What should I mean but that, much as I love you, it's impossible for me to marry you."

Her ashen pallor frightened him. He stopped, scarcely aware of what he had said.

"And you've made me say I loved you!" said Barry, in a choked voice. "You've tempted me on to show you all my heart; you've dared to kiss me— to put your arms round me—me, a good man's promised wife! Oh, you villain!" cried she, her voice rising to frantic fierceness. "You meant to deceive an innocent girl, did you? I tell you, Harrison Fairleigh, if I knew how to do it, I'd murder you where you stand—I would! But wait; God'll never let you off with this. He ain't so unfair as all that comes to. Look out—you'll suffer yet; and as heaven's above, I'll do my best to be at the bottom of it!"

For a moment she stood menacing him with her clenched hand, scorching him up with her blazing eyes; then she sprang off the bridge, and immediately disappeared in the forest, leaving the gallant to pick up his fishing-gear and trudge homeward with a very grim visage.

CHAPTER II.

RENSSELAER'S LANDING, on the Hudson, a pleasant sail from New York, was the scene of Dr. Hugh Wayne's labors. It was a bustling country townlet, possessing as yet but one or two manufactories, and nestling luxuriously in the lap of rich green meadows, under the shelter of the gloomy Thunder Peak.

The zig-zag road between Rensselaer's Landing and the few settlers' houses, hidden up in the forest, had for the last two years almost daily witnessed the passing of Hugh Wayne to worship at the shrine of the mountain maid; for he had wooed her long and patiently.

He was a fine-looking fellow, over six feet in height, lithe, and firmly-built, with ruddy face and the frankest eye imaginable. He had graduated creditably at Yale, gone to Berlin for a year, and returned to his native place, Rensselaer's Landing, to buy the prettiest cottage in the village, beside his father's, and to walk into an excellent practice, without any undue delay. Such a big-hearted fellow he was! Such a pretty, dainty home as he had! No encumbrance; the kindest, prettiest woman in Rensselaer, his sister, to keep house for him; and patients from north, south, east, and west driving in to consult him. No wonder the belles of Rensselaer's Landing blushed their prettiest when Dr. Hugh Wayne rode by on his dashing little mare, Coquette. He let them blush, while he climbed up the stiff hill-side with beating heart to court a smile from beautiful Barbara Pomeroy.

Now, Mrs. Pomeroy was that most indigent of ladies, a country minister's widow. Once she lived in that pretty parsonage in the heart of the village, surrounded with trim plots of flowers and furnished with the neatest of upholstery. But when good Arthur Pomeroy died she was forced to retire into veritable obscurity, hiding in the pine woods at the foot of Thunder Peak, in an old farm-house, with her crabbed step-brother, who, with his barns bursting, and his cattle browsing far and near, grudged the widow's pittance, and gave her the bitter bread of dependence to eat day by day. True, some there were who could recall the time when Arthur Pomeroy came to their little village with his lovely young wife; and these were fond of hinting at a pre-history more distinguished than usually falls to the lot of an

American citizen, at least as far as the young clergyman was concerned. At all events, he was an Englishman, but lately come from the Old World to seek
free breathing space in the New, and though absorbed
in his sacred duties, and satisfied with the love of his
charming American wife, he seldom alluded to his
previous life or family, the acute gossips had long
suspected that the reverend Arthur was the younger
son of some fine old house which all too probably had
been mortally offended by his democratic marriage.

However that might be, at his death his widow
made no appeal to her husband's relatives, but, churl-
ish as her step-brother was, appeared to prefer to de-
pend upon him to asking charity from those who
perhaps had more right to bestow it, and here West,
miserable old miser though he was, upheld her. They
were right, too, and in the exercise of their stout'
American independence, proved their claim to a
pride of spirit as deserved as any born of noble
birth.

Mrs. Pomeroy might or might not know her husband's antecedents. She never revealed them to her
neighbors, nor even to her daughter, but people can
have their impressions, you know, and so the ancient
fable had its place in the public mind, and Barry was
looked upon, therefore, with peculiar attention; while
the widow received much unspoken sympathy on ac-

count of the hard life she led with her only surviving relative.

The truth was, Richard West was a greedy, grasping old miser, half-killing himself every summer by trying to do all the work of his farm himself rather than engage hands; and starving himself and his household the year round in order to keep down the expense—and all this for what? For the miserable satisfaction of plunging his skinny hands into his bag of hoarded gold, and chuckling over the mere possession of a metal which was in effect as useless as a bag of stones to him, or to any one else while he was alive.

Perhaps he meant to leave it all to Barbara? Nothing of the sort: he never thought of leaving it to any one. The idea of his ever having the misfortune to die at all seemed so unnatural that he never entertained it for a moment.

· Meantime, the minister's widow and her lovely daughter clung together, and were happy and thankful to have each other to cling to and a roof to shelter them.

"Hugh must wait; I can't leave you, mother," Barry would often say, as she briskly stepped about in the kitchen. For, be sure, she was the household drudge, or how else could she pay her board? "It's all very nice for him to speak of your coming to live with us down in the village, but a wife can't be everything to her mother, as an unmarried daughter can; you'd have many a lonely hour, I know."

Yet Mrs. Pomeroy liked Hugh, and it would have pleased her to see her daughter married to him.

* * * * * * *

"What makes you so wan, child?" asked Mrs. Pomeroy, that evening, when, the tea-dishes washed and set away in shining rows behind the glass-doors of the cupboard, the floor dusted white as snow, and the lamp lit on the big wooden table, Barry sat at her side, her lap full of white muslin frilling, which her fingers were bungling badly. Dr. Wayne sat opposite, pulling his tanned mustache and eyeing her with uneasy wonder.

Nettie Wayne, his sister, and Lizzie Bright, his cousin, the prospective bridesmaids, were plying their needles on the simple *trousseau* behind a mound of gauzes and glistening ribbons, merrily chattering as they worked; and the master of the house, gaunt and hollow-chested, leaned back in his hard elbow-chair, with his cold feet in the ashes on the hearth, dozing and grunting.

At her mother's query, Barry started, and called up a smile of surprise.

"Nonsense, mother!" exclaimed she, "am I pale, though? Perhaps I got a sunstroke going out without a hat on to-day."

Dr. Wayne gnawed his mustache still more uneasily.

"What sent you off at that time, anyhow?" asked he, trying to catch a glimpse of Barry's down-dropped eyes.

"Yes, what on earth took you, Barry?" the girls chimed in. "You whisked off and down hill as if a rattlesnake was after you."

"Did I?" said Barry, with a dreary little laugh. "I guess I was tired sewing, and wanted a race. Hugh, would you like to read something to us?"

Obedient Hugh went to the hanging bookshelf, and taking down a volume of poetry—Mrs. Pomeroy's property—insinuated himself into the chair by Barry, and opened at a love poem, of course.

Dr. Wayne was an elegant reader, and he was profoundly in love; judge, then, how he read this fragment from Heine:

> "It's only an old, old story,
>   That there goes but little to make,
> Yet, to whomso it happens,
>   His heart in two must break."

"Don't," gasped Barry, rising hastily, and running from the room.

Mrs. Pomeroy's sweet, venerable face looked round at Hugh in startled dismay.

"She's ill, I think," muttered the young doctor, hurrying out after her.

He saw her leaning against the tumble-down gate-post of the little garden, which it had ever been her delight to cultivate—leaning with her dear face hidden in her hands, and the tears which dripped from between her fingers glancing in the effulgent moonlight.

At the sound of his footsteps she dashed away her tears, and looked up, laughing.

"Am I not foolish, Hugh?" said she, with nervous gayety. "All this fuss just because I can't endure the thought that love—that love—must—must break the heart that feels it!"

She burst into a wild fit of sobbing, and more painful than all, she mingled her rending sobs with hysterical laughter.

Her lover caught her hands and held them firmly. For the moment the lover was forgotten in the doctor; he thought she was ill.

"Let me take you back to the house, Barry," said he, tenderly. "By and by you must tell me what has upset you."

She forced back her turbulent emotion—she made a mighty effort and calmed herself.

"Hugh, dear, I'm only tired," said she; "nothing in the world is the matter else. Don't worry poor mother " (her voice shook, she coughed, and hurried on) " with my megrims, and don't you worry either. I ain't worth it."

He gazed wistfully into the white, averted face.

" Do you know, Barry, I begin to think I rather startled you this morning, hurrying on the wedding ? " said he.

She murmured something indistinctly, meaning, he thought, to reassure him.

" You know, dear, I wouldn't do anything to trouble you," said Hugh, his deep tones trembling ; " I love you too well for that. Dear Barry, I love you so well, that if I thought you would not be happy with me, I'd give you back your freedom to-night."

She stood motionless, pale as death, regarding him.

" Hugh," said she, at length, in a low, hard voice, " do you really love me ? "

" God knows I do," answered he, solemnly.

" And yet you'd give me up ! " she cried, breathlessly.

" If it made you happier," faltered Hugh.

" And you—what about your happiness ? "

" I'd bear the loss of it like a man, I hope."

She stood before him a moment longer, looking at him with her great night-black eyes as if she had never really seen him before. Then she clasped his arm with her two cold, shaking hands, and bent her face upon them, gasping:

"Dear, true-hearted Hugh Wayne! you deserve a better wife than I. Oh! why were you ever so unlucky as to care for me?"

"Hush! hush! Don't, Barry, my darling; you wring my heart when you speak so!" he exclaimed, shocked and alarmed.

"I'm bound to break it, Hugh!" wept Barry, kissing his hand in the wildest way. "Oh! you good, dear Hugh! if I ever grieve or wound you, will you try to forgive me, and to remember that I told you I wasn't good enough to be your wife? And will you never forget that I told you to-night I love and honor you so much that I wish—I *wish* I could die right here, with your good opinion of me unchanged?"

Her vehemence, her pallor, and the unwonted wildness of her words, completed his bewilderment. He could only stand there looking at her helplessly.

What did Barry mean? These were not the usual tender agitations of a bride-elect. Barry was not ill, she was in trouble. Good Heaven! was Barry *regretting?*

"You are not yourself to-night, darling Barry," said Hugh, in a hushed voice, through which the beating of his heart could be heard; "something has

happened to worry you. Have I said or done anything?

"No, no!" said she, shrinking.

"Has anybody else?"

"Hugh, don't—*don't* tease! I told you I was tired
to death, and nervous. There, I've spoken crossly to
him!" and she burst out sobbing again.

He took her in his arms, and bent to comfort her
with kisses.

What! Was this his bride-elect drawing back—
putting up her shaking hands to ward him off—covering her convulsed face lest he should read it?

"Oh, Barry, Barry! What have I done?" burst
from Hugh Wayne, with an exceeding bitter cry.

"For—forgive me!" stammered she, "I scarcely
know what I do or say. Come to-morrow morning,
and—and I'll let you know what worries me."

Leaning for support on the vine-draped gate-post,
the moonbeams falling full upon her pallid, disturbed
countenance and tear-filled eyes, she stretched out
her hand to her lover.

"Good-by—good-night, I mean," said she, huskily.
"You've always been so good to me that it hurts me
to wound you. No, dear—no kiss to-night. Spare
me; I'm very weak."

Grasping his hand tightly, she gave him a long,
heart-broken, despairing look, then turning away

with a choking sob, she slowly crept to the cottage door between the dew-diamonded flowers. Once she stopped, glancing back, with her hand pressed to her heart, but at his impetuous spring forward, she waved him back, and went in.

So then the young bridegroom that was to claim her in a week, rode down the leafy road with a heart as heavy as lead, and a mind as full of torturing forebodings as a mind might be.

    *   *   *   *   *   *   *

"Mother! mother!" whispered a faint voice in the dark.

Mrs. Pomeroy waked out of her first nap, and sat up affrighted.

"Goodness, Barry, is it you?" exclaimed she.

"Hush!" whispered Barry, "the girls will hear and be frightened. There's nothing the matter, only I can't sleep, and I thought I'd come and sit beside you for a minute or two. Lie down again, mother, it's cold."

"Have you and Hugh been quarrelling?" asked Mrs. Pomeroy, sweeping aside the curtain from the window beside her, that she might see her daughter by the last rays of the sinking moon.

"No, indeed!" laughed Barry, looking very beautiful and ghost-like in that magical light. "Mother, I wouldn't marry Hugh if I was not perfectly satisfied with him ; and you wouldn't want me to, would you ? "

" Certainly not ! " cried the mother. " No woman has a right to take advantage of a man's love to fool him so cruelly as that ! But you love Hugh, of course."

" Too much to be in any danger of fooling him as you say ; if I married Hugh without thinking him the best man on earth, I would feel as if I was just selling myself for the sake of a home."

" May you be as happy as you deserve, my darling ! " said Mrs. Pomeroy, kissing her tenderly. " What, crying ! What's the meaning of this, Barry ? "

" Did you never cry during the last few days before you were married ? " answered Barry, with a dreary attempt at playfulness.

" Ah, well, perhaps I did—perhaps I did ! " murmured Mrs. Pomeroy, " but it was for joy, Barry."

" You were sorry to part from your mother, I know," said Barry, almost inaudibly.

" I'm afraid I wasn't so sorry as I ought to have been," answered Mrs. Pomeroy, " and anyway, you're not going to part from your mother for very long. I'm coming to you soon."

Barry suddenly stooped and took the frail old

woman in her arms, lifting her to her breast in an impetuous way.

"Love me, love me always, mother," said she, trembling with suppressed feeling. "Whatever befalls me, mother, never let me go out of the corner in your heart where you have kept me so long. And now good-night—good-night!"

She kissed her once, twice, with a strange and solemn fervor, and laying her tenderly back upon her pillow stole from the bedroom.

*   *.   *   *   *   *

"Barry! Barry!" roared old West, as he stood in the red dawn at the foot of the stairs which led to the loft occupied by his niece.

The kitchen fire was unlit, the milking-pails were still on the bench, not a soul was stirring in or out, and it was an hour past the usual time for Barry to be up and doing. What in the name of sense had got into the girl?

"Barry!" roared the miser again, in a voice that shook the rafters.

A smothered giggle came from the room where the bridesmaids lay, and the floor of Mrs. Pomeroy's bedroom creaked, advertising to her scowling benefactor, that he had frightened her out of bed; but no whisper came from the loft.

"Blamed if the girl ain't turned deaf!" mumbled

the old man, mounting the crazy staircase, with limbs as creaking and sapless, and he knocked on the worm-eaten door, with knuckles as hard as iron, till the furious din brought Mrs. Pomeroy, deprecating and frightened, from her room, with the old wrapper thrown around her anyhow.

"Oh, don't, Richard! Barry must be sick, or she would have answered you long ago," said she; "I'll go in and see."

She went in, the miser standing outside to listen and muttering to himself; the room was neat, the window was wide, everything was in its place, even to the jug of flowers on the mantel-piece; but Barry was gone.

"She's out to her work," said Mrs. Pomeroy, with some resentment. "Barry never oversleeps herself."

"She ain't gone to her work," said West, roughly. "Everything's lying around higgledy-piggledy, and the cows are starving in the pen yet. Gone to her work, forsooth! If she ain't here she's gone into the woods to gather some of her rubbish. What's that letter I see lying on the bed?"

Mrs. Pomeroy picked up a little envelope, sealed.

"Mercy on us, it's for me!" said she, quite bewildered; "and I do believe—yes, it is from Barry! What in the world——"

"Open it, and see!" roared the churl. "There's some deviltry here, I'll bet."

Mrs. Pomeroy obeyed, her venerable face, lined with many an anxious thought and constant care for Barry, assuming a blank look of dismay.

This was her daughter's farewell:

"Mother: I've gone away. I could not marry Hugh. I never loved him well enough to be his wife, and I couldn't stay to see his pain and yours; and besides, mother dear, I'm best away while I feel what I do. Some day I'll come back, creeping like some tired, wounded bird to its forsaken nest, but not till I've made another home for you and me in a new place. Forgive me, mother dear, for this shock, and leave me to myself just now. Don't fret, poor mother, but try to believe this has all happened for the best. With love forever and ever, I remain your own sorrowful BARRY."

The aged lady took all this in, her brain reeled, her heart sickened, and, with a piercing cry, she fell as if shot.

CHAPTER III.

BARB, THE SECOND BARBARA.

A VERY different scene from that of Thunder Peak, with its sparkling streams, its forests, with the gorgeous colors of October, its solitary hush, and rose-perfumed zephyrs!

It was now November, and a chilling rain was falling in sheets upon the muddy thoroughfares of busy New York;—five o'clock on Saturday afternoon, and the matinée pouring out of the Grand Opera House.

Throngs of ladies, old and young, shivering under their rich velvets and still more costly embroidered cloths, hurried across the steaming pavement to their carriages; gentlemen, with trim mustaches and slender canes, rushed into the nearest oyster saloons; the more republican of the throng filled the horse-cars, or surged off the avenue into the streets; a very bustling scene indeed was that in front of the build ing.

A few minutes afterwards, and the little crowd of

dirty idlers, *blasé* men, rakish lads, and elfishly sharp street Arabs, which hung about the stage entrance at the rear of the Opera House, began to be rewarded for their patient waiting by the appearance of the actors emerging by twos and threes from the guarded entrance, to their cabs—the stars—that is; while the supernumeraries, lay figures, and ballet-dancers trudged afoot, in rusty waterproofs, under well-worn umbrellas, and so dispersed, hustled, and jostled by the very throng they had amused.

Last of all these a young girl stepped into the street, drawing her thin woollen shawl around her with a shiver, as the cold rain met her full sweep.

Poor little creature, as she stood there the object of as keen scrutiny as if she had been the principal actress herself, how helpless, defenceless, and young she looked!

On the stage, when girt with tarlatan clouds she spun behind the foot-lights on one toe, waving her well-powdered arms, and posin5 her well-padded figure in the so-called " poetry " of the dance, who could have imagined that, all the stage adjuncts laid aside, the airy, fairy *figurante* was only a slim, pale girl of seventeen ; narrow-shouldered, thin-armed, with no beauty to commend her but her sad misty-blue eyes, and her pale rings of flax-yellow hair?

As she mingled in the passing throng, she heard a

2*

lond laugh echo from the opposite side of the street, and as she ran along, hoping by the swiftness of her passage to make up for the lack of an umbrella, she observed at the first corner, in front of a lager-beer saloon, a considerable crowd, all seeming to be so well entertained that they cared neither for the biting wind nor for the soaking rain.

She was running by, not much interested in the cause of their merriment, when a low cry—a woman's cry—reached her ear. The little ballet-dancer came to a dead halt, gazing across the street with eager interest, and by-and-by, through a gap in the jocund throng, she caught a glimpse of a woman's crouching form, which was being rudely hustled and knocked about by the merry mob. This was a common enough spectacle; why, then, did the city girl, inured to sights far worse than this, stand on the opposite pavement as if chained to the spot, with her wide, innocent blue eyes filling and brimming over with tears?

She had caught a glimpse of the woman's face, flushed and weeping, as she raised it for a moment in supplication from her hands, and it was so young and beautiful that the ballet-dancer could not tear herself away and abandon this unfortunate on the brink of the abyss.

She looked up and down the street as if to call

for help, but she only saw the police hurrying from different quarters to disperse the mob. She gathered up her soaked rags and ran across the muddy street right into the middle of the laughing and half-tipsy wretches; at the same moment a policeman pushed his way through them and seized the young girl by the arm.

She uttered a scream; it was answered by a shrill cry from the ballet-dancer:

"Let her be, policeman—let her be!" she exclaimed. "Tell them to let me get to her; she's my sister, and she's sick!"

"Way, there!" said the policeman, waving apart the throng to let the wretched little figure join him. "Now, my girl, she's no more sick than I am; she's *drunk*, that's what she is."

The ballet-dancer threw her arms round her, forcing her to lean upon her.

"She *ain't!*" said she, stoutly. "Look at her! She ain't one of them kind!"

At the touch of a woman's arms and the sound of a woman's voice, the young girl uncovered her face and looked down at her protectress—for she was a head taller—with dark, terrified eyes and a distress in her beautiful face that was pitiful to see.

"I'm afraid I am drunk," stammered she. "I was looking for a place—and I'm not used to the streets—and I got so tired—they gave me some wine to drink—and I guess it went to my head—for I never drank wine before."

All this she uttered brokenly, evidently quite confused, but with such simple earnestness, backed by such a shrinking modesty, that it was impossible to doubt a syllable.

"Poor dear! poor dear!" murmured the ballet-dancer. "What would have come over you if I hadn't seen you? You won't take her to the station, policeman, will you?"

"I guess not!" said he, kindly. "Some folks are just idiots enough to give liquor to a tired girl, and then turn her out on the streets. You can help her home I, dare say, she ain't far gone. Here, clear out, will you?" he shouted to the gaping crowd, " and leave these girls go unmolested."

He was obeyed, and so the little ballet-dancer went off with her prize.

A queer pair truly! No wonder if the impatient passengers, pushing along under capes and umbrellas, glanced sharply at them, wondering at the rich beauty of the "unfortunate," as they styled her in their minds, and the loving care bestowed upon her by her wizened little protectress!

The helpless girl was well and neatly dressed; her waterproof was just the thing for such weather, her hat was quiet and becoming, her hands were nicely gloved; and the cherry-colored bow at her throat was tied as daintily as any lady's daughter could have tied it. All the more piteous was it to see the tears streaming over her flushed, distressed face, her black hair half uncoiled on her shoulders, and her unsteady gait!

Further and further east the ballet-dancer guided her; they soon had left the pleasant precincts of Broadway, Madison, and Lexington Avenues far behind, and were hurrying along the poverty-stricken, vice-haunted First Avenue.

Not a word was spoken by either, until the ballet-dancer drew the rescued girl into a long, dark passage in a tenement-house.

Then she said:

"I guess you ain't used to such poor doin's as I am, an' my crib ain't exactly a palace, 'specially when the old 'un is in; but she's out charring all day, so don't be frightened, my dear. Come right up, an' make the best of it."

The young girl clung to her, sobbing:

"Any place—any place to hide in! Only don't go away from me!"

They climbed the rickety wooden staircase, flight by flight, and at every landing, as they passed the doors of the lodgers, the ballet-dancer whispered her companion urgently:

"Cover your face, my dear, they're a bad lot here!"

And the lovely face of the stranger being concealed in a corner of her wet cloak, she would hurry her along as if Death strode behind them.

At last, having ascended to the very top of the house, the ballet-dancer produced a key from her pocket, and opening a door, pulled her guest in and locked it again.

Her first care was to take off the waterproof hat and gloves, and to lead her to a little narrow bed covered with a white dimity-quilt in a dark corner.

"Lie down, dear heart, and sleep till I get ye a cup of tea," said she, busily arranging the tiny pillows. "Don't cry any more now, by-an'-by you'll wake up quite bright. You're safe here, and I won't stir from the room, so jest go to sleep peaceful."

The young girl looked up with shining eyes, while a wonderful smile irradiated her whole countenance.

"You are the first who has shown me human kindness in this awful city!" said she. "I might have died but for you!"

"Lucky for you I happened by when I did," said the ballet-dancer, cheerily; and then she bustled off to light the fire and prepare her frugal meal, every now and then stealing to the bedside to feast her eyes upon the beauty of her guest, who slept profoundly.

"Oh, ain't she splendid!" aspirated the little creature, clasping her thin hands in ecstacy. "She's handsomer lyin' there without paint or pads, than Princess Exilda in her new diamond crown and satin court-dress. My! wouldn't she fill the house as the Grand Sultana!"

And having paid her the highest compliment her experience could suggest, the little *figurante* would steal back to her work, refreshed.

In a very short time, however, the wooden table was set, its gray old boards nicely concealed by a pure white cloth, as coarse almost as sacking, but none the less carefully starched and ironed for that; two or three cracked plates and old knives, three unmatched cups and saucers, a coarse loaf, and a scrap of butter,—these furnished the board.

The ballet-dancer gently awoke her guest, and led her to the table.

"Now, begin at the beginning, and tell me your name," said she, when, having placed food before her, she sat down behind the broken-nosed teapot, with her chin in her thin hand, and her earnest blue eyes fastened upon the young girl, feebly illumined by the one guttering tallow-candle.

The stranger threw back her splendid black hair, and passed her dark, shapely hands across her forehead. She was quite herself now, and looked about her with a calm self-possession in singular contrast to her manner half an hour previously.

"You have done me a kindness," replied she, fixing at last a grateful look upon the ballet-dancer. "I wish I could reward you, for you seem to be very poor; but I am worse off than you are, for I have no home. My name? Yes, I'll tell you that, so that ever after you'll know who thinks of you gratefully. My name is Barbara Pomeroy."

The ballet-dancer opened her deep eyes wider.

"*Barbara Pomeroy!*" echoed she. "You ain't fooling, are ye?"

"No," said Barry, astonished by her astonishment. "Why should I? What do you know of me? Have you seen any advertisements——"

She stopped, turning pale with alarm.

"I ain't heard anything about you," cried the ballet-dancer; "but ain't it enough to make one stare to meet a stranger with one's own name? I am Barbara Pomeroy, too. Barb, they call me, for short."

Barry eyed her with increasing alarm.

"Who are you? Where are you from?" asked she, faintly.

"I guess I don't know," said Barb, sadly. "I'm only a poor waif, kept by old Nan, the charwoman. I've begged with a basket ever since I could remember, till three years ago I was lucky enough to get a place at the Opera House as ballet-girl. Old Nan says she picked me up somewheres at Five Points when I was a tot in baby-clothes."

Barry gradually calmed down as she listened to this brief autobiography; and after a few moments' thought, she said:

"Dear Barb, you have had a sadder life than mine, yet I think you are a better and a happier girl to-day than I am. Listen. I had a pleasant home in the beautiful country; a dear mother who loved me, and plenty people to flatter and admire me. A good man fell in love with me, and I promised to marry him. I really meant to, you know, although I never cared, right down in my heart, for him; but mother liked him, and I supposed it was all right. I would have been, too, I dare say, if I had never met the man who stole my love from Hugh, and then showed me how little he thought of it by telling me he could never marry a poor girl like me——"

Barry paused, her cheeks ghastly pale, her teeth set, and her eyes flashing furiously.

Barb leaned across the rude tea equipage to pat her hand.

"You gave him his answer, I'll bet!" cried she, admiringly. "It's just the likes of you that can give 'em a lesson now and again."

"I did give him his answer!" exclaimed Barry, with a bitter smile. "But I ain't done with him yet, Barb; I was to have married Hugh three weeks ago : well, the very day the city gentleman affronted me—that was a week before my wedding—I ran away from home."

"What for?" asked Barb, wonderingly.

"To have my revenge on Harrison Fairleigh!" said the young girl, fiercely.

CHAPTER IV.

THE ballet-dancer uttered an exclamation of dismay.

"What do you mean to do?" asked she. "Nothing wrong, I'm sure—nothing that you wouldn't like to tell your mother?"

"Oh, keep quiet about my mother!" said Barry, tears rushing to her eyes; "I wouldn't have her know the deadly change in me for anything!"

"Seems to me, if I had got a mother, I'd just want to go right into her arms and tell her everything that troubled me," said Barb, wistfully; "wouldn't it do me good!"

"This," said Barry, looking up with cold, hard face, "I must bear alone. It was my own fault that I fell in love with a gentleman who felt himself so far above me that he could only insult me when he offered his. If I'd known the world better I would not have been such a fool. It's my own fault that I feel so bitter hard about it now; that instead of staying quietly at home and deceiving an honest man,

I've come, friendless and penniless, into this dreadful wicked city, upheld by the hope of meeting him again, and making him rue, to the day of his death, the wrong he would have done the simple country girl."

"But how do you think you can do that?" asked Barb, dubiously.

"If years of hard work and self-improvement can make me a lady," said Barry, "I'm willing to toil my fingers to the bone, to live on a crust, and to see nobody, if only in the end I can meet him on his own level, with my beauty as dazzling as he used to tell me it was, and my manners as perfect as his mother's or sisters'. Then I'll make him give me the same worship I once gave him, and when he feels he can't live without me, as I felt about him, then I'll laugh at him, and trample on his love as he did on mine!"

"Oh!" murmured Barb, with a shudder, shrinking back from the flaming eyes and clenched hands of her guest, "ain't it too dreadful to work hard for nothing but that?"

"'Nothing but that!'" reiterated Barry, passionately. "Oh, if I could see that day, I'd consent to die for it. I've gone through so much—so much already," said she, more gently, "I think I can bear almost anything now. Parting with mother and Hugh was the worst, for I daren't give them any notion what I went away for, or where I was going, and

I know that every day they hope to hear from me, and I daren't write lest they should trace me out by my letter, and make me go home, and all the while my heart is bursting to hear from them. When I left home I had a little money, and I took along one or two good new dresses ; but I thought sure I could get some sort of work right away, or I'd never have dared to come with as little as I did. I tried to get into a store first, for I understand figures and would make a good saleswoman, but nobody would have me without references ; the same with dressmakers, until, my money having run out, I had to quit the boarding-house for a cheaper one, and to sell my clothes to pay a week's board in advance. Every day of that week I've been on my feet from morning till night looking for any sort of work that I could do. I'd be glad enough to get a servant's place, so as I could keep a roof over my head, but it's all the same wherever I go ; it's nothing but ' no, no.' I can't cook French dishes ; I've never been in service before ; I ain't got no character to show ; I'm too good-looking to be good ; that's the sort of talk I hear ; and to-night I must turn out of the only place I can call a home, and then Heaven only knows what's to become of me. The last place I went to I was so tired out and disappointed when they said they couldn't take me that I fell right down in the slopping-wet area in a swoon. Oh, if mother could have seen me, how she'd have cried! So then the lady bade them carry me into the kitchen, and made me drink the wine herself; she meant it kindly, I know, but she didn't understand nor think how dreadful it would be if it was to go to my head in the street; nor I didn't understand either, till I got out into the air, and everything seemed to be pitching about like the trees in a gale."

For a few moments after Barry's recital was finished the two sat silent, Barb keeping her eyes fixed upon Barry with painful interest.

"What do they call you at home?" said she, at length. "I mean what's the pet name that your mother always called you?"

"Barry," said she, faintly.

"Well, Barry," said the ballet-dancer, earnestly, "I'm a poor, ignorant thing myself, and I ain't had any one to love me and make me grow up good like you had, but it seems like as you was going all wrong —all wrong, on this track. Why don't you let the bad man go his way, an' you go yours, an' be a good and happy girl all your life?"

"Don't speak of it!" said Barry, fiercely. "I live and breathe for nothing but revenge. "I'd kill myself, I tell you I would, if I didn't hope to be even with him some day!"

"No, no!" pleaded Barb; "you wouldn't be let to do that. If your mother's a good woman her prayers would drag you back again."

Barry turned to her, paling visibly.

"How do you know all this? You, a poor little ballet-dancer, when I, a minister's daughter, don't?" faltered she.

"Dear heart, you do know it, on'y maybe you haven't been let to feel it yet. I knowed all about the dear Lord Jesus long before I let Him right deep down inter my heart, an' now it seems to me it's about the only thing I do know as clear as day. I ain't much on the readin' or writin' line, an' I know I'm blind ignorant, but I tell ye all the wisdom an' larnin' in the earth couldn't puzzle me on that p'int. I love Jesus an' He loves me, an' for His sake I'll live jest as good as I can. An' you must try to do the same, Barry, dear. Leave it all in His kind hands, an' I'll bet ye won't hev much trouble any more!"

"Oh, do try to feel about it as I do!" exclaimed Barb, tears trembling in her great, hollow eyes. "You're far too innocent and too much thought of at home for to go astray like this."

"Child," said Barry, turning away bitterly, "you don't know what a woman of spirit is when her pure love has been trampled upon. Say no more. *You* can't turn me from my purpose. Perhaps mother's prayers will; but if they do, I hope—I hope God will take vengeance in His own hands, and make Harrison Fairleigh far more miserable than ever I could."

Barb had stolen round the table to her guest's side, and was about to lay her hand on her shoulder and continue her entreaties yet more urgently, when a heavy step became audible in the creaking passage without, and a heavy hand rapped boisterously on the door.

"It's Nan," whispered Barb, shrinking back with a look of fear. "I didn't think it was so late, or I'd have got you away before this. But don't you mind her, dear, and promise me you won't go, without I can go with you, for I'm blessed if I'll let you sleep in the streets alone to-night."

"Barb, Barb! What are you about?" bawled a hoarse voice from the other side of the crazy panels. "Are you deaf or dumb, gal? Let me in before I drop, you lazy hussy!"

Trembling visibly from head to foot, Barb unlocked the door, and was immediately seized by the slight shoulder and shaken so violently by a frightfully stout woman, whose Cyclopean arms, bared to the elbow, and hard, wicked, slate-blue eyes, surrounded by a nest of wicked little wrinkles, were sufficient to strike Barry with consternation.

"Laying around asleep, I suppose, eh?" panted the woman, throwing the light form of the ballet-dancer from her with a violence that sent her half across the floor. "Now, then, who's this?"

She stood before Barry, her fat, purple hands resting on her hips, her little, satanic eyes peering at her as she cowered there, her face and figure indistinctly seen by the miserable light.

"She's a friend of mine, Nan," said Barb. "She only came in for a minute; she's going away with me when I go back to the house."

"A friend o' yours! Highty-tighty!" cried the old woman, raising her voice and scanning the speaker over her nose with the most imperious scorn. "And what right have you to bring home friends to eat up my bread and butter and drink my tea? Ain't it enough that I keep yourself out of my hard earnings, you good-for-nothing young beggar?"

Perhaps Barry Pomeroy had heard such words herself too often to be daunted by them now, and perhaps the cruelty and oppression had taught her a perfect unity of feeling on this point, at least, with this, her humbler sister. Certain it is that, with a bound of her old grace and a flash of the old spirit, she took her place by Barb, and, putting her arm round her, said, proudly:

"Woman, I shall allow no abuse of this girl for

my sake. She has done me a service which I shall never forget, and as long as I live I mean to be her friend. Now, ma'am, what you have to say, say to me!"

This address seemed to take the old woman's breath away; she stood for a full minute glaring speechlessly at the intruder; then she bethought her of her spectacles, drew them from their worn case, and re-examined Barry from top to toe. At last she spoke in the mildest, blandest accents, a propitiatory smile hovering about her odious features, and a cringing courtesy prefacing her remarks:

"I beg your pardon, miss—miss, ain't it? I see no marriage ring. I wouldn't have spoke so, not for the world, if I had seen you clear at fust. I thought you was one of them low street wagrants that Barb had picked up, for she's always a poking her nose into other folk's business, whenever their luck's down upon 'em, 'stead of cottoning to well-dressed, well-to-do folks like you, my dear, good, pretty young lady, with a face as sweet as a daisy. And won't you break some 'arts yet, is all I say!"

"Don't listen to her; don't listen to her," whispered Barb, who was ghastly pale.

"What's that?" cried the woman, sharply.

"You're very civil," said Barry, somewhat bewildered between the fervor of her address and the vehemence of Barb's adjuration ; " but perhaps your civility won't outlive the honest truth. Barb, here, is rich to what I am, for she has work to do that pays her, while I have neither work nor one cent in my pocket. Now, ma'am, I'll go; I have no idea of sponging on you."

The old wretch drew close to the beautiful girl as these words poured from her, and with a grin of surpassing oiliness upon her evil mask of a face, she answered, sweetly :

" Dear young creetur, you mistakes Nan Devlin. There ain't a more feelin' heart in Noo York than hers. You're welcome to your bed an' board here till I finds ye a nice, snug home I knows on——"

" Take care!" shrieked the little ballet-dancer, pulling Barry violently out of reach of Nan's great purple hand, and intercepting her own tiny figure. " Take care, ye wicked woman! Say one word to soil this innocent lady's ears or heart, an'—an' I'll run away from ye an' let ye starve, I will ! "

The giantess glared down upon the poor little, panting, trembling, bright-eyed coryphée, and a demoniac flash broke from her half-closed lids.

" It ain't worth while to tackle ye now, you precious limb," said she, actually gnashing her teeth, " cos you wouldn't be fit fur your night's work ; but ou'y wait till you come home—on'y wait, I say, an'

I'll sarve ye out handsome for this; so's you'll dance for a fortnight to come as if the devil switched ye up to it! Now you be off, an' this young lady and me'll soon come to terms."

Barb, pale as death, pulled Barry with her to the peg where she had hung their wraps.

"Barry," whispered she, "ye don't know what danger I've took ye into. Forgive me, dear! An' mind, ye must stick by me close as wax, or—or ye'd best kill yerself to oncet!"

"Wha-at? Eh? eh?" cried the old woman's discordant voice, as she strode between them and the door with arms akimbo, and a ferocious grin upon her swollen lips. "Young miss, come away from that viper; she's telling ye lies!"

Struck to the heart with a nameless fear, Barry gazed from one to the other, and silently took down her waterproof and hat to put them on.

"No, no, ye don't leave this to-night, my love," said Nan, advancing upon them. "I has views for you which I asks your company for to hear, an' takes no denial."

Barb sprang forward—a fine bound it was—such as only the flexible limbs of a practised *danseuse* could make, and landing full on old Nan's capacious chest, she felled her to the floor.

"Run now!" screamed she to Barry, opening the door.

Hand-in-hand they flew into the black and loathsome passage, and down the treacherous stairway, but had not reached the next landing when old Nan's voice, hoarse with rage, was heard shouting:

"Tim! Tim, I say! stop them gals! Tim Polson! stop them gals!"

Barb drew Barry on only the faster.

"If he tries to stop us, don't give in!" was all she said, but her eyes glinted in the dark like live coals.

They flew down another flight, but now the coarse voice of a man yelled a response to old Nan's vociferations; doors high and low flew open, letting out streams of sickly light, and men and women of terrible aspect, wickedness, poverty and filth striving for the mastery in their appearance.

"Stop them gals!" rang through the house, and was taken up by a babel of voices; but still the girls flew down, winged with fear, and pushing their way through the fast-filling stairways and passages, burst at last through a knot of idlers arrested on the pavement by the boisterous sounds in the old tenement-house, and so darting across the street and mingling among the rough passengers on the opposite pavement, they escaped.

Barb drew Barry into the first street, which seemed quite dark and solitary after the roar and glare of the avenue, and hurrying her along, they soon left that quarter of the city behind them. Then they stopped in a quiet place, and Barb began to fetch her breath and to explain matters.

"Maybe you don't understand what all this fluster was about, Miss Barry," said she, looking up into the face of the beautiful woman with sorrowful eyes.

Barry returned her look, horror and bewilderment in her glance.

"No, you don't; I see you don't, dear soul," resumed Barb. "Oh, I wish I didn't either! You needn't shrink away from me, Miss Barry, though," she added, straightening herself proudly. "I'm only a ballet-dancer, and maybe you thinks there's nothing so low as that; but it's miles and miles above what old Nan would have had me be if I would, which I never did, miss, God he knows, nor wouldn't if she had beat me to death!"

Barry drew her to her breast with a sudden revulsion of feeling.

"I believe you, you poor dear little soul," said she. "You're a good girl, a brave girl! But what did the woman want with me?"

Barb clung to her with trembling hands.

"I daren't tell you," whispered she. "Don't ask me again. Only if she could have kept you, it would have been no sin for you to take a knife off the table and kill yourself with it!"

A long shudder shook Barry Pomeroy from head to foot, for a moment her very heart stood still.

"Oh, mother! oh, Hugh!" she moaned in horror.

"Barry," said Barb, tenderly, "go back to 'em, do! Twice to-day you've been saved by a miracle; oh, be warned in time, and go back to them as loves you true as gold."

"Wait a moment," said Barry, faintly; "let me think over it again."

Barb busied herself in adjusting Barry's and her own disordered dresses.

"You can't go back to that woman after this?" asked Barry by and by.

"Oh, yes, I must," replied Barb. "I've nowheres else to go; but never mind me. Have you made up your mind, dear?"

"No," said Barry, weeping. "My heart fails me for the first time."

"Be quick then, deary love!" said Barb, leading her on again. "We'll soon be at the theatre now, and in twenty minutes I must go on. Before we get's there, I want to have your consent that you'll go back to 'em in the morning, and then I'll know what I must do for you to-night."

"Let me think," said Barry.

They walked on in silence while the angels of Good and Evil fought in the young girl's breast for mastery, and the fagged dancer thought dismally of the brutalities in store for her.

When they came to the back street and the stage entrance, Barry said, tremulously:

"I haven't decided yet; I can't decide. He broke my heart. Am I to have no satisfaction?"

Barb took her hand between her own two cold, slim ones, saying, with a strange rich gush of music in her voice:

"Dear love, ain't we always a breakin' of the Master's heart, and does He ever want any satisfaction except to forgive us?"

At this, coming from the lips of an ignorant city waif, the carefully-trained maiden broke down, and wept bitterly.

"Let me stay with you a little while longer, Barb," sobbed she. "You're so good, that maybe I'll do as you say."

Barb led her in, explaining to the porter that she was a friend who came to help her dress in a hurry. Being an old hand in the business, this irregularity was permitted the little coryphée, and she conducted Barry through intricate and winding passages to a large dressing-room, where a crowd of young women were dressing themselves in silk tights, short, spangled skirts, etc., and carrying on the while a perfect babel of clatter, some of which made the pure-souled

Barry's cheeks tingle with shame, until her eyes rested upon the white, childlike face of little Barb, who busily went on with her toilet, mindful of nothing else.

"It rolls off her like rain off a leaf," thought Barry. "What's that about the 'pure in spirit'? "I wish I was like Barb!"

In a few moments the call came for the ballet-corps. Barb tripped, in her silk sandals and gauze petticoats, to her friend's side. Not a poor little haggard drudge now; no, no; the Lady of the Air was lovely as any fairy of poet's dream!

How richly her cheeks glowed!

How gracefully her long flossy hair waved! How sylphine was her figure—how delicate her limbs!

"Miss Barry, dear love!" murmured the coryphée, leaning on her glittering wand, while the playful elf-like strains of the fairy dance stole in from the orchestra, and the people applauded the fairy cavern at the rising of the curtain, "you've no right to be running about the world with that there pretty face of yours, an' mark my words, it'll be your ruin if you do. Now, don't stir till I come back."

She floated away, closing the door behind her.

Barry Pomeroy sat thinking, with set face and troubled heart.

What a struggle was there!

3*

A thought of Harrison Fairleigh, and hell raged, all its demons broken loose! Hatred, vengeance, despair!

A thought of her old mother, saintly in mind and life—her venerable face a benediction—the clasp of her hand a caress—and tender love, remorse, penitence pressed around her with wooing whispers!

The door opened—a jaunty face peeped in.

"Doves all flown, by Jove!" exclaimed a voice which pierced her like an arrow. She turned her back to the door, and drew her thick vail closely.

"Bah! the old duenna is on duty, too; no use waiting!" replied another voice. "Come on, Fairleigh."

A few minutes afterwards the dancers trooped in and threw themselves panting upon the chairs and floor.

"Decided yet, dear?" whispered the Lady of the Air, fanning her hot face with her shining shield.

"Yes!" said Barry, looking up with a dreadful smile. "I am going to hunt him down!"

CHAPTER V.

BARB and Barry sat together in the window of a wide, bright room. Two rows of immaculate narrow white beds stretched along the snow-white floor to the distant door; some prettily framed Scripture texts adorned the walls, and a soft warm atmosphere cheated the occupants into a momentary forgetfulness of the chilling wind which blew against the frozen windows, and of the first fall of the December snow which was whitening the busy street below.

The fugitive and her friend had found a safe asylum in one of those Homes for Friendless Girls which adorn the Christian city of New York far morethan do the noblest palaces of Fifth Avenue.

On that night when Barry Pomeroy had declared her unalterable resolve, Barb, very sadly, but firmly, had said:

"You're in a bad way, Barry Pomeroy, an' I daren't desert you—wherever you go, I go."

"I've nowhere to go," Barry had answered in a hard, indifferent way. "I guess I've got grit enough to fight along by myself; you take care of yourself; it ain't your business to look after me!"

"Maybe not, Barry, but I know more about the town than you do, and you can't make me leave you if I won't—so there's an end on't."

So Barry, thinking of other things, had let her have her way.

Well, how had they fared, these straws cast into the vortex?

The first night Barb had conducted her friend to a station, and, demanding a night's lodging by right of poverty and homelessness, had enjoyed at least a shelter among the vagrants of the most revolting character; yet this was the best the poor little dancer could do at such a late hour. In the morning, one of the constables gave them the address of the Home referred to, and there they had been taken in with Christian charity, and made welcome until they should find situations.

Barb could easily have got an engagement in another theatre, for she dared not return to the Opera House lest old Nan should trace her; but the matron advised her so tenderly and faithfully against her old profession, encouraging her to remain in the Home and learn sewing or running a machine, that she stayed cheerfully with Barry, who was qualifying herself as fast as she could for a place as nursery-governess or lady's-maid.

How often had Barb entreated Barry to tell her the name of her native place, thinking with simple wile to put her in communication with her mother, and so to break the deadly spell which bound her! But Barry kept obstinate silence on that point, and, worse than that, refused to give her own name or history to the matron, so intimidating Barb with the threat of running away if she ever betrayed the confidence she had reposed in her, that she held her peace perforce, fearing to consign her friend to destruction should she go against her.

"Mind, Barb," Barry had said, with that eerie glint in her dark eye, "my name—till I've got my heart's desire—is Marah Leith. I used to read in my Bible that 'Marah' meant 'bitterness,' and oh, it suits me right well now!"

As they talked softly by the window that morning, both plainly, but pleasantly dressed, with pure white aprons on, and hair demurely coiled in a simple knot behind, the matron came in, her gentle face wreathed with a smile of pleasure.

"Girls," said she, beaming upon them, "go down to the parlor; a lady is there who wants to select, from among my girls here, one to take right home with her. She's a dear good lady, and whoever she chooses will be a happy creature, I know."

The two girls went down stairs hand-in-hand, and entered the parlor, where they found three or four of the other inmates of the house; and, seated by herself, with pale and gentle face turned attentively toward them, a beautiful aged lady, richly dressed.

"These are all I have at your command," said the matron closing the door. Barb and Barry glanced at each other with rising color, for the lady, seeing them enter so lovingly, had given them a long, wistful look, and then a smile of surpassing kindness.

"Oh!" sighed Barb, in her heart. "If she'd only let *me* be her servant!"

The lady spoke in a gentle, velvet voice, and with a high-bred accent which carried a peculiar charm with it.

"My girls," she said, "God has been laying His hand heavily upon me. My daughter, whom I loved too dearly, is dead. In my sorrow, God has put into my heart to take another child, this time not born in luxury and bred in fashionable ease, but snatched from poverty and temptation. I want a daughter whom I can love and cherish for my dead daughter's sake. The more helpless, friendless, weak, and discouraged she comes to me, the more gladly will I open my doors to her. Girls, who will come to the

aged mother who mourns her lost darling, and uphold her tottering steps to the grave?"

These few simple, but heartfelt words seemed to
stir the little assembly like the breath of some ma-
gician.

They were all girls gathered in from the streets—
some rough and ignorant, some positively vicious—
all but Barry; and yet, while they wept in a burst
of pity, she stood like a stone, white, yet perfectly
calm. For, through this gentle stranger, did not
her mother's heart-broken cry come up to her ears?

Oh, Barry, Barry! listen to that pleading whisper
in your breast—return—return!

"Lady," said a low, tremulous voice, breaking
the sobbing stillness, "do, do take this poor dear;
she ain't fit to rough it among the bad folks here.
Look how pretty she is!"

It was Barb who spoke: it was Barry she drew
forward, while the matron's eyes glistened upon her.

The lady beckoned both the girls to her side, and
again she gazed upon them earnestly.

"You are not of such stuff as outcasts are usually
made of," said she to Barry. "What is your
history?"

The others drew to the further end of the room,
leaving the three apart.

"It is a bitter story, ma'am," answered Barry,

stonily. "I'd rather not tell it. There was no shame in it, either, leastways not to me; but there was cruel, cruel wrong done by others!"

"You speak bitter as gall, my girl," said the lady, slowly. "Have you left your home in revenge for some fancied slight?"

"I have no home till things come right," said Barry, in her hardest voice.

The lady turned her heavenly eyes—for all peace and purity dwelt therein—from the beautiful frowning face of Barry to the meek, emaciated one of Barb.

"Little girl," said she, tenderly, "you are not this poor soul's sister, are you?"

"No, indeed, ma'am; I'm one of the roughs—she's most a lady."

"Don't you want to come and be my daughter?" inquired the lady, passing her soft old hand lightly over the flaxen curls of the blushing creature.

"Oh, jest don't I?" Barb burst forth in ecstasy. Then she checked herself, and cast a glance of piteous entreaty toward Barry. "But it ain't the likes of me that wants such a angel as you to guide 'em back to good," she added, earnestly. "I'm used to going round on the loose an' takin' good care of myself, but she ain't. She's innercent as a sparrow, ma'am, an' any rogue might harm her for all the suspicion she has of their wicked ways. Oh, do take her, dear lady!"

"Do you wish to come?" asked the lady, turning from Barb, with great tears in her eyes, to Barry.

"Yes, I wish to go, but Barb is a far better girl than I, and far worthier your kindness," answered Barry, in a low voice.

The lady covered her face and mused deeply for some time; then she beckoned the matron, and after conferring with her, said:

"My heart goes out to the one you call Barb, rough-spoken and untaught as she is. She is young to have fought such a hard fight. Oh, I want to have her! But the other, Marah; I don't know what to think about her. There is a latent power— I might almost say a ferocity—under her rigid self-possession which repulses me. She is most in need of a safe home though, with that beautiful face and bitter spirit of hers. Alas! my duty is plain. I choose her who needs me most. May God smile upon us both!"

The matron recalled the young girls, who had stood aside during this conference, and leading Barry forward, presented her to the lady with a few sincere and touching words.

"I choose you, Marah Leith," said the venerable lady, solemnly, "and I charge you, by your mother's memory, to give me no cause to rue my choice."

"I promise to devote myself to you as long as you keep me," said Barry, with her cold gaze on the ground.

*　　*　　*　　*　　*　　*　　*

The next evening, as Barb sat plying her little sewing-machine among some dozen other workers, the matron came in with a quiet sparkle of satisfaction in her kindly eye.

"Barbara Pomeroy," said she—and all the machines stopped—" your friend, Marah Leith, has come back to see you. You see she hasn't forgotten your kindness to her, my child," added she, as the eager Barb hurried out with her. "It's pleasant to see gratitude," she soliloquized, "and to know there is such cause for it."

Barb flew into the parlor, and found herself alone with Barry.

What a transformation !

Her splendid form was draped in rich cloth folds, which did its massive beauty justice at last; costly furs shielded her throat, her wrists, her delicately-gloved hands; her blue-black hair was brushed and coiled by artistic fingers under her heavily-plumed hat; with her scarlet cheeks, glittering eyes, and

white teeth flashing between her parted lips, she per
sented a spectacle of glorious beauty!

She stood before Barb motionless, gazing at her
with a strange, reckless mirth in her sparkling eye,
and Barb, standing off in innocent awe and venera-
tion, sighed out:

"Oh, ain't you just splendid! Oh! deary love,
ain't you going to be happy!"

Barry's features contracted in a sudden fierce
scowl.

"Happy!" said she, between her grinding teeth.
"Scarcely! Another mother-heart to be crushed in
my path to vengeance. Oh, silly little Barb, why
didn't you go there yourself? Why didn't you save
her—why didn't you save me?"

"What's—what's wrong?" gasped Barb, terrified
by her manner.

"The lady who has adopted me for her daughter,"
said Barry, in an unnatural voice, so stern, so fearfully pitiless, that Barb shrank back in utter horror,
"*is Harrison Fairleigh's mother!*"

CHAPTER VI.

FAIR FACE, FOUL HEART.

YEAR has passed since Barbara Pomeroy entered the home of Mrs. Fairleigh, under the false name of Marah Leith, to be educated as her own daughter had been. She has improved as only one could whose purpose is to be gained by improvement; she uses no longer the homely colloquialisms which stamped her as plebeian; she has cultured her tones to imitate the sweet melody of the ladies-born who surround her; she has drunk in all knowledge, all learning, all accomplishments with a never-to-be-satiated thirst—in one year the mother who bore her would scarcely recognize in this well-trained city beauty the Barry who carried the milking-pails and sang in the vine-wreathed kitchen.

In all this time she has never once seen Harrison Fairleigh. Indeed, she never entered his mother's house until he had left it for the Eastern Hemisphere, languidly hoping to enliven his idleness by the new scenes of European dissipation and pleasure. But the mother has kept her well-informed of all his movements, for she loves him as only good mothers can love wayward sons, gifting him with many a noble quality which dwells but in her own pure breast, and incapable of comprehending in her innocence the actual deformity of his heart and mind. She has written to him, too, of her new daughter such generous and glowing praises that, could bitter Marah have read them, her proud lip would have curled with yet fiercer triumph, and she would have turned her to her chosen path with yet sterner purpose.

Harrison has been lazily interested in Marah Leith ; has even asked his mother for her picture, but this Marah has sedulously guarded against, for she will not suffer herself to be photographed.

Truth to say, the sweet old Christian lady scarcely understands the daughter whom she has taken for her dead Maud's sake. She admires her noble beauty, her docility, and her insatiable craving after knowledge, but she can never get her heart to heart with her ; whenever she would draw her close, longing to give and receive some token of affection, an invisible wall rises up between them, high as heaven, and they look through it at each other, divided as by the bars of a castle.

Her past history Marah Leith has locked away in

her own breast; Mrs. Fairleigh scarce ever expects to hear it now, and yet she believes her *protégée* as innocent of guilt or shame as if she knew all. Erring she knows she is, and it is her constant endeavor to pour upon her darkened soul light from that Lamp which leads the most erring back to the fold.

Barry has not yet so deteriorated in heart that she can live this easy, luxurious life without satisfying herself how her poor old mother is bearing her sadly clouded one. She has not dared to trust herself to write to her, nor to expose herself to the pain of receiving letters in return, filled with vain prayers and questions, and yet she knows that her mother is comparatively well, and looking day by day with an exhaustless hope for Barry to come back. Money can do anything; Barry has plenty of it now, and she has easily found an unsuspicious messenger to send on some ostensible mission to Thunder Peak, and to bring her back the news she craves to hear.

Meantime, patient little Barb's fortunes have also improved. Partly through the bounty of the matron's friends, partly by Mrs. Fairleigh's aid, she has by this time a business of her own, where, in a pleasant, quiet street, not far beyond the radius of fashionable custom, she runs a machine, assisted by two smart apprentices, all day long, diligently improving her mind in the evenings at a night-school.

She and Barry see each other frequently; indeed, she is the only soul on earth who knows the workings of her friend's mind; and if warnings can save her, of Barry there is no fear.

We come now to the night when, tired of his gay wanderings, Harrison Fairleigh is expected to arrive home.

Barry stands at the window of her own room; the snow is falling softly, softly outside, like silent blessings upon that sacred home; the street-lamps burn with a blur about them, and every passer-by seems robed with ermine.

Is this the calico-clad Hebe who stood on the crazy bridge under the Thunder Peak, confessing her love to Harrison Fairleigh, this splendid empress of beauty, with snow-white, massive shoulders gleaming through priceless lace; magnificent bare arms, adorned with rare gems; statuesque figure, enrobed with sweeping black velvet; dusky tresses massed in a royal coronet upon her proud head, with one burning geranium above her small white ear?

Is this the arch, passionate, innocent face that blushed at his praises—this icy, pure, stately countenance, with the curl of scorn upon its rich red lips, and the glimmer of wild cruelty in its glorious eye?

A carriage rolled to the door and stopped. Trunks

loaded the box; a traveller, wrapped in a splendid cloak of Russian sables, descended.

Barry dropped the curtain with a slow, gasping sigh.

"He has come," she muttered. "Let me play my part now, bravely, recklessly."

She stood a few moments before the mirror, examining herself with an intense scrutiny which left not the smallest flaw unscanned, instantly to be set right with impatient hand; then she threw herself into a large satin easy-chair before the slumbering fire, and with her teeth set, and her hands pressed upon her bounding heart, she waited until at length a servant tapped at her door, with the message that Mrs. Fairleigh desired her to descend.

She swept down the broad, velvet-covered steps; bronze nymphs, filling niches in the stairway, shed soft, lustrous beams upon her from their silver lamps; snowy Venuses and Junos looked down upon her, not half so beautiful as she, from their carved pedestals in the tesselated hall; a footman flung wide the noiseless door, and in she passed.

Three people occupied the drawing-room.

Mrs. Fairleigh, in her dead-black silken train, and crape cap, pure as the driven snow, resting on her silver-bright hair, sat on a crimson sofa; at her side, with her hands in his and his bold bright eyes dwelling fondly and proudly upon her, sat Harrison Fairleigh ; and, standing apart by the exquisitely designed mantelpiece, with an admiring gaze fastened upon the other two, a gentleman, tall, dark, and young, listened silently to their rapid and eager conversation.

Upon these three came Barry, with the step of an empress.

With one accord they looked at her; with one accord they fell into breathless silence.

Mrs. Fairleigh, just about to greet her with a loving word, stopped, awe-struck by the wonderful *diablerie* of her rare beauty ; the stranger could but stare in bewildered surprise ; and Harrison? A glare of astonishment, of consternation broke from his arrested eye ; then the quick blood surged to his bronzed face like a crimson mask, distorting and transforming the elegant languor of his well-trained features ; then he grew white to ghastliness, and a convulsive shiver ran through him.

Sideways he glanced at his mother and the stranger; they were still intent upon the marvellous vision which had made him quail.

He glanced back at her ; he met her great, gloomy eyes; fixed in a sort of royal scorn and pity upon him.

Harrison collected his thoughts.

4

He passed his delicate hand across his damp brow, and said, with a smile:

"This, I suppose, is Miss Leith, of whom I have heard so much?"

"Yes," answered Mrs. Fairleigh, rising as if some evil spell was broken. "Marah, this is my son—your brother."

Marah put her soft hand into his, and smiling into his eyes, said:

"I feel as if I knew you already, Mr. Fairleigh; you are, I know, worthy of all the sisterly affection *I* can bestow."

Slight as the emphasis was, it made him wince like a pin's prick.

"And I am sure," replied he, "I shall find you all my dear mother *believes* you to be."

It was her turn to wince, but if she did, she hid it with a deep bow, the stately grace of which might have been copied by any tragedienne on the boards.

"Allow me to present my friend Mr. Roscoe, an Englishman whom I met in Paris," continued Harrison, with a careless wave of the hand; and having thus disposed of his adopted sister, he turned again to Mrs. Fairleigh.

Barry entered into conversation with Mr. Roscoe, easily, gracefully.

Had she not made golden use of every moment

since she had entered these walls to garner in her mind all information, to teach herself to understand every classical, scientific, and erudite allusion in which elegant conversationalists might indulge?

Mr. Roscoe, accustomed to the less ready and more reticent English lady, was enchanted. From time to time he cast a glance toward Harrison Fairleigh, as if inviting his admiration also.

Harrison was absorbed in some recital which his mother was making. He neither noticed his friend nor his adopted sister.

Barry knew what that recital was, and her burning heart writhed in its chosen flame.

Mrs. Fairleigh was telling Harrison where she had found this lovely girl, Marah; and Barry was waiting for the moment when he would turn with angry disdain to her, crying:

"Barbara Pomeroy, what does this imposture mean? Why are you here under a false name?"

She was waiting, with pulses all throbbing, with heart on fire to avenge its wrongs, with this answer trembling upon her lips:

"You stole my love, intending to trample it, dishonored, in the dust. Through you my mother's heart is broken; and now through me your mother's heart shall break, as I denounce her son, villain and *roué!*"

While these terrible thoughts occupied her mind, her rich, ripe lips were wreathed in smiles, and her discourse was of themes a duchess might choose for graceful discussion.

Suddenly she caught the eyes of mother and son fixed upon her—they were listening, Mrs. Fairleigh with a proud satisfaction, Harrison with an astonished and uneasy air.

Barry thought:

"He shrinks, coward-like, from exposing me, fearful of reprisals. Come, I must force him to speak."

She turned her splendid face, devil-possessed, full toward her benefactress and her son.

"You have been telling Mr. Fairleigh my story, have you?" said she, silver-voiced; "confess now, Mr. Fairleigh, are you not aristocratically shocked to find such as I installed in your home?"

Harrison glared at her in a sort of startled admiration.

"You are certainly a singular production for plebeian soil to have the honor of growing," answered he, rising and sauntering over to her. "Roscoe, will you give my mother a *résumé* of our travels, while I devote myself to my new sister? Thanks. Now, Miss Marah, if you will bestow your company upon such an uninteresting personage as myself, I should like to see what strange and foreign flowers my mother has been adding to her conservatory. *Who knows? she may have been deceived by some poison- ous weed,*" he added, significantly.

For the moment she sat speechless, her busy mind running over the probabilities of such an interview. Did she comprehend the wild bound of her heart at the thought of once again standing face to face with this man, alone? No!

"He hopes to induce my silence by some of his old flatteries," she mused. "Let him try: he shall find the lowly maid as bent upon avenging his insult as any princess born!"

She put her hand upon his arm, and, smiling strangely, led him from the drawing-room, down-stairs, through the marble halls, and so into the conservatory, dimly lit to-night, full of monster shadows thrown from giant plants, and odorous with the breath of invisible blossoms.

Yes, these two were alone once more!

And not more dissimilar were the rickety old bridge spanning the opalescent stream, with the giant peak behind and the burning sun overhead, and this hushed, fragrant, dusky home of the flowers, than were the Barry of the bridge and the Barry of the conservatory.

The door was closed, the velvet curtain dropped over it; only the crescent of taper lights above them and the great fiery-throated passion-flowers beside them saw and heard.

"Barbara Pomeroy!" whispered Harrison.

"Yes, Barbara Pomeroy!" answered she, calmly.

A deep breath escaped him ; he leaned somewhat heavily against the back of the rustic seat near, and looked at her in growing astonishment and uneasiness.

"Have—have you told my mother that you and I were old friends ?" stammered he at last, awkwardly enough.

"I have not," smiled Barry, with cold amusement.

"Then why are you here ?" said he, flushing suddenly. "Did you expect me to come back and fall in love with you again ?"

Barry gave him one look—a flash of unspeakable scorn.

"I expected you to come back," said she.

"I don't understand it," said Harrison, flushing now with mortification. "What madness could have possessed you to come to my mother's house under a false name ?"

"Cast me out now if you wish to do so, you have the power," said she. "What better could be expected from a girl who was considered fit only to be a rich man's toy ?"

"You mean that if I speak you'll tell my mother

the facts of the case?" inquired he, more and more thunderstruck.

This was the moment for which she had waited. Why then did she not flash forth her well-conned answer and listen to his entreaties to spare his mother with pitiless indifference? This was her moment for revenge. Why then did she pause, her flickering eyes passing slowly over him, and the rich blood receding from her cheek and lips? Now, had she stopped to analyze her emotions she might have learned that the foul flame of revenge had not yet succeeded in comsuming her maiden love for this man—she might have learned, and stayed her foot on the brink of a chasm.

"This would be but a poor revenge," thought Barry, hurried on by her passion. "I would only have crushed his mother with the knowedge of her idol's villainy, while he would escape scot-free, for it would be no pang to him to lose me; no! this shall not satisfy me; I must teach him to suffer before I strike."

"Harrison," said she in a soft and altered tone, "if you have the heart to thrust me forth, do so; I shall not say a word in my own defence. I fled from home because I dared not marry a good man with the stain of your proffered love fresh upon me; I would have died at home of grief and shame. I preferred to die elsewhere, that your name might never be coupled with my sufferings."

Harrison shifted his position again and again, as if her words were stings, and she, observing her power, continued with yet more luring deceit:

"Was it my fault that you had stolen my love from the man whom I was contented enough to marry? Was it my fault that when I learned your purpose my heart broke, and I wished only for a place to hide myself? I came to New York and was chosen without any agency on my part by your mother, whose very name I did not know until I was fairly installed in her house. As for my false name, I assumed it only to escape the pursuit of my friends."

"But when you knew all," said Harrison, "why did you remain? You must have known that, sooner or later, I would come home, and then what did you expect?"

"I expect to be turned adrift," answered she, giving him one of her old-time glances, and noting with exultation that she had the power to move him as of old.

"And you were going to submit without a word in your own defence?" asked he.

"Without a word," said she. "Harrison Fairleigh was sent into my life to be its blight and curse, and sooner or later he will be the cause of my death; it matters little when."

Harrison approached her with impulsive hands outstretched.

"My poor girl," said he, "I have injured you, but I shall injure you no more; forgive me for the past, and let us be friends for the future.

She laid her hands in his; she called a dewy moisture to her triumphant glittering eyes, and a gentle humility to her too-smiling lips.

"You will not betray me to your mother?" she asked.

"No, no! Dear Barry! Poor Barry!"

"You will not send word to mother or Hugh where I am?"

"Never, my poor wronged darling!"

Imperceptibly he was drawing her closer, ardently he was bending over her, his eager breath already on her lips. Oh, for one kiss of reconciliation!

Her wild heart rose to meet his, a splendid blush suffused her charming face, she was yielding—yielding, when the handle of the conservatory door turned, and the voices of Mrs. Fairleigh and Mr. Roscoe were heard.

She tore herself from his detaining clasp with a choking gasp:

"No, no, Harrison!" said she, in thrilling agitation. "Never that again, or you would madden me indeed! Yet, let us be friends!"

4*

"Yes, Barry, yes!" muttered Harrison, crushing her hand in his.

Next moment the venerable old lady stepped down the marble steps, assisted by the handsome Englishman.

CHAPTER VII.

WOMAN'S LOVE VERSUS MAN'S PASSION.

IT is perhaps a week afterward, and on a bright winter afternoon, Barry is seated with her friend Barb in the beautiful room which has been assigned her as her *boudoir*.

If Barry has improved so has Barb. She is fair and meek as the Grecian Slave, to which she bears no small resemblance. Her misty blue eyes are innocent as ever, her smile as tender, and her speech as simple; but she is no longer rough, ragged, or forlorn; she is as comely as a sweet wild rose, and just as single-hearted.

In her neatly-fitting winter dress, adorned with a simple knot of azure at the throat, she presents by no means an incongruous appearance in that dainty chamber, even though her friend's robes are of the richest purple velvet, and her jewelry worth a year's income of the busy little needlewoman.

At present a perfect aurora of smiles are chasing each other over her attentive face, while Barry, with the soft lustre restored to her eyes, and womanly blushes on her cheeks, speaks softly and tenderly of —Harrison Fairleigh!

"He is sorry, very sorry, indeed, for what he did," she is saying. "He could not treat me with more respect if I was the greatest lady in the land. He is kind, too; oh, so kind! He could not give me so much pleasure if he did not love me, could he, Barb?"

"No, of course he couldn't, dear," cried innocent Barb, surveying Barry with beaming admiration. "How could he help loving you, now that you are a lady in his own station, respected and loved by his mother? Oh, I hoped it would turn this way all the time, Barry! I knew it would! He'll ask you to marry him in right-down earnest now; and won't you—won't you be happy!"

"Oh, hush!" whispered Barry, trembling with soft rapture. "Perhaps he will; but, oh! perhaps he won't—and then——"

"Nonsense!" flouted Barb. "Of course he will, if he has really repented of the wrong he sought to do you. Now, Barry, dear Barry, do write your mother," added Barb, timidly, for this was a forbidden subject.

Large tears gushed from Barry's eyes, a tender smile quivered on her lips.

"Dear mother!" breathed she. "Yes, I'll write to her the very hour I've promised to be Harrison's wife. I'll set her poor heart at rest at last—oh, I've been a bad daughter—I don't deserve God's blessing now! Hugh Wayne, too; good, constant Hugh, he'll be glad to hear that his cruel bride-elect is not dead or gone to destruction. He was always so un-selfish—always so unselfish. The night I ran away he offered to give me up if it would make me happier, and I didn't dare to tell him that he must, Barb, dear. I don't deserve this happiness, I don't, indeed."

"But you're grateful for it, aren't you?" said Barb, wistfully. "And even if it didn't come, you'd never be as hard and vindictive as you were, would you?"

"Even if it didn't come!" echoed Barry, in a faint, low voice. "Oh, don't say that, my dear! It must come, for if it doesn't I sha'n't be able to bear it. If he deceives me now it would be worse than the first time—far worse; for he has told me over and over again that I was the one woman in the world for him, that I was formed to make him angel or devil, and that we must never part. No, he dares not deceive me a second time. Oh, no! oh, no!"

She laughed a little wildly, then putting a check on herself, took Barb in her arms, and kissed her in a burst of proud humility.

"You are so much better and nobler than I, my darling girl," said she, "that you can't begin to imagine the terrible thoughts that sometimes crowd into my mind like imps from Satan. How can you love me so much, you pure child?"

Barb was about to answer, when a tap at the door interrupted her.

"Ah! he is here," said Barry, turning from her friend with radiant face. "This afternoon will decide all; I know it will. I feel a strange, mystic excitation at my heart here that never came to me before. Kiss me, Barb—kiss me, dear! There, thank you. If I return a happy woman, I vow to live a good one; but, if not—if not—O God! have mercy upon me!"

The last shuddering sigh was still on her lips when Mrs. Fairleigh entered.

Harrison Fairleigh being a gentleman of independent means, chose rather to live in a fashionable hotel than in his mother's house; but he and his friend Roscoe, who had put up at the Fifth Avenue Hotel, spent many hours each day walking, driving, or chatting by the glowing hearth with Mrs. Fairleigh and her adopted daughter. And there had been other interviews, not so public, when Harrison and Marah lingered together in the library, or walked by themselves in some quiet up-town quarter, when words were spoken and looks were exchanged that surely were sacred to the expression of but one passion on earth.

Mrs. Fairleigh had not been unobservant, and it was a part of Barry's boundless gratification that she had looked on with evident pleasure, being just unworldly enough to prefer for her son one whom she believed would make him a good wife, to the most illustrious belle whom fashionable society could offer.

Harrison had invited Barry out driving in his elegant new equipage, and Mrs. Fairleigh, hearing, had given her consent to the arrangement with a smile of peculiar approbation.

"Are you ready, dear?" said she, scanning Barry's well-chosen toilet with careful eye. "Harrison is to drive you himself, and he and his horses are impatient to be off."

"Yes, yes, thank you, Mrs. Fairleigh. Help me, Barb," murmured Barry, in a soft flutter; and Mrs. Fairleigh, taking a seat by the window, where she could command a view of the departure, watched with radiant interest the sweet, fair-haired girl as, with skilful fingers, she threw round the shoulders of her more beauteous friend her purple velvet carriage-cloak, lined and trimmed with ermine, and placed on her glossy black hair her ermine trimmed hat.

A few moments longer, and Harrison's mother and Barry's friend watched from the same window the regal beauty step into Harrison's glittering carriage, her cheeks blushing with richer bloom, and her soft smile answering his eager greeting.

Then they dashed off, and the rich lady drew the little sewing-girl close to her side, and began to chat with her as she loved to do: for when these two talked together, they spoke on a theme which placed them on the same level, daughters of the same Prince, aspirants for the same crown.

As Harrison and Barry drove out to Central Park to join the gay stream of equipages there, a slight constraint seemed slowly to gather like a cloud over his gay spirits.

Barry noted, and her heart fluttered with rising excitement. She took refuge in her most brilliant mood to hide her breathless anticipation of what was coming.

Never in his life had Harrison sat beside a more fascinating woman. The cloud darkened on his brow; he glanced at her once or twice strangely, then lashed his horses into flying speed, only to rein them up again with savage strength.

They joined the fur-filled turnouts of the New York aristocracy; they passed many a radiantly beautiful woman, many a magnificently handsome man ; then glancing at each other, their passion-filled eyes said :

"None so beautiful ; none so fascinating—as you !"

They chose anon a quieter drive, where few met them, and the naked trees arched overhead their twigs, all cased in ice, a glistening tracery of most minute and exquisite delicacy against the deep blue sky.

Here the jet-black horses walking along the frosty road, Harrison took the reins in one strong hand, and, placing the other on Barry's wrist—for her hands were nestling in her costly muff—he burst out fiercely :

" Barry, I'm the most miserable man on earth? I'm a fool, an idiot! Oh, I wish I had never been born ! "

An encouraging preface to a declaration—was it not ?

She gazed at him perplexed, yet smiling ; convention had taught her to keep her countenance ; yet the sight of these gloomy eyes and whitening, compressed lips sent a chill to her heart.

" I thought you seemed quite satisfied with your lot in life," said she. " What do you lack to make your happiness complete ?"

" I want *you*," said he, " and—and you've denied me ! "

Her heart stood still. It had come !

"I have denied you," said she, a heart-beat in every faltering tone; "but that is all forgotten—forgiven."

Harrison seized both her hands, crushing them in such a fierce grasp that her diamonds pierced her tender flesh like pins. She scarcely felt the pain; she drooped toward him, a beautiful woman, her love in her eyes.

"I said I couldn't marry you then," muttered he, with an angry oath. "Conceited ass that I was! I might have seen in you the material for the glorious creature you are now!"

"Forgiven, Harrison! Believe me, all forgiven!" whispered Barry.

"And you love me as well as you did? Yes, you do, better, far better than you did!" exclaimed Harrison, with burning earnestness; "for your mind is expanded, you are mistress of the whole range of the emotions. They are at your command, and, too, you are at theirs. Your capacity for loving has grown with your power to inspire love; you are Love's queen, but also his slave! Oh! Barry, Barry! Why didn't you beg me to marry you a year ago, and shame me into it, or when you failed bury yourself where I could never behold your tempting loveliness again? Perhaps I could not have withstood you. You love me, don't you, Barry?"

Perhaps it was a whisper of woman's dignity; perhaps it was the sight of his haggard, anxious face, that held her dumb. This time she did not answer that question. She shrank back from him, trying to release her hands.

"You won't say? Well, it would be poor consolation if you did," remarked he, bitterly. "I know you do, and I love you better than any woman in the world, and I would marry you, oh, proudly, gladly, *if I were not engaged to marry another!*"

Barry sat dumb-smitten, gazing at him like one risen from the dead.

"Don't—don't look at me that way, my poor darling!" faltered he—miserable tears coming to his eyes. "I should have told you at first, and saved you this, but, as usual, I was a selfish beast, and thought only of basking in your wonderful new charms."

Barry opened her lips to speak, but they were dry and rigid; she could not utter a syllable.

"I thought when I saw you first," continued he, "that you had schemed to get into my mother's house in my absence, to meet me on my return home with the bitter revenge of telling my mother what I was, and I begged you to stay in the hope of conciliating you, but now—now, I adore, I worship you, Barry, you are the one woman in the wide earth for me, and I've PROMISED TO MARRY KATHERINE HENDRICK!"

She made shift to speak this time, but in a voice so strangely unlike her own, that he started in horror as these hollow tones fell upon his ear:

" When are you to be married ? "

" In a month. For mercy's sake, don't talk about it!"

" Who is she ? " next asked Barry.

" You've heard of Baron Hendrick, the millionaire ? His daughter. I met her in Paris, passing the winter with her relatives, the Roscoes. Oh, she's a beauty and a belle, I tell you ! " But I wouldn't give her whole delicately nurtured, diamond-bedizened body for your little finger, if you were a beggar in the streets, Barry Pomeroy."

Barry's eyes flashed.

" You are sure of my love; you are sure of your own ? " said she; " why don't you tell Katherine Hendrick the truth, and marry me ? "

His clasp relaxed. It was his turn to shrink back with a scowling and disconcerted air.

" What a question ! " exclaimed he. " I do think a woman the most unreasoning creature on the face of the earth. Here is this lady, a splendid match; everybody dying for her; the favorite toast in the highest circles of Paris, London, and New York; and here's you, a nobody; picked up out of the streets by my poor Quixotic mother—with but one endowment—a sort of demon's fascination that, Circe like, turns men who drink of it into swine, satisfied with nothing else. Why don't I drop her? you ask, to the scandal of the social world, and court its ridicule and derision by marrying you! I can't tell Katherine Hendrick the truth—I won't!"

"And what, may I ask, was your purpose in speaking to me this afternoon?" said Barry, a scarlet spot burning in the middle of each white cheek.

"What's the use of my telling you?" said he, harshly. "Like all your sex you are incapable of disinterested love. You'd be right glad to be a rich man's wife, doubtless! But you wouldn't for love of him give up a few wretched conventionalities."

"Stop!" shrieked Barry. "My God, this is the second time!"

That tingling cry sent the pacing horses bounding forward, and off like the wind, the reins on the ground at their heels, but Harrison scarcely noticed them, for with her words, Barry Pomeroy had hurled herself from the carriage, and now stood alone in the middle of the leafless avenue, gazing with set face after her insulter, as he leaned over the back of the carriage with arms stretched forth to her!

*   *   *   *   *   *   *

No wonder the people stared after that hurrying figure as it sped through the gathering night, trailing its sumptuous skirts in the frozen street, covering its bent face with a handkerchief of costly lace! A velvet-robed lady, with jewels worth thousands of dollars twinkling in her ears and at her throat, flitting alone through the lonely wilderness of unoccupied lots which surround Central Park.

It was Barbara Pomeroy, the Barry of Thunder Peak, two hours after Harrison Fairleigh had for the second time blasted her ears with his accursed love.

Where had she been all that time; and whither was she flying now?

· Ah, the despair-filled heart recks little where the swift feet bear it, only bidding them fly! fly! and leave its agony behind! Round and round those interminable walks had she strayed, unconscious of the passing time; and her frenzied thoughts had by this gradually shaped themselves toward one fell purpose.

Cruelly, cruelly wronged she had been, had she not, oh, sisters?

Who that has lavished the purest, the noblest, the most generous love of her nature upon man at his fervent entreaty, would not deem herself debased forever, cheated, fit for life no longer, when with words like Harrison Fairleigh's upon his shameless lips, he showed her that her god whom she worshipped was but a loathsome demon, tempting her to depths of unutterable infamy?

After this, either revenge or death!

Barry thought no longer of revenge. Ah, no! Her heart had died within her; revenge needs life, fierce vitality, to nurture it!

As she had sat exhausted upon a bench near one of the park entrances, a policeman had come to her, saying, respectfully enough, but significantly:

"Madame, shall I get you a carriage?"

She had roused herself then, to observe that it was nearly seven o'clock, and that the park was deserted and night deepening.

"Thanks!" said she, in a quiet, dull way. "I shall walk."

She passed out, crossed Eighth Avenue, and, taking Seventieth Street, rapidly disappeared.

"Looks badly," muttered the policeman, taking up his march again. "She was as white as a ghost!"

She looked all along the quiet streets—every door shut—no shelter for her! She looked up to the cold, violet sky—the doors of heaven were like the doors of earth—locked against her! She muffled her stricken face, and ran down toward the river.

As its chill breath came up to meet her, and she felt it on her burning brow, she uttered an inarticulate cry.

Rest lay in its cold bosom—ah, how near!

She quickened her steps.

At that moment Something laid hold of her skirts and dragged her back. She stopped and looked round. Not a soul visible—nothing!

"Feverish delusions!" muttered she, and sprang on again.

The strong smell of tar came to her nostrils, with the noisome odors of shipping and river mud; she saw the masts and ruddy lights about the margin, and caught the smooth glisten of the water beyond.

"I wonder if he is dead, and if I shall meet him before God right now!" thought Barry, and she flew over the slippery pavement.

And again Something laid hold on her floating skirts and held her back.

She looked about; she put down her hand and shook her robe. No one had touched her; nothing was near her.

She put both of her shaking hands to her forehead and began to moan.

"I am mad—mad—mad! God won't judge me now for this last sin. He'll know my brain was turned."

She staggered on and reached the river's brink, at a quiet place shut in by a crazy wooden fence. A shadow black as ink lay on the water here, cast from the hull of a vessel at the next wharf, and although there was the hum of voices all around, and the glare of the low taverns and dance-houses across the street, neither voice nor light intruded here.

Barry Pomeroy leaned over the black water.

"You let me love him, God," she muttered in bitter reproach; "and you let him do this to me. You've made it impossible for me to live here any longer; now let me get into another world. I don't know which, and I don't much care. This one is about as terrible as any you've created."

With these fearful words upon her lips, she was just poising herself for the fatal leap, when, for the third time, that mysterious Something laid tight hold upon her, and tore her back from the black verge of suicide.

She gazed about wildly. Nothing, nothing to be seen!

An awful panic seized her; the flesh of her crept; the hair upon her head stood upright.

She flung herself upon a heap of loose stones and rubbish, panting, ready to die with supernatural horror.

And then she seemed to hear two voices speaking close beside her, and the first was her own. It said:

"*I'd kill myself if I didn't hope to be even with him some day.*"

And the other was Barb's. It answered:

"*No, no! You wouldn't be let do that. If your*

5

mother is a good woman, her prayers would drag you back again!"

* * * * * * *

"Oh, great God!" shivered Barry. "Is mother praying for me? Then I dare not try to die! Cruel, cruel Creator, I will live, then; but I tell Thee this: if Thou hast not avenged me already, I will only live to avenge myself!"

CHAPTER VIII.

IT was about nine o'clock of the night when Barry alighted from a street cab at Mrs. Fairleigh's door. The footman who opened the door expressed his relief at her appearance.

"They've been out searching for you ever since Mr. Fairleigh was brought home: Mrs. Fairleigh and young Mr. Fairleigh are in a sad way about you, miss."

"Tell them I'm safe," said Barry, and immediately passed on to her room.

Harrison Fairleigh was not killed, then!

As she laid aside her torn and draggled clothing, the unearthly glitter of her eyes might have daunted the bravest heart, and yet how soft and gentle grew that livid face of hers when Mrs. Fairleigh hurried in to clasp her in her arms, breathing joyful thanksgiving that she was unhurt!

"But where were you, dear? You must have passed a terrible time!" exclaimed she, taking the cold face between her soft hands and gazing into it with eager questioning. "Harrison has suffered the keenest anxiety about you ever since he was brought home, poor fellow; if he had not been really too much shaken to stand on his feet, he would not have rested a moment until he had found you."

"When the horses ran away I sprang out, and was stunned by the shock," said Barry, in measured tones. "It was a long time before I thought of leaving the park, and then I was too bewildered to take the right direction home. However, no harm came to me, and I'm quite myself now; don't worry about me at all, dear Mrs. Fairleigh. How is Harrison?"

"Not badly hurt, I hope," answered Mrs. Fairleigh, cheerfully. "There are no fractures, but he must lie still for a day or two. The horses fetched up at length against a wall, and one of them was killed on the spot, poor animal; Harrison was dashed out with great violence, and was picked up insensible, and cared for in the nearest drug store. Then he came home to me. I am so glad that he did not go to the hotel instead. He has been so uneasy about you that I could not soothe him. Marah, dear, you must have both been very much absorbed in conversation to let the horses run away," added the lady, with a searching glance.

Barry cast down her eyes modestly.

"Yes, we were exchanging confidences on a very interesting subject," said she, "and in his enthusiasm Harrison dropped the reins.   No, no; you misunderstand," she added, quickly, as Mrs. Fairleigh, with a bright smile of triumph, made a movement as if to embrace her, "*I* was not the heroine of Mr. Fairleigh's romance."

"Marah!" gasped Mrs. Fairleigh, "you don't mean to tell me——"

"I can tell you nothing," interposed Barry, taking the soft old hand in hers with a graceful tenderness. "Harrison will, no doubt, tell you all himself."

Mrs. Fairleigh looked puzzled and disappointed.

"My dear," said she, presently, "I am forgetting my orders.   Harrison insists upon seeing you the first moment you can go to him, that he may assure himself that you have suffered no harm from his folly, as he calls it."

Barry paled a little, but being fully dressed, and having no excuse ready, she said, without the slightest appearance of embarrassment:

"Oh, I shall certainly obey! I shall go now;" and down she went forthwith to the parlor, where Harrison lay groaning upon the sofa.

He turned his ghastly face as she came in so coolly and calmly with his mother, and a cold perspiration broke out on his forehead.

"I want to speak to Marah," he said, hoarsely. "Only a few words, Marah; I owe you some apology, you know," he added, with a sickly attempt at a laugh, "for giving you such a scare."

Mrs. Fairleigh stole out, hope in her smiling eyes.

Barry went near the sofa, and stood with dark gaze fastened upon the writhing young man.

"Barry!" he burst forth, feverishly, "can you ever, *ever* forget this second insult? I don't defend my conduct—you see I've suffered for it pretty dearly, and serves me rightly; but what are broken bones or the loss of a dozen blood-horses to the loss of you? I see too clearly what a blind beast I was ever to hope to win you by any but the regular way; and, confound it! it's too late to try that now."

The loss of a horse comparable for one moment with the eternal loss of a woman! Was this the man she was ready an hour ago to drown herself for? Barry's lip curled with ungovernable contempt, but she merged the curl into a pathetic droop, and veiled her scintillating orbs with pathetically dropped eyelashes.

"O Barry!" entreated the victim of his own selfishness, "if you knew how passionately I love you, you would forgive me. I've been almost frantic about you ever since that wretched accident; a thousand times I heartily wished I had been dashed in pieces instead of Giaour, fearing you would never come back."

He groaned again with physical as well as mental pain, and feebly stretched out his hand to the glass of water at his side.

Barry swept forward, sank on her knees, and passing her beautiful arm under his head, placed the glass to his lips, and, with a smile enough to make one's brain whirl with pleasure, bade him drink.

"Trouble yourself no more," said she, in velvet accents. "Love prompted your fault—true love forgives it. If I must lose you so soon, Harrison"--a peculiar expression flashed over her well-ordered face, as if some restless fiend had peeped out—"so soon, my dear, I sha'n't embitter our last hours together. In a month Katherine Hendrick will claim your duty. Till then I hold you mine."

Harrison, hearing this wild instance of woman's devotion, felt a warm glow of exultant satisfaction steal over him, even while he laughed mightily in the secret recesses of his worldly-wise heart over its mad and fatal folly.

"Done!" said he, grasping her with greedy hands, and wasting not a thought on the ruinous consequences to her. "Till marriage parts us, we belong to each other. Kiss me, Barry."

Obedient, she bent her blushing lips to his, but long,

long he remembered the mystic thrill of unreasoning
terror which ran through every fibre of his being at
their burning touch

*　　*　　*　　*　　*　　*　　*　　*

"Ah, come in, Barb; you're cold, ar'n't you? Miserable day."

"Yes, Barry, it is snowing some, but I ran all the
way here in such a hurry that I'm as warm as toast.
You didn't come this morning to tell me about the
drive, after all."

"No; we met with a disagreeable accident which
put a summary stop to marriage proposals; besides
which, a new feature made its appearance not exactly
conducive to comfortable love-making."

"Mercy, Barry! how queerly you do talk! And
now I see you clear, how queerly you look! Is—is it
all gone to smash, dear Barry?"

"Good little woman, don't worry over it—I don't.
I'm resigned, perfectly. Yes, my hopes in that direction have all gone—as you put it—to smash. My
cavalier is engaged to another lady, 'fairer and better
than I,' as Joaquin Miller has it. Ha! ha! A millionaire's daughter, my child—worth thousands!
What would you have? A year ago I was milking
cows!"

"Don't, Barry! You don't speak in earnest, I
know; this is all bitter chaff, you couldn't smile with

them white lips of yours if you let your real feelings speak. Mr. Fairleigh has played the villain, and I know you too well to believe you are going to take it as quietly as this. Oh, my dear! my dear! tell me everything, and let me at least cry for you!"

"There's nothing more to tell, except that in the heat of the discussion he let the horses run off. I jumped out and found my way home by one road, and he was dashed out, and brought home hurt, by another."

"Is he here—under the same roof with you?"

"He is."

"And you intend to stay here?"

"Yes, and to assist at his nuptials. Ah! ha! ha!"

"Oh, don't laugh, Barry!"

"And don't you cry, Barb. There's nothing worth crying over. All is going merry as a marriage bell!"

"I never saw you so hard, so—so *terrible*, Barry. What are you going to do?"

"To study how to live comfortably without the inconvenience of feeling. There, there, don't wear the subject threadbare ; let's drop it."

"No, dear Barry, I can't drop it. You are not like yourself, and I'm afraid of you. I'd rather see you as you used to be, ramping and raging—I knew what to dread then, but now—now—for my sake—for your *mother's sake*, beware where your evil heart leads you!"

"Stop! mention my mother's name to me again, and you'll never see me more. Let me go my way, Barbara, and you go yours; we are not likely to agree well henceforth."

"You tell me that, Barry! Oh, my heart! what is she going to do?"

"To bear the cross which God has put upon me with a quiet spirit, and to thank Him for it, as the palpable means of my salvation."

"My darling, you scoff, but He is very sorry for you just now."

"Enough, Barb, I can't stay with you to-day, because I think it my duty to practise the sweet graces of a forgiving spirit, and to crucify the flesh with its affections and lusts, by devoting myself to the amusement of mine adversary who has smitten me so sorely. Don't come to see me again, Barb, until you've made up your mind to let me bear this my own way."

And so they part, Barry to sweep down in her lustrous robes to the sullying presence of the man who would destroy her; Barb to creep out into the whirling snow, with her little hands clasped and the sobbing cry upon her lips:

"Sweet Jesus! melt her heart!   Sweet Jesus! melt her heart!"

*   *   *   *   *   *   *   *

"So my son is engaged to Miss Hendrick!" exclaimed Mrs. Fairleigh, eyeing her adopted daughter wistfully. "And he has told you all about it.   Well, well, she is a beautiful girl, and a highly accomplished one; I hope they may be happy together."

"Amen!" murmured Barry, looking up from her delicate silken fancy work.   "They love each other so devotedly, that they deserve to be happy—at least so I gather from Harrison's enthusiastic descriptions of her devotion, beauty, and worth."

"We must go and call upon the bride-elect.   We should have gone before had we known of this engagement.   I wonder why Harrison did not announce it at once."

"Perhaps he felt the subject too sacred to be discussed before outsiders," said Barry, with an innocent smile.   "I know if I loved any one with the reverential idolatry which he lavishes upon her, I should feel a certain hesitation about airing my passion or analyzing it, even to my mother, if I had one."

Mrs. Fairleigh dropped the subject; it was difficult to carry it on with such a tyro in love matters as this inexperienced maiden; besides which, it was a painful subject to her, and caused her some uneasiness.

It was very singular, very, that Harrison should have delayed so long announcing his engagement to a lady to whom he was to be married in a month. She was an unexceptionable match in a worldly point of view, and he was none the less eligible; they had been engaged for several months already, and had appeared openly together in Paris and London, why then this uncomfortable secrecy, and this unpleasant ignoring of his only relative? Above all, why should he have sedulously concealed the matter from his mother and her adopted daughter, for a whole week after his arrival home, while the bride's friends were busily engaged in preparations for the ceremony, and were doubtless marvelling much at the unwonted delay of his relatives in recognizing the connection about to be formed?

"No time is to be lost, Marah; we must call this afternoon," said the ruffled lady. "If we had known we should have gone down to the steamer to meet Miss Hendrick. What must she think of our negligence?"

Miss Hendrick had crossed the ocean under the protection of a wealthy New York lady acquaintance in the same steamer with her betrothed, Mr. Fairleigh, and her cousin, Mr. Roscoe; indeed, she had spent many months in almost daily companionship with the gentleman who was about to claim her hand, having travelled with the Roscoe party, of which he and she formed members, all over the European continent, not to speak of the gay season in Paris, and the familiar communion afforded by the voyage across the ocean. She ought to understand his nature well, if any woman could!

About half an hour subsequently the two ladies were being ushered into the reception-room of the elegant white marble mansion of Baron Hendrick, where the baroness and her daughter sat in state, receiving.

A word or two about this rival of Barbara Pomeroy's.

A pampered baby—an indulged child—a selfish woman.

Beautiful? Yes, as beautiful as if an Angelo's hand had sculptured her, and yet a Greater than Angelo created that lovely face, and it wanted loveliness.

Soul, there was none; gentleness, humility, maiden tenderness, were gems that all her wealth could not buy Katharine Hendrick.

And men raved over her "rust-red locks," twined in burnished masses round her queenly head; over her pure visage, rendered haughty, said they, only by the delicate aquiline of the nose—for the mouth was small and red as rose-leaves, and the eyes were humid hazel;—over her long neck, white as sea-foam, her sylphine figure, stately only in its regal poise; in fact, over all the outward clothing of the small, chill heart and dwarfed soul which made the real woman.

Her mother? Well, there are thousands such—tens of thousands. Filled with vaunting pride of wealth and station, with vaulting ambition, never to be satiated, superficial observers, measuring all men by the length of their purses. Oh, she was not the mother, I tell you, to yearn over the future of her one fair child with brooding anxiety and tender prayers—of far greater consequence to her was the precedence of her haughty Katherine in society than mere vulgar heart-ease!

Having made the acquaintance of their specially interesting visitors, the four sat down to take stock of each other, and while the elder ladies glanced with intense curiosity at the younger ladies, these fastened their eyes upon each other with a keen scrutiny scarcely disguised. And as each felt the power of the other's wondrous beauty, one little lightning flash of scorn darted from each pair of eyes, and a faint defiant smile curved each perfect lip.

"Miss Leith is—a—your adopted daughter?" drawled Baroness Hendrick, folding her large white hands in her silken lap.

"Yes; a charming girl, and a great source of pleas-ure to me; but let us talk of your lovely child, she is perfectly radiant. It seems heartless to steal her from you, you must love her so dearly," answered Mrs. Fairleigh, who was quite moved by the sight of her son's choice, and felt her warm heart going out to her already.

Meantime, Miss Hendrick was saying, in a voice like some sweet silver instrument:

"You were long in coming to see me, but now you've come, I can't be angry with you. I daresay you were so glad to have Harrison back that you could not be troubled making formal calls."

To which Barry answered, perceiving distinctly the little shaft of jealousy shot at her, and glorying in her power to sting:

"Mrs. Fairleigh never makes formal calls, and does not consider this one; but, as you say, we were very glad to have Harrison back, and he was so glad to be at home again that we could scarcely get him to con-sent to our leaving him to come to-day."

For a moment Miss Hendrick sat mutely gazing at her as astonished as if she had struck her in the face; but the bold eyes met hers unflinchingly, and the splendid woman before her seemed to her, in that first instant of wondering terror, as strong, as hard, and as inaccessible as a tower.

"You never saw my *fiancé* before, did you?" demanded she, a strange quiver in her silver tones.

"Never before," answered Barry, with a cruel smile; "but I know him pretty well already, and he is such a finished courtier that I do not wonder in the least at his victory over your heart. He has almost won my own, ha, ha! Really I envy you, Miss Hendrick."

"Ha! ha! ha!" laughed Katherine Hendrick, softly, while her flashing eyes said: "War to the death, Marah Leith!"

"Ha! ha! ha!" echoed Barry, as softly, while her taunting eyes took up the challenge.

CHAPTER IX.

ARRISON FAIRLEIGH was back in his hotel again, having quite recovered from the effects of his accident, and having nc excuse to stay longer under his mother's roof.

He had been wonderfully loth to leave, however; for once in his life he sincerely enjoyed the quietness and seclusion of Mrs. Fairleigh's home, and turned with an internal shudder of disgust to the fashionably fast life to be led in his hotel. But he had no excuse to stay, and Roscoe waited impatiently for his friend to rejoin him.

One morning, sauntering out to Madison Square to smoke a sulky cigar, and to muse uninterruptedly upon the tempting fascinations of—well, not exactly his bride-elect—he was stopped by a little vailed figure wrapped in a thick shawl, which rose from a seat at his approach.

"Mr. Harrison Fairleigh?" said she, interrogatively.

Her voice was tremulously sweet, fresh, and young, and the tip of a wind-blown tress of pale gold hair was visible under her veil. Harrison thought it would be interesting to stop, so he did so.

Had some wrinkled, helpless old woman slipped upon the frozen pavement and fallen at his feet, he would have passed on with a shrug and a muttered "Poor old mummy!" but this being, whom he firmly expected to beg some sort of assistance from him, was young and (he hoped) pretty, and on the whole, Harrison did not mind paying something for the pleasure of talking to a handsome woman.

"Yes, madam, that is my name," replied he, lifting his hat with his most easy grace. "Have I the honor of knowing you?" and he gazed hard at the black veil.

She drew it aside, exposing a delicate, small-featured countenance, with large misty blue eyes, and a pure, earnest expression.

"You don't know me," said she, quietly, "but I know you and *Barbara Pomeroy*."

He started, and a dark glow overspread his frowning face.

"You do!" exclaimed he, "and who are you?"

"Never mind that; I have watched for a chance of speaking to you unobserved, for several days."

"You must have something tremendous to say, or

you wouldn't freeze yourself hanging about here on that slim chance! Come, young lady, what *do* you want with me?"

For a few moments they walked under the leafless trees, side by side, in silence; Harrison casting side-glances at the sorrowful young face of the girl, and racking his brains to conjecture what she might have to communicate, while she walked on wrapped in thought.

Presently she turned to him, scanning him with a timid yet earnest air.

"You have done such harm to Barbara Pomeroy, that you've changed what, I am sure, was a good nature, into a vindictive and revengeful one. I don't know what to say to you about her, except to entreat you to leave her alone, and to beware of her." She stopped, tears rushed into her eyes, her gentle lips trembled. "I can't bear to speak so of Barry, for I love her very dearly," faltered she, "and it breaks my heart to see her so bitterly wronged that she should turn as hard as a rock."

Harrison listened in astonishment.

"Who are you?" he burst forth, "and how do you come to know all this girl's secrets?"

"I needn't tell you;" said she, firmly, "and you needn't ask her neither; I've no business to interfere in the matter, for I'm no relation to Barbara, but I love her too well to stand by and see her destroy herself for the sake of a man who isn't worth her love."

"Thank you! thank you!" said Harrison, satirically. "I perceive why you preserve an incognito; behind it you can say a good many things you would not venture upon else."

"You mistake," said she, with simple dignity. "I have no wish to reproach you; that would do no good; but I must save her from you, and from herself."

"I would advise you not to meddle," said Harrison, irritably. "Barbara and I can get along well enough, I dare say, without your assistance."

Her sweet blue eyes flashed upon him with a sudden loathing.

"What do you call 'getting along'?" said she.

"You want a definition?" laughed he, with a shrug of the shoulders. "Well, here's one that will suit your unsophisticated ear. Barbara and I have agreed to forget the past, forgive each other, and be friends for the future. That's pretty well on the square, isn't it?"

She did not heed his taunting manner or his mocking tone: her whole attention was fastened upon the true meaning of his words.

"You know, sir, that she loves you; you've made her say it often!" exclaimed she, in an agitated voice.

"And I've returned the compliment; so we're quits!" jeered he.

"How do you think she will bear your marriage with Miss Hendrick?" continued the young girl.

"As well, I dare say, as I shall," answered he, gnawing his flossy mustache impatiently. "I can't marry a country girl from Thunder Peak, you know——"

"*Thunder Peak!*" whispered the young girl to herself.

"And she's quite convinced of that by this time, and is far too sensible to throw up her comfortable home with my mother for any stupid sentiment regarding me."

"Oh, how you have mistaken her character!" cried the girl. "What a pitiful sham your love must be, when you could think her so shallow! Now listen, Mr. Fairleigh."

They paused close by the basin, under a stout tree which somewhat shielded them from the observation of the passers-by.

"I have often heard her threaten you with her vengeance because you insulted her at Thunder Peak; but these threats were nothing, meant nothing, I am sure, and would have proved mere idle words had you given your love to her honorably at last. But ever since that day you and she went out driving, I have trembled for her and for you. Oh! she is hard and bitter! I would rather see her dead than following the promptings of her own heart now! I don't know what she means to do, but I know she means to take a fearful revenge, and what I say to you is, Beware!—beware of Barbara Pomeroy!"

She uttered these last words in a raised and excited voice, retreating from him as she spoke; and with a slight parting wave of her hand, hurried away.

"What's all the mystery?" cried a laughing voice.

Harrison looked round with a whispered execration, to see his friend Roscoe almost at his elbow.

"'Beware of Barbara Pomeroy?' And who's Barbara Pomeroy? A very pretty little escapade, my gay Lothario!"

"Hang it!" muttered Harrison, completely covered with confusion, "who was to suppose you were dodging one?"

"Eh! 'Dodging?' No, no, Fairleigh, that's too bad!" remonstrated Roscoe, staring in some dismay at the visible perturbation of his friend. "I saw you strolling along in this confoundedly draughty place, with a nice-looking young lady beside you, and strolled after you, in the natural hope of sharing in a pleasant episode. You seemed so absorbed too——"

"And how much of our absorbing conversation did you overhear, may one know?" interrupted

Fairleigh with disagreeable defiance in his manner.

"Nothing, 'pon my word, but the words, 'Beware of Barbara Pomeroy.' There, you needn't cut up rusty about it; if you choose, I'll never again mention the mysterious Pomeroy. Only I'd advise you not to meet her in public parks, if your meetings are intended to be *sub rosa;* and, further, if they are *sub rosa*, I'd suggest the decency of breaking off with my cousin, Miss Hendrick, before you take up Miss Pomeroy."

Harrison glanced uneasily at the stern face of his friend, and burst out laughing.

"Bah! there's nothing in it—a mere bagatelle—never saw the young woman in my life before; was mistaken for another fellow by her—that's all!" cried he, volubly. "Don't take up the matter in that high-tragedy spirit, or I'll expire, I vow! Come on, let's spend the morning with Katherine."

But as they walked away, arm-in-arm, chatting merrily, an unwonted cloud lowered on each brow.

*   *   *   *   *   *   *

The wind blew moaningly around the lonely cottage at the foot of Thunder Peak, rattling the windows in their loose casements, and whistling drearily through the keyholes, like shivering spirits supplicating a shelter that bleak winter night. The snow lay knee-deep round the house, and a great drift ran right across the little garden where the rose of Sharon, and the magnolia and the lily-of-the-valley bloomed in summer time.

In the wide, old-fashioned kitchen, a ruddy fire flashed and flickered, showing the snow-white floor, the empty arm-chair, and the tall eight-day clock pointing with stout hand to the hour of twelve.

A door stood wide upon the kitchen, and now and again the rising flames gave a glimmering glimpse of old Richard West's sharp white face as it lay upon the pillow;—of his bony hands toiling ceaselessly upon the patchwork quilt, and of the wearily drooping figure of Mrs. Pomeroy seated at his bedside, with her face buried in her lap.

Midnight, alone with the dying, in the depths of the forest; the roads drifted impassable; an old woman, infirm before her time with sorrow and suspense. Ah! that was a fearful night!

Yes, Richard West was dying at last. Three days ago he was struck with paralysis as he sat in his elbow-chair, fiercely denouncing Barbara Pomeroy to her mother in words which touched her writhing heart like flame; and now he was sleeping his life away, his loud and stertorous breathing echoing through the hushed house, and mingling weirdly with the moan of the wind and the rattle of the case-ments.

No one had come near the house since, for the snow-storm had blocked the roads, and the nearest neighbor was miles away; the pantry was empty—when had its bare shelves ever held more than a day's provision at a time?—and poor old Mrs. Pomeroy, as she cowered there, shuddering with cold, felt faint and giddy from the want of food, and sometimes dozing, sometimes awake and praying, saw strange visions all around, and half thought them true.

And ever her husky, half-spoken and half-sobbed plaint was:

"Barry, Barry, come back to me! O dear Lord! bring Barry back to me!"

And at the strange sound of her hollow voice the airy shapes which peopled the dim air would all float close around her, holding out their shadowy arms, some with harps and some with crowns, but all with the faces of those she had loved and lost long, long ago; friends she had parted from, babies she had buried, brothers, sisters, husband—all beaming upon her with blessed smiles of welcome!

But she never could see among them the one she yearned for most, and so she would moan again:

"Barry, Barry, come back to me! O dear Lord! send Barry back to me!"

And at last a sweet, sweet ringing of bells came to her wondering ear, and she thought:

"They are ringing ·in heaven for me! O Barry! make haste!"

And the kitchen-door stole open, with a rush of bitter wind and a drift of needle-sharp snow; and, lifting her heavy head, she saw—oh, wonderful vision! —a tiny woman form, with face as angelic as face might be, and long, loose, bright hair blown back like a golden halo, and misty blue eyes brimming with tears—standing in the doorway, looking in.

But when she saw that it was not Barry yet, the weary mother moaned, weeping:

"Barry, Barry, come back to me! O dear Lord! bring Barry back to me!"

And a human voice said, brokenly:

"Just listen to this, Dr. Wayne! Oh, come in quick!"

And the little figure ran across the glimmering kitchen, and flung its arms, all snow-clad as they were, about the trembling old woman, murmuring over and over again in her gradually deafening ear:

"The dear Lord has sent me instead of your Barry to look after you, and to give you news of her!"

So, when the mother heard that, her joy struck her senseless in little Barb's faithful arms.

* * * * * *

A gala night at Baron Hendrick's.

Have we told you how Bernard Hendrick obtained

his title! Hush! it is one of the *on dits* only whispered—true, though, as the Ten Commandments. Bernard Hendrick began life as a tutor in private families; rose to be travelling tutor to a German gentleman of distinction; continued to rise until his charge was an archduke; learned some shady secret of his patron's; traded upon it so successfully that but two alternatives arrayed themselves before the illustrious victim—disgrace, or a title for his aspiring instructor. And so—Baron Hendrick retired to New York, a made man!

Everybody likes to be asked to the baroness's receptions; but catch her ask any but the very top of the cream of good society! Still, to-night the whole street is made lively by the roll of carriages and the continuous bang of unfolding carriage-steps, and reverberating double-knocks at the baron's grand entrance.

Quite a crowd of street Arabs and sewing-girls have collected, intent on enjoying their part of the spectacle, that is, the passing of wondrously habited ladies and gentlemen over the velvet carpet spread under an awning from the curbstone to the marble steps.

The baroness is giving a fancy ball on the eve of her daughter's marriage; it is Miss Hendrick's last appearance, and brilliant indeed is the assembly gathered to do her honor.

Statesmen, poets, literary stars, princes (of the purse, not of the blood), notables of every species; in they pass, with their ladies on their arms, a constant stream of fantastic figures.

The usual magnificence of appointment awaits the brilliant throng inside; the usual concourse of gay, grotesque, and majestic figures incident to a *bal de fantaisie*, fills the baron's halls; the usual grand reception by the host and hostess, under a perfect arcade of flowers; the usual soft, entrancing strains of orchestral music, furnishing a delicate accompaniment to the hum of the masquer's voices.

There are many distinguished toilets there, at which all eyes glance with admiration, while numerous guesses at the identity of the wearers pass from lip to lip. But the two who are entering the grand drawing-room by different doors at this moment, elicit a murmur of applause which not even the general hum and the sound of the distant music can cover.

Who that has visited Booth's Theatre during the winter of 1875 can fail to recognize that tall, queenly figure, clad in white satin, seeded with diamonds, with court-train of brilliant green velvet and royal cloak of purple edged with ermine—with Britannia's crown upon her red-brown locks, and Britannia's sceptre in her slender hand?

Or that gliding figure entering at the opposite door

in long, limp robes of white, with rich dark hair dishevelled, and trailing dark cloak, half enshrouding her white form as she advances with unsteady gait and drooping attitude?

Queen Elizabeth and Amy Robsart!

The murmur grew to a perfect round of applause, as the two masquers advanced to meet each other—Queen Elizabeth, with quick and haughty step—Amy Robsart slowly, tremblingly.

The group of cavaliers, attired in the rich old English garb, who accompanied her Majesty, hurried after her, uttering audible exclamations of surprise at the apparition of the injured Amy. One of them, on whose arm she had entered, said, nervously:

"Now, who is this that has guessed your Majesty's intention to appear to-night?"

"Ah, Leicester!" said the queen between her teeth, "we fear thou knowest too well!"

They met. With one accord the throng stood silent, looking on with amused interest.

Amy Robsart knelt at Queen Elizabeth's feet, and throwing back her cloak, revealed the sumptuous arms and shoulders of a Juno.

"Justice! justice, your Majesty!" she cried in ringing accents; and at that cry there was a stir in the throng, and an aged Mother Superior, leaning on the shoulder of a white-veiled nun, pushed their way almost into the clear space occupied by the queen and her train. "My lover has forsaken me in order to marry a richer lady than I. Justice, O Queen! Command him to return to me!"

The slight, proud figure of her majesty towered over the suppliant in such a menacing attitude, and with such a visible quiver running through it, that the startled interest with which all had listened to the pathetic—nay, the anguished—accents of Amy Robsart, deepened into speechless wonder; and when the queen burst forth with a shrill cry of wrath, followed by a torrent of furious words, not a rustle could be heard in the great reception-room.

"Ay! And who art thou?" cried Queen Elizabeth, touching the kneeling maiden with her satin slipper, with a gesture so bitterly disdainful that consternation seized the onlookers. "And what dost thou here, thou insolent country wench, with thy shameless tears and supplications? What do we know of thy faithless gallant? If thou hadst not wit enough to keep him, how darest thou bring thy 'plaint to us? Can we turn men's hearts to that which is beneath them?"

"Be patient, your Majesty," murmured the courtier beside her; "this is but a mummery to make you smile. The maiden does but jest. Command me to lead her aside."

"Does she but jest?" cried the queen, looking at him fiercely, if her small clenched hands and quivering tones indicated her mood aright. "Methinks we see some meaning in her jesting neither palatable to us nor safe for her and thee."

"Your Majesty is cruel!" murmured Leicester, with such well-dissembled perturbation that one might swear the farce was all reality. "Why should your Majesty connect this suppliant with me?"

"O Leicester! Leicester! Dost thou think us blind and deaf?" cried she, in rising fury. "Have we no eyes to note the frequent absences of our truant knight? Have we no ears to hear the rumors of his constant intrigues with milking-maids and such like mud-made deities?"

At this the kneeling Amy Robsart raised her head, and, in spite of her mask, the blaze of her eyes was seen and marvelled at by many of the baron's guests.

"One word, your Majesty," said she, in a choked voice. "My lover, who has deserted me, still holds me in his heart, and deems me nobler far than the proudest and richest lady in the land!"

"Maid, thou art mad!" interposed Leicester, in a horrified tone, and stooping, he seized her by the arm to drag her, unbidden, from the royal presence.

"Ha, traitor! Dost thou forestall our commands!" uttered the queen, furiously; and, with a spring, she seized Amy by the other arm, hissing out:

"Speak the truth! Is this man your lover?"

There was an instant's deep hush, for now there was not one in the room who was not convinced this was a drama in real life, and no preconcerted piece of acting; but in that instant a new character appeared upon the scene.

The bent, black-draped figure of the Mother Superior came forward trembling; with one wrinkled hand she held back her shrouding vail, and the other she placed on Amy Robsart's head.

"*My daughter!*" said she, in tones that thrilled every heart that had a spark of human pity in it.

Amy Robsart sprang to her feet with a shriek that rang out wildly and terribly in the intense stillness, shaking off the hands of the queen and Leicester as she did so. For a few moments she gazed as if transfixed into the worn, deathly-pale face of the old woman, whose features worked with convulsive emotion, then she flashed round upon Leicester and looked upon him in the same breathless way, then upon Queen Elizabeth, who was looking on in an attitude of haughty disdain.

And when her eyes met hers, Amy Robsart burst into a peal of taunting laughter.

"My Lord Leicester was right," said she, "this was

but a jest—a play meaning nothing, I have no lover; 'twas but a device to escape the convent, to which this holy abbess would consign me."

Uttering these words, she was turning away with a laughing reverence, when again the feeble and tremulous voice of the old woman was heard:

"Oh, Barbara Pomeroy, come back to me!"

Leicester uttered an audible hiss, an execration bitten in the middle, and made a stride forward, but at that moment the little nun ran to her, saying, with urgent entreaty:

"Here I am, dear mother! Here I am! Let these gay folks go. Barbara Pomeroy will never forsake thee."

Still the old woman stood with one hand stretched toward Amy Robsart, who, leaning lightly upon the arm which Leicester had offered her, with an imperious gesture, exclaimed, audibly:

"Excellently well acted! Only the holy mother mistakes me for some one else," and with this she obeyed the urgent movement of Leicester, and swept away with him, laughing and chatting.

The Mother Superior gazed after her with such an anguished and despairing wonder, that again that ungovernable thrill ran through all hearts; paler and paler she grew, till, with great tears coursing down her withered cheeks, and her poor faded lips quivering convulsively—enough to wring the heart of a Nero—she sank back in the young nun's arms in a swoon.

CHAPTER X.

EICESTER hurried Amy Robsart through *salon* and corridor, until he found a deserted parlor in the upper story, where, the gas turned down and the furniture in some confusion, it was evident that no guests were expected to intrude.

He locked the door, turned on the gas, tore off his mask, and confronted Amy, who, with her mask also in her hand, stood in defiant silence, awaiting his pleasure.

"Barry, how *dared* you!" hissed Harrison Fairleigh, scowling like a demon.

"Now, now, what have I done next?" cried she, flashing her bewildering eyes at him, and pouting most alluringly.

But he was neither to be glamoured nor tempted yet.

"Are you bent on ruining me?" muttered he.

"Oh! ha, ha! No, Harrison—oh, no!" laughed she, wildly.

"You—you Jezebel, I sometimes think you capable of murdering me in some of your mad moods!" exclaimed the young blood, staring at his uncanny prize in some anxiety. "What could have possessed you to wear that dress, of all dresses in the world, when you knew that Katherine was dressing as Queen Elizabeth, and insisted on me appearing as Leicester?"

"Wasn't it a bright idea, and so naturally acted!" exclaimed Barry, with a fearful gusto. "Once I thought she was going to strike me. O—h! how jealous she is of me!" and her eyes shone like two diamonds.

"Barry," quoth the too irresistible gallant, not ill-pleased, "you've no business to make her so jealous. You're always at it. I believe there will be some mischief yet between you, for Katherine is just as much in love with me as you are."

And he stroked his elegant mustache with considerable complacency, feeling inclined to chuckle over the infatuation of the two finest women he had ever yet seen.

"But you ar'n't as much in love with her as you are with me," retorted Barry, her full lips wreathed with a reckless smile. "You are always bored with her; you are never, never with me! Are you now, Harrison?" and she leaned toward him in a perfect abandon of Delilah-like witchery.

"Never!" breathed the man, yielding himself up wholly to her spell. "You make me forget everything in the universe but yourself. Oh, Barry, I don't think I can give you up!"

"Nor I you!" responded she, with a passionate intensity. "I love—I love—I love you! I want no happiness but you; I want no life unshared with you! The day you give me up for her, I swear I will not outlive it!"

"Hush! hush!" cried he, in horror. "You curdle my blood. You would not give me that agony to bear through life? Barry, speak! Don't look at me in that awful way! Do you intend to take revenge upon me by killing yourself and leaving me to die of remorse?"

"No," smiled Barry; and then she hid her too expressive face upon his shoulder, and a little shiver crept through her. She looked up anon, blanched and solemn.

"Harrison," said she, in a hard voice, "you've made a terrible wreck of me. I used to be a good girl, as far as high principles and truthfulness were concerned. That was before I knew you. Look at me now! For your sake I have denied my own mother!"

She hid her face again, shuddering convulsively. Harrison glared.

"Great Heaven!" muttered he, recoiling, "was that old woman actually your mother? And—and —you could pass her without acknowledging her! Why, Barbara, you've acted like a monster! I thought that part, at least, was all farce; but—her poor old mother came to take her home, and she denied that she knew her! Oh, you miserable girl, after that you'd do anything!"

"Yes, anything!" hissed Barry on his breast. "Talk of moral deterioration! Here it is—innocence and truth transformed into imposture and brutal cruelty! Here it is!" and she beat her breast with her clenched hand, looking heavenward with a wild, defiant smile carved upon her bloodless lips.

Harrison Fairleigh felt a stab of conscience for the first time in regard to his dealings with this girl. Well he knew the tender bloom of that purity which he had brushed off her character with his base love; it had been the charm which first enslaved him. It was gone now, and in its place had come a wild demoniac fascination which charmed him yet more with its subtle spell; but, alas! look close, and how black was the spirit which had been so radiant in its guileless simplicity!

Yes, for once conscience spoke to Harrison Fairleigh in whispers which stabbed him with stinging pain. And because he acknowledged that this sadly erring woman was the creature of his own making, he yielded yet more wholly to her royal sway, dimly dreaming of compensation.

He gathered her back to his heart—he had never in his life held Katherine there—and he smoothed back her rich, unbound tresses with tender hand.

"My poor Barry!" murmured he with a break in his voice, "I've been but a curse to you ever since you knew me. No use now to regret the part I've played—regrets are but mockery. Guiltless as we are, in one respect, we are traitors to Katherine Hendrick in our hearts. I am as bad, I am worse than you are, for it was I who wooed and wooed your unsuspicious love, only to madden you with the sight of it lying sullied under my feet when won. On my head lies the guilt of your deterioration ; for my sake you have become what you are. Oh, my poor, poor girl, what can I do now but crown my madness by one last act which will make the world ring with derisive laughter ?—and let it ring ! "

"You mean——" panted Barry, a flame on each cheek—her eyes ablaze.

He folded her in his arms, and whispered what he meant in her tingling ear !

*   *   *   *   *   *

Meanwhile the excitement caused in the drawing-room by the brilliantly-acted episode of Queen Elizabeth and Amy Robsart, was forgotten in the arrival of some specially illustrious guests, and when the baroness had again leisure to turn her jewelled eye-glass upon the spot where she had last seen the fainting Mother Superior being lifted in the arms of several of the gentlemen, Amy Robsart and Leicester sweeping out at the door arm-in-arm, and Queen Elizabeth standing among her courtiers as if struck to stone, not one of the actors of the late scene was visible

The baroness was decidedly ill-pleased.

What was the meaning of that horribly natural delineation of jealousy and fury ? Why had Katherine seemed so uncomfortably in earnest ? And who was this who had appeared in the character of Amy Robsart, ruffling Katherine's imperious and jealous temper almost to the point of a disgraceful exhibition ? Then who was the mysterious old lady whose feelings had overcome her so inopportunely, and the young nun who had supported her ? Not guests invited by her she could have sworn. She summoned a gentleman, and on his arm made the tour of all her apartments, with the determination of solving these successive mysteries, and with but poor success. Not a trace could she discover of Leicester, whom she knew to be her daughter's *fiancé*, or of his companion,

Amy Robsart. The Mother Superior and the nun had vanished as mysteriously as they had appeared, and she could only find Katherine, lying on the carpet in her own dressing-room, her laces torn, her dress disordered, and the foam of an ungovernable fury upon her bitten, bleeding lips.

Madame the baroness whipped the door shut just in time to prevent the Austrian Minister, who had escorted her thither, from witnessing this appalling spectacle.

"Katherine! Katherine! rise instantly, I command you!" exclaimed she, hurrying to the prostrate form, and endeavoring by main strength to drag her from the floor.

Katherine shook her off, uttering only a growl like a young tigress, and burying her face in the thick, soft carpet.

Baroness Hendrick glared aghast, her empurpled visage paling; then she threw her massive form into the nearest chair, and applied her diamond-encrusted vinaigrette to her nostrils.

Horrors! Here was Katherine in one of her tempers, three hundred people congregated downstairs to witness her conquests and triumphs for the last time before she married the wealthy Harrison Fairleigh, best *parti* of the season. What was to be done?

She invoked all her gods to help her in this dire strait, and began in the supplicatory vein:

"Dear child, be calm! compose yourself, for my sake—for all our sakes! What will they think downstairs?"

"Think!" shrieked Katherine, shrilly, rising to her knees, with convulsed face and rich hair streaming where she had torn it down with reckless hands. "Let them think the truth—that I am defied and taunted in my own father's house by my bridegroom's latest conquest, Marah Leith!" and she sprang to her feet, her magnificent robes floating wide around her, and, gritting her teeth and tearing her hair, she passed in rapid haste to and fro, her ungovernable passion and haughty beauty lending her no small resemblance to some insulted queen.

The baroness tried the soothing vein.

"Marah Leith! Nonsense! You insult yourself by putting yourself in the same category with her! And how do you know she was Marah Leith?"

"Know her! I would know her among ten thousand!" cried Katherine, stopping to grind her slender, satin slipper into the carpet. "The wretch! don't you see how she lures and wiles him on to neglect me and lavish all his attentions upon her? Have you not always seen this from the first day we met them walking together? Oh!" screamed Katherine, wringing her hands, "what does he care for me beside her, with her daring, demoniac beauty—the base vagrant, whom nobody ever heard of till his idiot mother picked her up from some charitable asylum! Nothing—nothing! Oh, mother, I could shoot them both as they gaze into each other's eyes in my very presence! I could laugh to see the blood flow from their treacherous hearts!"

"Don't rave now, you'll only be ashamed of yourself to-morrow!" urged the mother, who, accustomed to the various moods of her high-spirited daughter, seldom felt any alarm, except, as in the present instance, when exposure seemed to threaten her. "Think a minute how tame it would be to lose such a match on account of a nobody, as you justly call her."

Katherine's delicate face kindled up with indomitable resolution.

"Lose him! Ah, no, I shall not lose him!" said she, with a fierce quiver in her soft tones. "You are wise to remind me; an exhibition of jealousy would only drive him from me; his heart is in the balance; one foolish word and look from me and she will win it and him! Mother, I am calm; help me here, where is my crown! Ah! how ghastly white I am!"

She gazed mournfully at herself in the great mirror, then seized a rouge-box and dashed some living color on her bloodless face, and called a faint smile to her quivering lips. Meanwhile, the baroness, with much secret thanksgiving, rearranged her *toilette* with anxious care, doing her best in passing to soothe her agitation and infuse as much pride and defiance into her mind as should support her through the rest of the evening.

Quarter of an hour afterward Queen Elizabeth, sailing into the dancing-hall on the arm of an inconceivably grotesque satyr, beheld Leicester leaning with folded arms and moody attitude against a pillar. She flashed a lightning glance round the hall for Amy Robsart, but her scrutiny was interrupted by the approach of a magnificent Mary Queen of Scots, who, making a splendid court bow, said, in Marah Leith's voice:

"And do we at last meet our royal sister on common ground? We salute thee, Virgin Queen, mistress of legions—wife to none!"

"And we salute thee, unhappy Queen!" retorted Katherine. "We read thy dire future, when, stripped of youth and flatterers, thou shalt pine alone and die detested!"

CHAPTER XI.

POOR little Barb, how bitterly she wept as, with Mrs. Pomeroy lying insensible in the corner of the carriage, and one of the gentlemen who had assisted to carry her out of the baron's house supporting her heavy head, she returned to her quiet boarding-house defeated, heartbroken !

She had been so sure that Barry had but to see her mother to melt and fly to her breast; and, lo! what unutterable cruelty had she discovered in Barry's heart ! She had turned with a lying laugh from the mother who had stretched out her yearning hands to her; from the mother whose hair was whiter, whose face was more furrowed, whose form was more bent because of her desertion !

Yes, fond little Barb's cherished plan had failed miserably, after all the trouble she had been at to carry it into effect.

She had nursed Mrs. Pomeroy back to a remnant of

her once vigorous strength—she and patient Hugh Wayne. In the interim Richard West had passed away and been buried in the frozen ground—no harder than his granite heart—and no hoarded treasure nor any will having been discovered, the house and farm were put up for sale.

Then Barb and Hugh had brought Mrs. Pomeroy to New York, and Barb had for the last time implored Barry to leave her life of imposture and return to her mother, only to be icily bidden to hold her peace, or see herself the cause of such fearful doings as should make her ears tingle when she heard them.

"There is but one chance more," thought devoted Barb. "If she knew what I had done she would never let her mother have an opportunity of seeing her. I will bring them face to face at the fancy ball at Baroness Hendrick's; her natural feelings will be touched at last, and before them all she will confess her deceit and repent of it."

This experiment failing, what hindered Barb from declaring the truth before them all, with her own lips?

There is one bright gem which the lowliest may possess as well as the noblest, and that is—honor.

Barry had confided her history to Barb. Barb would die before she would betray her confidence.

No, Barb could never expose her erring friend;

she might warn her and others; she might try in her simple way to combine circumstances so as to force Barry to confess and repent; but to betray her never once occurred to that loyal soul.

And what now was to be done?

Look at the stricken mother, but lately drawn back from the yawning grave for this cruel blow to be struck at her by her Barry's hand!

Barb's sorrowful thoughts were interrupted by the voice of the baroness's guest, a handsome, dark-haired young gentleman, whose rich violet velvet doublet and glittering orders were but half concealed beneath his ample cloak. He had been one of the courtiers in Queen Elizabeth's train.

"Young lady," said he, leaning forward to gaze curiously into her tear-wet face, "have I not seen you once before? Is not your name Barbara Pomeroy?"

"Yes," answered Barb, timidly. "Where do you think you have seen me?"

The gentleman's handsome face seemed very cold and stern by the glimmering light of the carriage lamps, as he replied, briefly:

"In Madison Park, a fortnight since, talking to Mr. Harrison Fairleigh."

Barb started perceptibly, and returned his piercing gaze in silent agitation.

"Miss Pomeroy, I wish to be frank with you," said he, in an authoritative manner, which almost took her breath away. "Mr. Fairleigh is to be married to Miss Hendrick in ten days. I am Miss Hendrick's cousin, and I have a right to ask this question. Have you any claim upon Mr. Fairleigh?"

Barb, just about to exclaim, indignantly, "No!" paused in bewilderment. A host of future possibilities rushed into her mind. Should she disclaim all knowledge of Harrison Fairleigh, how could she account for the conversation which this gentleman had doubtless overheard pass between her and Barry's selfish lover? His suspicions would inevitably point at Marah Leith—the other Barbara Pomeroy; his interference might hurry Barry on to the execution of her mysterious purpose. No wonder the little sewing-girl hesitated!

"Very good, madam," quoth the gentleman, between his teeth, "your silence answers me. I shall now know how to deal with Mr. Fairleigh; and if you would like to communicate any particulars to me in future, this is my name and address."

He put his card into her hand, and as he did so the carriage stopped before the door of Barb's boarding-house, and a young man hurried out.

"Has she come?" asked he, eagerly, as he dashed open the door.

One glance at the occupants of the carriage, and he turned aside with a groan.

Only for a moment though; the next he was helping the gentleman to carry the inert form of Mrs. Pomeroy into the house.

When Hugh Wayne was on his knees beside Mrs. Pomeroy trying to restore her, and the stranger was gone, and there was nothing now to do but wait and weep, Barb looked at the card.

On it she read this:

"LIONEL ROSCOE,

"*Combe-Roscoe,*

"*Devon.*

"*Fifth Avenue Hotel.*"

*   *   *   *   *   *   *

Next morning Barb sat by Barry's bed telling her all this, and imploring her to fly before she brought shame and misery upon all who knew her and Harrison Fairleigh.

"And your mother—oh, she has never spoken since you turned your back on her!" wept Barb. "She lies there so pale and strange—it kills me to watch her! Come to her, Barry—Barry!"

And Barbara, like one possessed with a devil, rose on her elbow in her dainty couch, and answered, with the shiver of delirious laughter;

7

"By-and-by, Barb!—by-and-by! And you have brought Dr. Hugh Wayne, too, have you? to track me down! Poor Hugh, he's made of different stuff than Harrison Fairleigh; they make saints out of such stuff."

"Come home, Barry—end it all, my dear, this morning!"

"And Lionel Roscoe is on the trail, and the baroness and *you!* Heavens, they won't give me time!" muttered Barry, rending her long purple-black tresses with savage hand. "Barb, I want to think of this," said she, turning abruptly to her with a startling change of manner—so soft her tone, so gentle her smile, that Barb's hopes rose. "Give me the day—give me till this time to-morrow morning to consider—but mind, Hugh Wayne must go back to Rensselaer's Landing, and never dare to meddle in my affairs. He must go to-day. I can't see my mother till he is gone. Tell him that, will you? And now, child, leave me—don't—*don't* touch me!"

Her vehement words rose to a muffled scream, as Barb in her gladness attempted to take her burning hand.

So little Barb left her, with a backward look of love and pity which an angel might copy.

Barb sat alone by the bed of Mrs. Pomeroy somewhere between midnight and the morning following that eventful day. Hugh had received Barry's message, and was gone; and the unhappy mother had been told with anxious carefulness to expect her daughter's return any hour of the twenty-four; so she had not closed her eyes since.

It was very still outside and in. Barb's boarding-house was in a quiet neighborhood, and had no other inmates but the family of the proprietor. Her room was on the second story, with the window looking on the street.

Anxious that the invalid should not work herself into a state of anxiety by straining her ears to listen to every passing sound, the sweet girl had taken down her little Bible, and had been reading aloud such comfortable and dearly familiar passages as she thought would catch her friend's attention, and beguile her from the present suspense.

Mrs. Pomeroy lay looking at Barb's small, *svelte* figure and dove-eyes, she all unconscious of the increasing interest of the gaze.

Suddenly the old woman's quavering tones interrupted the low musical ones of the reader.

"Child, stop a minute," said she earnestly, "the more I look at you, the stronger the resemblance grows."

"What resemblance?" asked Barb, meekly laying aside her book to bend tenderly over the bed.

"It is not only that her hair is fair, and her eyes

blue like his," resumed the venerable lady, a far-away look in her own dim orbs; "she has the same trick of expression, the same cast of features,—they might be of the same race! and why not? It could be no mere accident that gave her the Pomeroy countenance along with the name of Arthur's mother!"

"Are you speaking of me, dear Mrs. Pomeroy?" asked Barb, wonderingly, "and if you are, who is it that I resemble?"

"My husband, Arthur Pomeroy," replied the elder woman with some agitation; "if I had not been so engrossed in my own poor Barry's affairs, I should have been struck with it long ago. Little Barb, I doubt not that you are of Arthur's kindred. He had brothers, one older than himself, the heir of March-Common, the Pomeroy estate in Devon, and one younger, a wild young rake in the army, who married a lady of wealth but low birth, squandered her money, and then deserted her. My husband kept out of their way, all of them, because they thought he had married beneath him, but probably if Henry, his youngest brother, had known where to find him, he would have confided you to his care. I believe you are his daughter, child."

"I should like to belong to you," said Barb, wistfully, "but I fear I shall never be able to prove it. You see, old Nan Devlin got me when I was a baby, down at Five Points, and I suppose she couldn't have got me if anybody had been alive to claim me."

"Do you know where to find her?" inquired Mrs. Pomeroy.

"Oh, yes, in Cardinal Court, ever so far down First Avenue,—and I wish she may never know where to find me!" exclaimed Barb, nervously.

"When this trouble is over, if the dear Lord pleases that it should pass away," murmured the old lady, meekly looking up, "we must look into this. But hush! Did you hear a ring? There, Barb—there! at last, thank God, at last!"

Yes, at last, when the street was quiet, and every light in the neighborhood was out, a gentle ring came to the door-bell.

Barb passed one eloquent glance with the agitated invalid, and, throwing a shawl round her shoulders—for the halls were cold as the grave—she flitted down-stairs with a candlestick in her hand, and softly, so as not to disturb the other inmates of the house, undid the bolts and opened the door.

A man, muffled completely in a driver's cloak, powdered with snow, stood on the steps, and behind him a carriage was drawn up to the pavement.

"You are Miss Pomeroy, are you?" quoth he, indistinctly, as if he feared to rouse the neighbors.

"Yes!"

Barb's eyes were glued to the window of the coach.

" Lady wishes to speak to you," said he, stepping aside to let her pass.

Barb hesitated, a vague fear at her heart. Was this Barry, determined not to alight till she knew that her deserted lover was gone, or Miss Hendrick, resolved to learn the truth ?

A female head appeared at the carriage window, veiled.

Barb flew down the steps, the driver hurrying after; the carriage door was opened, and two hands as strong as iron seized her by the arms.

Barb, violently startled, made an effort to free herself from the woman's vice-like grasp, and in the struggle the woman's veil was wrenched from her face.

Barb uttered one wild scream of horror—a scream that rang through the street and up the open passage to the room where poor Mrs. Pomeroy lay with ear strained to catch her daughter's voice.

" In with her! " muttered the woman, with an oath ; and the driver, clapping his hand upon her mouth, forced her inside, jumped up to his seat, and, lashing his horses to their fleetest speed, tore down the street just as the policeman's warning whistle sounded, and Mrs. Pomeroy appeared at the open window, holding on to the sill, and feebly calling:

"Help! help! Oh, Barry!"

In vain Barb struggled madly in the brutal grip of the detestable woman; she held her as if she was a child, almost smothering her with her coarse hand in order to keep her quiet; and soon, with a wail of despair, Barb sank down in the bottom of the carriage, all her strength quenched in a moment by the appalling thought: "*Barry has done this!*"

Who but Barry knew enough of her life to set old Nan upon her, aided by her horrible accomplice, Tim Polson—the ancient terror of Barb's childhood—Nan's aid and abettor in every villainy which required two to carry it out? Yes; Barry had invoked their aid to rid her of this too faithful friend who would have saved her from the commission of some dread crime!

Sweet, loyal, tender little Barb, waif of the streets, taught by God alone, now may He guard and succor thee, thou beloved of His angels!

They stole her thus from the modest home she had made for herself, and consigned her to the loathsome den she had rescued Barry from one year ago.

Her hand had led Barry out from dangers worse than death, now Barry's hand thrust her back into them!

Fitting return, was it not?

Yet, base as this act of ingratitude may seem, when offered by one human being to another—how natural, how customary, how excusable such acts are when offered by mortal to his Creator! Ay, so says the World, but one day the Heavens shall be reddened with shame for the World, as it burns on the Day of its Doom, and by that last great conflagration we shall see things differently!

*   *   *   *   *   *

The frantic scream of the kidnapped girl brought help anon to Mrs. Pomeroy.

And when they found her lying like one dead beneath the open window, with the snow drifting over her, and the house door left wide to the wall, they thought she had risen in delirium and that Barb had fled in terror for a doctor; so that when half an hour later another carriage arrived, with a beautiful young lady in it, who gazed like some one struck to stone upon the senseless face of the invalid, and in a brief sentence explained that Barbara Pomeroy had fled to her for help for her friend, and that she had come with her servants to remove her at once to her own residence, they let them go without cavil, more especially as all expenses were paid in the handsomest manner.

But when Mrs. Pomeroy opened her eyes again upon the world which had darkened so dreadfully for her, and found herself in a beautiful chamber surrounded with all the luxuries and elegancies of life, with a neat old nurse in attendance, and the noon sun shining cheerily upon silken curtain and marble statue, she wailed:

"Where is Barry? Where is Barb? Alas! I am bereaved—I must die in a stranger's arms!"

"Madame," said the nurse, approaching with velvet tread—a womanly smile irradiating her comely features, "I not Inglis—no, I German."

*   *   *   *   *   *

Ten days only, and then comes the wedding morn, on which Katherine Hendrick and Harrison Fairleigh are to be united in the holy bonds of matrimony.

The bridal *trousseau* is completed, and is the envy and admiration of Katherine Hendrick's innumerable lady friends. The bridal presents are arriving, jewels, plate, triumphs of art and taste; already they say that half a million of dollars would not buy them. The chamber devoted to their display looks —say they who have seen it—like a section in Tiffany's.

The invitations to the wedding have been out for some time, and the feminine *monde* is in a perfect fever.

The baroness is truly happy at present. Never has she felt the dignity of her position as she feels it now. The baron—to whom we have never as yet been personally introduced—in public, bears the honor of this

7*

projected alliance with all the *sang froid* of one born to the purple, but in the privacy of his own *sanctum*, as he lolls back in his easy-chair, with legs crossed, and fat finger-tips meeting over his ample person, he sends up, with every curl of pale-blue vapor from his excellent cigar, a mental thanksgiving to the god whom he adores—Success.

"Ha! ha!" exults Bernard Hendrick. "Nothing succeeds like success. Had the archduke succeeded in concealing that *faux pas* of his from me, where would my rank and wealth be now? But my god smiled upon me as it frowned upon him! Republican society crouches at my feet; the best match in the market bears off my daughter. I have nothing before me but serene old age and happiness. Once I thought I should have had to enter the church for a living!"

The beauteous Katherine, too, is almost complacent. How can she find room for dissatisfaction with fifty new *toilettes* in her wardrobe; new jewels worthy of a princess in her caskets; the handsomest man in New York visiting her, with ardent protestations of devotion, three times a day; a grand six months' European tour in contemplation, every lady of discrimination bursting with envy, and, best of all, Marah Leith in disgrace with Harrison!

"I confess I used rather to admire the gypsy beauty

of the jade," the bridegroom-elect sometimes says; "but since I discovered that she had fallen in love with me, and had a devil of a temper besides, I've lost all interest in her. I think Roscoe's smitten in that quarter—he's always dangling after her."

The latter clause of this sentence was the only portion of it which was founded on fact.

Mr. Roscoe *was* singularly attentive to Miss Leith in those days, and, what is more, she seemed to encourage his attentions.

"The tragedy ends in comedy," thought Katherine. "Despairing of Harrison, this adventuress will set her snares for the next best match. But wait until I'm safely married, I'll see that Lionel does not make such an absurd *mésalliance !*"

This comfortable arrangement of past perplexities —namely, the dispersion of Barb, Mrs. Pomeroy, and Hugh, and the reassurance of the baron, baroness, and the bride-elect—wanted but one manœuvre to make it complete.

Roscoe's suspicions had to be allayed, and Barry found herself equal to the task.

She went to Harrison and retailed the evidence given her by Barb—Roscoe was on the trail, how was he to be set at fault?

Harrison, aghast, could think of nothing but immediate elopement.

"Impossible," said Barry, her long lashes hiding the inscrutable smile in her eyes. "I've had to dispose of our evil genius—the other Barbara Pomeroy—for a time, and to conceal my mother where Dr. Hugh Wayne won't find her, and where I can see her every day. She's desperately ill: I can't leave her—I won't leave her until I'm forced to go!"

"I thought you said you loved me above anything in heaven, earth, or the other orthodox locality," said Harrison. "Having made up our minds, why do you put me off now? You won't go with me till you are forced, you say. What will force you, then?"

"Your marriage-day," said Barry, glancing up with luring wile. "Whatever happens, I keep my promise before that."

A short interruption for lover-like raptures on Harrison's part, the tropical ardor of which would have set the cold blood of Katherine leaping like fire through her veins.

Barry drew back with a gasp.

"Reserve all that," said she, in a breathless way. "Time enough after the fifth of February;"—this was Katherine's wedding-day—"yet," she added, with a sudden glance of fire, as she held out her beautiful hand, "don't feel disappointed in me, Harrison; you know I love you as woman never loved before."

He seized it and covered it with mad kisses. Ever luring, ever repulsing him, she held him like a chained lion, with her foot upon his neck; but, oh! her promises for the future were enough to compensate for all her present niggardliness.

"There, that will do," said she presently, withdrawing even her hand from him. "Let us to business. Lionel Roscoe suspects a past history, in which Barbara Pomeroy and Harrison Fairleigh were the sole actors. He will run the mystery to the ground for Katherine's sake! Something must be done."

"Yes, indeed!" responded Harrison, pulling his mustache savagely; "but what can that something be? Dashed if I have the ghost of an idea."

"Well, if you can suggest nothing, I must," said Barry, shrugging her shoulders. "Turn him over to me; I'll undertake to throw dust in his eyes. Oh, what an ugly frown! Ha! ha! How absurd to see you jealous! Perhaps some day you will wish you had turned him over to me in earnest."

"All right, Barry! I suppose I can trust you. It would be a queer thing if I couldn't, eh, after all that's passed between us."

"'Twould be as unnatural and unexpected as death," said Barry. "We never look for that, you know."

"Yet it always comes," said Harrison, gazing at her nervously.

"Always! Always!" breathed Barry, flitting away.

"How she talks!" aspirated Harrison. "She's always sending this horrid creep through me now. If she wasn't so desperately in love with me, I'd sometimes think there was mischief brewing. Somehow I don't much care—I only want to win her now."

CHAPTER XII.

THE bride-elect had long ago declared her dislike to residing in Virginia, and the bridegroom-elect had gracefully given up his dream of restoring the old manorial house of his fathers, and installing her as mistress of his Southern principality. Instead, he had taken a fine house an hour's ride up the Hudson, and fitted it up royally for her reception at the close of the wedding-tour.

Mrs. Fairleigh and Barry went to see this palace where Wedded Bliss was to reign; they passed from bottom to top and down again, viewing nothing but prodigal splendor.

"Is anything lacking?" asked Harrison of his mother with his lips, but of Barry with his eyes.

"Nothing," smiled Mrs. Fairleigh; "all is perfect. May the bride's gratification be equally so!"

"One thing—a trifle scarce worth mentioning," smiled Barry—"do you see that panel?"

They were standing in the bridal chamber, and she was pointing at a court beauty in diamonds and point-

lace, who looked down from the panel exactly opposite the grand mirror, as if eternally admiring herself
therein.

"Well?" demanded Harrison, eagerly.

"Have that, the symbol of social rank and pride,
taken down, and in her place paint with your own
brush a Maud Muller, symbol of beauty and worth
without birth or wealth. The bride will recognize a
subtile compliment to herself—an unspoken assurance
that had she been a very Maud Muller, standing
breast-high in the corn, her lord would have loved
her all the same."

"Impossible, my dear!" cried Mrs. Fairleigh,
laughing. "The idea is pretty, but where is the
time? Three days!"

Barry lifted her great, velvet-soft orbs to Harrison's
conscious face.

"Is it impossible?" said she.

"No, no; nothing *you* ask is impossible!" answered he, with a passionate glance. "It shall be
done; but I must work day and night to achieve the
task, lady fair."

"That will but prove your devotion!" murmured
she.

He turned away, that his mother might not see the
flush of adoration rise to his cheek and burn there.

Mrs. Fairleigh let these two please themselves in

the matter; she thought her Marah's wish an eccentric one, but she had a deep respect for her taste, and enjoyed Harrison's admiration of it.

So Harrison shut himself up in the empty mansion, with paint-box and palette, and in spite of all he could do to keep her off the canvas, painted a Barry Pomeroy among the corn.

Would the reader know Barry's reason for this whim? She wanted him to place in her hands a *written declaration of his perfidy to Katherine.*

The day before the wedding he received this letter from Barry:

"HARRISON: Lionel Roscoe is mysterious. I distrust him exceedingly. He is evidently resolved to bring Barbara Pomeroy and you together if he can, before it is too late. Tell me once more how you love me—how you honor me. Let me read with my eyes what I have so often drank in with my ears— all you intend to do for me for true love's sake: and if my heart echoes to your words, as I hope it will, you shall find me in Room No. 71, —— Hotel, at midnight of this the 4th of February, ready to go where you will.

"For the last time, I remain

"Your faithful

"BARBARA POMEROY."

*   *   *   *   *   *

And so these last days dropped one by one into the
past, without a perceptible cloud upon their tranquil
skies to warn the doomed ones of the lowering storm.
One by one, in halcyon calm and shining content;
and beneath, above, from every side, sped the coming
horror, too awful to be dreamed of by the unsuspect-
ing victims.

*   *   *   *   *   *

The night before the wedding! Poets have sung
of it, artists have painted it, lovers have raved of it—
the beautiful night before the wedding!

The bride-elect sat alone in her perfumed chamber, and it seemed as if the deep joy and triumph
which irradiated her features glorified that perfect
face into supernal beauty.

She had come from his arms with a thrilling
"Good-night for the last time, beloved," to muse here
in breathless rapture over the swiftly approaching
culmination of all her hopes. For once the cold and
haughty Katherine was in the melting mood; great dia-
mond-bright tears threaded her down-dropped lashes;
delicate gleams of carmine came and went upon her
cheeks; her proud lip quivered with tender emotion.

The love of her life was stirring in her long-locked
breast, and before his magic wand all baser passions
were falling from their pedestals.

Who could have recognized in that dreamy, bending figure, its purple-tressed head resting upon its lily hands, and gentle tears dripping from its half closed eyes, the imperious Katherine Hendrick, who queened it in the world?

Katherine and Harrison had parted in the drawing-room at ten o'clock that evening, after an hour's interview—the only interview held between them since the day his mother and Miss Leith had gone with him to see his castle on the Hudson. This seeming neglect had been more than satisfactorily explained by the lover's ardent whisper:

"I was doing something with my own hands for my bride!"

And the baron and baroness peering down the long vista of drawing-rooms to that semi-darkened one where the stately pair stood together, he bending over her in loving tenderness, and she drooping in love's languor under his gaze, had glanced at each other over the solemn game of chess which they were playing, and nodded their mutual approval.

*   *   *   *   *   *

Katherine's reverie was broken by the gentle click of the key turning in her chamber door.

She looked, and half rose with a faint ejaculation. A woman, muffled from head to foot in an ample mantle, and deeply veiled, turned from the door,

putting the key in her pocket, and stood before her
with folded arms and eyes glittering through the rich
lace which shrouded her face.

And when Katherine saw the grand height, the
massive mould, and the full curving outline of that
noble form, an icy bolt of terror shot through her—
she sank back with a deep breath.

For a few moments she was silent; then her spirit
came back to her, her quick wrath leaped up, she
cried out, in a bitter voice:

"I know you, Marah Leith! Miserable adventuress, what insolence is this? You have the *entrée* to
my privacy, forsooth!"

And her enemy brushed aside her veil, cast off her
mantle, and showed her the face of Marah Leith
with a fatal smile upon it; and the form of Marah
Leith towering above her in magnificent strength and
scorn.

"Katherine Hendrick," said she, with an exultant
mirth in her tones, "I pay you this visit in confidence, out of respect to your feelings. I would not
have the world witness the first moments of your
agony. I alone shall be present to console you."

Katherine's delicate features assumed a livid pallor, but, with a single glance of disdain, she rose and
swept toward the bell.

Barry's low, derisive laugh stayed her hand; Barry's next words sent her back to her chair, with a fierce determination to wring the truth from her for once and all.

"Ha! ha! ha!" exulted Barry. "You prefer the public exposure of your so-called bridegroom's infidelity, do you? Good! I am ready to give it publicly or privately. What! you have changed your mind once more."

"You wicked woman!" exclaimed Katherine, between her teeth. "I feel myself as much insulted by your presence as if I had proof that you were the lowest *traviata* that prowls in Water Street. From the first I have suspected you to be imposing upon Mrs. Fairleigh's credulity—to be a mere charlatan, determined upon marrying her son—and now you've given me confirmation of my suspicions. If I had you thrust forth by my father's footmen I should but treat you as you deserve, but I shall not do so yet. You have come here to say something. Proceed—I'll hear it."

A strange sight, truly, these two beautiful women confronting each other in that dainty room; softest luxury and rarest elegance all about them—savage passions raging in their souls!

The scathing words, the lady-like stings of high-bred Katherine, were scarcely less terrible than the quiet, slow scorn and visible strength of the country girl;

but the first was as the light arrow-shaft glancing off the impervious steel of the amazon.

"To-morrow is your wedding-day," said Barry, her rich contralto tones contrasting forcibly in their even tranquillity with the shrill and tremulous soprano of Katherine's. "To-morrow at eleven o'clock you are to become Harrison Fairleigh's wife. You exult in the thought—you glory in it. Katherine Hendrick,"—she bent over her with a sudden wild pity in her lowered tone and softening eye—"*do you love him?*"

"What is that to you, wretch?" retorted Katherine, recoiling.

Oh, Katherine! had thy heart been womanly it would have spoken then, and thy evil pride would have been mute!

"Love him!" cried Barry, with a burst of vehement contempt. "Yes, as beasts love those who treat them best—as fools love the jewels which excite other fools' envy. *Love!* O God! that's her kind of it! If he insulted you, if he trampled on you, if he changed you from a simple, pure, kind, credulous girl, into a fiend in woman's shape meditating murder, would you still love him?"

"I am well rewarded for my clemency by this violence," said Katherine, bitterly.

"No, your love would not outlive the smallest

slight, nor the discovery of the most trivial imperfection, because you never had it in your tiny ice-house of a heart!" resumed Barry. "You marry him to gratify pride, ambition, and such poor substitutes for holy conjugal affection; nor would you give him up should you see her kneel at your feet in whom he has wrought the fell change I have described, and who loves him still, poor madwoman,—ay, and will love him forever!"

"You mean yourself, of course?" said Katharine, flashing into ungovernable rage. "Shameless wretch, that degrades the name of woman by wearing it. I don't know what infatuation forces me to listen to you! Do you mean yourself?"

"I mean one named Barbara Pomeroy."

Katherine uttered a gasping cry.

Twice had that name been spoken in her hearing; once when the Mother Superior at the masked ball had wailed, stretching out her arms toward Marah Leith:

"Oh, Barbara Pomeroy, come back to me!"

And again, when Lionel Roscoe had one day lately asked:

"Katherine, has Fairleigh ever mentioned a girl of the name of Barbara Pomeroy, to you?"

She fastened her bewildered eyes upon Barry's stony face.

"Tell me the truth," [illegible]
mistaken all this tim[illegible]
whom he has loved [illegible]

"What is that to [illegible]
late harsh words as harshly. [illegible]
won the love of an innocent girl, [illegible]
erably played with it that she is no[illegible]
as once she was pure."

"Are you the woman?" dema[illegible]
trembling with excitement.

"Never mind! there is such a woma[illegible]
"Would you marry a man whom you [illegible]
this?"

Katherine relinquished her point in [illegible]
terest of this question:

"I have nothing to do with his past [illegible]
haughtily; "I shall certainly marry [illegible]

"But not if you knew that your [illegible]
consign another woman to perdition [illegible]

Katherine Hendrick flashed a light[illegible]
at the dark, fierce face before her, and [illegible]
lines of cruel pain imprinted upon it[illegible]
most unreasoning of demons, Jealousy[illegible]
heart, and with a wave of his sceptre [illegible]
and all her train.

"Ha! You can't deceive me!" she cried, shrilly.
"You are the woman yourself! I thought I was not

swindler, impostor! Your real

And you have dared

ful to me!”

ever saw your face,”

“He has made me what I am. Silence!
insults, madam. The mask is dropped; you
hear the truth.”

“If it can be told by such as you!” sneered Kath-

a minister’s daughter. I was brought up
said Barry, turning pale, “I was engaged to
good man; my poor old mother leaned on
the joy she had on earth; he beguiled me
heart before I knew it; from the first moment
wicked love fell upon me, I began to sink.
false to my betrothed in heart before a word of
spoken, and when he did speak and I ac-
profession in good faith, and he made me
the true nature of his accursed passion, in
moment I fell from my high paradise of girl-
down—down to the depths of the degraded
had blighted me with a word. I’ve never
since! Try to comprehend me, you,
a lady’s life, into which such foul in-
intrude; I am debased by Harrison
Fairleigh, not in deed, but in mind—in deed I am as
pure as you!”

Katherine interrupted her here, exclaiming in breathless eagerness:

"What do you want, then? You are not really injured? Why do you make this outcry?"

"O! God! listen to this woman!" cried Barry, with fierce bitterness. "I am not injured! Is it no injury to have the door of heaven shut in my face? No injury to be sent to the eternal companionship of devils, as black-hearted as they? Katherine," she cried, clasping her hands, "nothing can save *me* from that which lies deep as the pit before me; but *you* can be saved from the shameful crime of thrusting me on. Give up this man Fairleigh at my request, write him your contempt and loathing, and send the letter tonight—you will thank me to-morrow for having given you the chance. I don't desire vengeance on *you*, you have done me no harm hitherto, not knowing my history, but deny me now, and eternity will not be long enough for your frantic repentance! Will you do this?"

They gazed into each other's steadfast eyes; neither shrank nor flinched.

The madness of jealousy blazed in Katherine's; the gloom of death filled Barry's, and Pandemonium raged in each heart.

"If he had wronged you a thousand times, that would be your care, not mine nor his," said Katherine, with curling lips. "Fool! you are simply love-crazed. Begone, I'll give you no such promise."

"You mean this?" said Barry, in a suppressed voice, a terrible smile gathering about her whitening lips.

"I'll never give him up! never!" cried Katherine Hendrick, rising and raising her shaking hand toward heaven. "I swear to marry him if my path to the altar was strewn with victims of his fascination! Now, go."

Barry drew from her bosom an open envelope, and laid it on the gilded tea-poy at Katherine's elbow.

"I would have spared you this," said she, laughing deliriously, "but you will have it. Farewell; you are a wickeder woman than I after all. We shall meet ere long in our master, Satan's realms. Till then, farewell!"

Katherine seized the packet, and recognizing the writing, uttered a sharp cry, and turned to detain her visitor.

She found herself alone.

CHAPTER XIII.

TEN days ago poor little Barb was stolen from her home with cruel violence, and consigned to a dark, loathsome closet off old Nan's attic, with the key turned on her.

How has she fared since then?

As she lay weeping in the dark upon the heaps of old straw and sacking under the eaves that first night, she overheard old Nan and Tim Polson chuckling together over their potations a little after the following manner:

Old Nan: "Good stroke of business for us, eh?" Didn't think the young sinner would ever have brought us such luck. Twenty dollars a week for her board and attendance—he! he!"

Tim Polson: "Boards indeed—I rayther think there won't be too many feathers nor springs between! An' attendance—guess she'll sometimes wish she had less of it when you're at her heels, old girl—ho! ho!"

Old Nan: "Confounded pity we couldn't ha' found

out who the fine young madam was that wanted to get rid of her. That was your fault, old man; you was too drunk to folly her straight. Jest think—we might have nosed out a secret that would ha' kept you and me comf'able for many a day. You're sure she got inter a carriage?"

Tim Polson : "Yes, a reg'lar bang up crack affair; horses, coach, and servants, all as black as coal, with gold mountings. But, Lor'! she was up to me, an' wouldn't let me get nigh her! Never mind her; we've got the cash for one week, an' the young minx inter the bargain. Tell yer wat, old Nan, Barb's spruced up wonderful. As salable a piece o' goods as one might see on Fifth Avenue."

Old Nan : "I wonder if she's as stubborn as she used to be! I've a mind ter break her in, Tim. She *is* as handsome as a daisy—an' too valiable for to let out of our hands agin. Eh, Tim?"

Tim Polson : "True for you, comrade. Let's drink to little Pomeroy, the future Trump-Card of Polson's Dance House!"

But here the trembling listener stopped her ears with her fingers, sobbing out :

"Father, do you hear them? Save—save—save me!"

The next morning, a fearful scene with old Nan took place in the locked garret.

The wicked woman made her proposals, leering and wheedling, painting according to her coarse fancy a life of ease and splendor, of admiration and pleasure ; this to be won by the toil-worn girl at the small expense of—Virtue.

Barb Pomeroy, her pure soul inspiring her tiny delicate frame, and flashing from her gentle eyes, until she towered formidably over the wondering wretch, sternly refused to accept a life of infamy, however splendid, at the inestimable loss of Virtue.

Then threats, violence, brutal cruelties were resorted to—but why needlessly distress the sickening reader ?

As she lay half insensible on the vile heap which formed her bed, alone in the dark, bruised, shivering with cold, fainting with hunger, what did brave little Barb think of cruel Barry who had consigned her to this ?

"Oh, good Lord !" she moaned. "She couldn't have thought of this ! Forgive her, dear Lord, and make her sorry, and don't—*don't* let her do what her heart is set on, for Jesus' sake—amen !"

And she fixed her fainting eyes on the boards above her head, where a glint of the dark-blue winter sky shone in, and the chill drops from the thawing ice dripped coldly on her miserable bed. And she held sweeter communion through that crack with the Father she loved so well, than does many a silken-clad worshipper kneeling on velvet cushion in the sanctified gloom of some old cathedral, while the white-robed altar-boys chant sweetly the strains of heaven; for He spoke to her then, Spirit to spirit, with never a jarring voice of man between.

This sort of thing went on for three days. They starved her, they beat her, they used every sort of cruelty they dared without maiming or disfiguring her, to force her into obedience to their infamous plans; then they were obliged to desist in terror at what they had done, for though she had the indomitable spirit of one of the ancient martyrs—a spirit like theirs given just when needed by the Great King whom she loved to glorify—she had but a poor constitution, and broke down alarmingly before the first sign of concession had appeared.

Then the cowards drew her out out of the den, and in much consternation at the consequences in store for them should she die in their hands, anxiously did their best to restore her exhausted strength. They succeeded; their rough nursing brought her back from the very gates of Heaven, and poor little Barb took up the burden of life again, meekly and patiently, though her dim eyes were still dazzled with the glimpse she had had of the glories within those open gates, and her sad heart yearned for the great peace that awaited her there.

And the days were hurrying by, bringing closer and closer that day which of all she dreaded the most—the fifth of February, Katherine Hendrick's wedding-day.

What was it Barry had said in that last interview, when Barb had warned her that Lionel Roscoe was on her track? Tearing her long black tresses, and writhing on her delicate couch in fierce impatience, she had exclaimed :

"So Lionel Roscoe is on the trail, and the baroness and *you*. Heavens, they won't give me time ! "

And then had come the promise, uttered with Jezebel-like gentleness, that she would go and see her mother, on condition that Hugh Wayne would return home, leaving her and Barb to her mercy.

What was it she meant to do ?

Amidst the worst of her sufferings, Barb thought almost constantly of this. What fearful vengeance was Barry about to take on Harrison Fairleigh, or possibly on Katherine Hendrick, before their wedding-day?

As her strength returned her suspense became intolerable, and she worried herself incessantly trying to devise some way of sending a warning to Fairleigh or Miss Hendrick, or of communicating with Dr.

Wayne. She was at her wit's end how to do either, for she was never allowed outside the garret door, no visitor was received inside it, and she was never left a moment alone.

Waiting impatiently for her recovery, that their persecutions might be resumed, old Nan and Jim Polson guarded her by turns, taking excellent care that their unknown patroness's orders should be obeyed—that she should hold no communication with the outer world—and that she should not slip through their fingers.

And I truly believe they would have succeeded in at least one part of their schemes—that is, in preventing her from meddling in Barry's affairs until it was too late, had not a tiny crumb which Barb had thrown upon the waters long ago come back to her now, as if by chance, in the very nick of time.

> "Chance sped the dart,
>   But God that chance did guide!"

Old Nan was out on some evil errand, and Jim Polson was on duty.

Disagreeable duty he evidently found it, for as he shuffled his greasy cards and slapped them down upon the blackened table beside the wretched fire, a mumbled curse escaped him now and again, and he darted glances of vindictive spite at his prisoner through the coarse mat of hair which overhung his beetling eyebrows.

Barb, pale and pure as a dove-eyed nun, sat in the rickety chair by the window in the corner of the room farthest from him, shivering a little as the keen air sifted in through the shrunken sash, but sewing busily on some rag of old Nan's, and singing very softly—that she might not feel so badly when Tim swore—these words:

> " God is near thee,
>   Therefore cheer thee,
>   Sad soul !
>   He'll defend thee,
>   When around thee
>   Billows roll ! "

"Stop that confounded whining!" roared Tim at last. "Who wants ter feel as if they were in meetin'? There's One-eyed Sal a-playin' 'Oh, ain't I orful!' down street; let's hear her—she's more to my taste."

Barb laid down her sewing in her lap, and turned to the window with a sudden flush in her wan face. The reedy strains of a miserable hand-organ floated above the din of the drays, the jingle of the street car-bells, and the hoarse shouts of vehicle-drivers on the street five stories beneath. The same old dreary round of tunes she had heard for years from One-eyed Sal's dilapidated organ—they distinctly brought up before her the familiar figure of the starved, weather-beaten, wan widow, who, having lost her eye by the exploding of a shell while searching for her dead husband's body on the outskirts of the battle, had been forced by grizzly want to do the only thing she could with impaired sight, for the sake of her puny child, a cripple for life. Time had been when little Barb Pomeroy—old Nan's foundling—had stopped by the hand-cart in which Sal wheeled her organ and her child the livelong day, and had spoken such words to the mother and given such smiles to the child that the weary woman thought her like an angel, and had looked for her day by day to come, the one glimpse of heaven thrown across her bleak life-path.

A kind word—oh, inestimable gem! For gold may rust, and favors corrupt the heart, but a kind word is like the sunbeam imprisoned in the opal, and once received into the warming bosom, shines there forever with inextinguishable ray!

Barb knew that One-eyed Sal loved her, and a great hope made all her pulses thrill.

"She's coming this way; I'll open the window," said she to her jailor. "Seems to me it would cheer me up a bit to hear the old songs."

"If anything would banish your blue devils it would be a mercy!" growled Tim, who had a decided *penchant* for music of the jovial order himself; "only don't let old Nan catch ye poking your head out there."

Barb opened the window and leaned out.

There was the poor old organ-woman half a block down the street, grinding away at her wheezy instrument, and there was her poor little boy, rolled up in rags in the end of the cart, his face as thin and blue as want and cold could make it.

Barb's pulses beat faster. In a few minutes Sal would pass under her window.

"If she would only look up and see me," thought Barb, "may be I could let her know that I want to get away from here. I know she'd help me if she could."

The organ stopped playing, Sal wheeled the cart a few houses nearer, and began again.

Barb looked back into the room, and through the blue smoke from Tim's pipe saw him lolling back in his chair, with his feet braced against the wall and his back to her, enjoying the music while he turned over the filthy leaves of a dog-eared song-book.

"If I only had a pencil," thought Barb, "and a bit of paper, I'd write something to Sal this very minute. I have some cents in my pocket, and I could roll 'em up in it and pitch it down to her easy."

As this sigh escaped her, she noticed the litter of cards and half-burned matches—both being the usual evidences of Tim's protracted vigil—lying temptingly on the table between them.

Barb like a spirit crept noiselessly to the table right behind Tim, selected a few of the cleanest cards and as many burnt matches as she could catch up, and, creeping back to her seat, leaned over the window, her little heart beating like a trip-hammer.

She laid a knave of hearts face down upon the grimy sill, and delicately removing the soft ash from the end of the match, she wrote the following upon the back of the card, as like print as she could make it:

"DEAR SAL: Barb Pomeroy is in trouble; send word to Dr. Wayne—Rensellaer's Landing, on the Hudson—that old Nan has her, and that Barry is worse. Dear Sal, do this right quickly for

"LITTLE BARB."

It took more than half a dozen matches to indite this epistle upon the back of a knave of hearts, an ace of diamonds, and ten of clubs, and by that time Sal was under the window, commencing her little round of popular airs.

Barb took the few cents from her pocket, and rolling the three cards carefully round them in a compact bundle, pinned it securely together; then tied the end of the reel of cotton from which she had been sewing round it, and all was ready.

But now, how was she to attract Sal's attention, that she might see the tiny packet about to be lowered to her, and prevent it from being snatched up by some hurrying passenger?

Barb peeped back into the room for some small object which she could throw down, but seeing nothing movable, caught up the scissors and cut a button off her own dress. She aimed it at Sal, but it missed fire, and dropped on the little boy's face as he lay fast asleep, with his head against the asthmatic organ, and it was evident by Sal's quick movement towards him, that he had awakened with a cry of fright.

The little prisoner watched with breathless suspense, while the woman, dropping the handle, picked up the button and looked hither and thither in angry surprise, to see who had thrown it at her darling; but as she did not chance to look up, another button, better aimed, dropped upon her shoulder, and at last she did look up from window to window of the whole five stories, till from the very top she saw a white face looking down, with a great mass of yellow hair floating about it—for Barb had pulled it down

in a mighty hurry, that Sal might know her better—
and a little white hand waving and gesticulating to
her. And as she stood there, gaping and wondering,
a tiny white speck dropped from the waving hand,
and came down, down, down, spinning round and
round, and growing bigger and bigger, till she
caught it in her own hand—a small, hard lump of
paper, tied about with a white thread.

"Shet the winder, will yer!" exclaimed Tim, in a
rousing voice. "Sal's gone, and the wind's like a
knife. What in thunder's come of them cards?"

Barb shut the window in trembling haste, and
turned back into the cheerless room to see her jailor
in vain endeavoring to play his solitary game without the knave, ace, and ten.

"Seems as if you was 'livened up a bit," said he,
staring at her. "All right, my gal, the sooner the
better, so's we'll go on with that little argyment of
ours!"

CHAPTER XIV.

WHAT DEVILS DID WITH HER.

NEXT morning Barb's persecutions began again, but she had not lain awake all night for nothing; she was ready with a proposition which, if conceded to, would stave them off till Dr. Wayne arrived.

"Get me my old place in the opera house," said she, "and I'll give you every cent I earn; but don't waste your time and ruin my health trying to force me to do what I never will, though you should tear the flesh off my bones."

"All very fine!" flouted old Nan. "You won't run away nor nothin', not you!"

"I dare say you'll take care of that," said Barb; "and it'll come to about the same thing in the end, I guess, whether you try to keep me here or to keep sight of me on the streets."

Old Nan's eyes glistened with cupidity. Barb was so wonderfully improved in appearance that perhaps they'd give her a place as principal of the ballet corps ; in time she might even rise to be a walking lady or a posturante, and then what a mine of wealth she would be to them!

"If you will promise faithful not to run away from us," said Nan, "I'll let you do as you like."

Barb turned a shade paler, for a struggle began in her mind ; at last she said, huskily :

"I'll promise not to run away if you'll just give me one afternoon to myself to go where I like."

A derisive shout from the twain checked her. Old Nan and Tim Polson were in convulsions of merriment at her simplicity.

"No, no! Yer don't try that on!" said Tim, when he could speak. "You was put here jest for to keep you out o' other folks' business, and it don't suit our book to break faith with the parties what handed yer over to us. Promise not to run away, and we'll let you go back to the theatre—that's square, ain't it?"

"Very well," said Barb, reviving again. "You let me earn my living honestly, and I'll work for you till I'm twenty-one, but try to drive me to do wrong, and I warn you I'll make my escape the first chance."

After considerable discussion this was agreed to, the wink which was passed between the comrades in crime testifying to the fidelity with which they intended to keep their part of the bargain, and the sparkle in Barb's downcast eye denoting how clearly she read their treachery, and how determined she was to frustrate it.

Nan went anon to the manager, and having succeeded in bringing little Pomeroy to his mind, easily obtained her re-engagement, and returned home elated.

And now commenced Barb's rehearsals of her half-forgotten art, when, hurrying off to the theatre at half-past seven of the morning, with her arm securely locked in that of the detestable old Nan, she practised poses, pirouettes, entrechats, and weary balancings on the tips of her toes till eleven o'clock, to be dragged home again to her meagre dinner, escorted back by Tim Polson at half-past one to perform her part in the matinee, returning at five to a still more meagre supper, and back again at half-past seven, as weary a little coryphee as one might find the world over, to embody the " poetry of motion " with what enthusiasm she might to please the devotees of Terpsichore.

And what sustained our good little Barb through this slavery? The hope of gaining an opportunity to send some word, before it was too late, to Katherine Hendrick.

She frequently met Sal, the organ-woman, loitering in the street, but one significant glance warned her not to accost her, and it was the third of February before, in passing her, Sal was enabled to thrust into her hand, unobserved, a crumpled piece of paper, which told her that Sal had written to Dr. Wayne as directed, and that Dr. Wayne was in town, waiting for a message from Barb as to what he was to do; that Sal had told him to keep in the background, knowing what "Turks" old Nan and Tim Polson were when anybody meddled in their business, and that there the matter rested.

It was that very same night, when Barb was lying awake in the dismal closet thinking, that she overheard a whispered conversation in the garret that made her blood boil.

Nan was confiding to Tim, as an excellent piece of news, that some "swell cove" had fallen in love with Barb as she danced that night, and had gone round behind the scenes expressly to see her, but had been taken in hand by Nan herself, who soon made a "stunning" bargain, and he was to run off with the poor little ballet-dancer next night. And while Tim Polson chuckled in fiendish exultation, and Nan set forth her own superior generalship, their intended victim lay quailing and weeping, till the thought of the Hand that held her ever calmed and comforted her, and then she smiled at their foolish triumph and went to sleep like an infant on its mother's breast.

The morning before the wedding-day, little Barb, on the way to her morning's practice, stopped obstinately beside Sal's hand-cart, and stooping, kissed the child.

"Stop that rot!" growled old Nan, dragging her on. "Folks don't care much for your fussing over them if yer don't give 'em nothin'. He! he! didn't I say so? Jest look at Sal grubbin' among the rags to see what yer gave Jimmie beside soft sawder!"

Yes, she was grubbing earnestly for something else, and she found it, too; a note written in pencil to Dr. Wayne.

"DEAR DR. WAYNE," wrote Barb as prettily as freezing fingers, no desk, a crumpled scrap of paper, and a blunt pencil would permit. "I am in great trouble. Nine days ago—the night of the very day you went home—I was kidnapped from my boarding-house by the people I used to live so miserably with, and have been kept so close ever since that I could scarcely get word even to you. I am afraid Barry is in terrible danger, but it's no earthly use for me to tell you what that danger is, or for you to try and see her. I must escape somehow and do what I can myself. Will you be at the Grand Opera House to-night in the first row of the orchestra chairs, and when a ballet-dancer comes forward to the foot-lights and kneels, drawing a silver tissue-scarf over her face, you'll know that that's me, and that I've

made you a signal to go round to the stage entrance
and meet me there. Old Nan and Tim Polson are
sure to be at hand, for they are always on the look-out
lest I escape; but I must give them the slip to-night,
for they have plotted my ruin, and I dare stay with
them no longer. Altogether I am in such a way
about Barry and Mrs. Pomeroy, who was so ill when
I left her, and about my fears for the future, that I
scarcely know what I am writing. I do hope you'll
get this, and understand it.

" Yours, very respectfully,
Barb."

And Dr. Wayne, who had been half beside himself
with bewilderment and anxiety, not knowing what
to think of the strange state of affairs, having read
this note, prepared to do Barb's bidding, devoutly
hoping that in his first interview with her light would
come out of darkness.

*   *   *   *   *   *

This is really fairy like, is it not?

The lights are lowered through all the house, and
a soft, tender radiance illumines the stage, which re-
minds one of the wonderful caverns under the sea,
with their rocks of gold, and coral sprays of blushing
rose; their fretted fronds of silver and pale amethyst,
and lurid fire, and rich, red bronze, their floors of

glistering sands, gem-bestrewn, and the faint green haze of the deep sea waves floating over all !

There are glittering white stalactites and stalagmites in this mermaids' cave, and great brown rocks weed-swathed, and wet green banks of ocean mosses, and heaps of starry shells, and the loveliest sylphs float in and out among the jagged columns—bound upon the rocks, recline smiling upon the soft moss couches, and bedeck their long yellow hair with the starry shells—singing all the while, with shut mouths, the sweetest, *delicatest* wave-song ever you heard in a delicious dream !

And in their midst rises, from glistening floor to weed-hung vaulted roof, a pyramid of fairy women, kneeling, reclining, standing on the opalescent rocks which form the central object in the cave, the three at the very apex upholding on their clasped hands an earth-maiden, a tiny, white-robed creature, who gazes in wonder upon the pretty mysteries of the deep.

To the sound of the mermaid song she floats down, stepping, with delicate foot, from hand to hand, until she reaches the floor, where, with a gliding-grace, she begins her dance, at which all the lovely mermaids gaze in admiration.

Suddenly she unwinds her scarf of silver tissue from her slender waist, and floating in a passion of pirouettes right up to the lowered footlights, she sinks slowly, deliciously, down to one knee, drawing her gleaming vail over her strangely solemn face.

As she does this, two gentlemen rise simultaneously, one from his place in the front row of the orchestra chairs, the other from his place in the right-hand stage-box, and precipitately leave the auditorium.

As the *figurante* whirls off the stage she catches a glimpse of each retreating form, and bounds behind the scenes like a veritable creature of the air.

*　　*　　*　　*　　*　　*

"Hello! Barb, what are ye after? You ain't nigh through, are ye?"

Old Nan sat half asleep in the dressing-room usually occupied by the ballet corps, and Barb—the earth-maiden—was tearing off her spangled robe, her silk tights, and all the adjuncts of her impersonation.

"Get your needle and thread quick!" cried Barb, tossing the heap of tarletan into her lap. "I'm torn to pieces and haven't ten minutes before I go on again. Ugh! how I shiver? I'll put on my dress while you mend me up."

With trembling fingers she did so, old Nan, meantime, pottering over the lamentable rents these same little fingers had deliberately made in the airy toilet of the earth-maiden, and then, throwing her shawl about her, she ran to the door, saying:

" I must have a look at 'em between the flats ; it's as pretty as a picture."

" You jest keep where you are !" bawled old Nan; but she spoke to the wind. Barb was gone; and the distinct sound of the key turning in the lock told old Nan that Barb was gone for good !

She raved, she swore, she shouted. Nobody heard or heeded her in the din of the " Sea Storm " which was transforming the Cave of the Mermaids into a seething maelstrom.

Barb, threading her way among the carpenters, the scene-shifters, the waiting actors, and such miscellanies as peopled that mysterious region behind the scenes, was congratulating herself that she was getting along beautifully, being neither accosted nor detained, when, opening the door and springing into the street, she was met by a man in a footman's livery, 'who pinioned her arms in a moment and held her fast.

By the light of the opposite street lamp she could distinctly see a handsome close carriage drawn up exactly in front of the stage entrance, a tall gentleman standing by the open carriage-door, and Dr. Wayne hurrying along the pavement toward her. Several figures she was aware of lurking in the shadow of the carriage, and she perceived in a moment that she was almost in the power of the man to whom her persecutors had sold her.

"Help! help!" shrieked Barb, struggling like a little tigress.

The footman attempted to close her mouth with his hand, and was reinforced in a moment by the men who were in waiting. Hugh Wayne darted forward, with one vigorous blow felled the man who held her to the ground, and seized her in his arms. She clung to him frantically, continuing her shrill cries for help, while Hugh fought off his assailants as best he could retreating step by step back to the stage entrance, Meanwhile the tramp of feet hurrying toward the spot, and the distant whistle of a policeman, warned the combatants that there was no time to be lost.

"Dash it all, colonel!" roared Tim Polson's voice, "ye see she won't come by fair means. I'll *hev* to settle this business my own way."

"No violence, my man," returned the gentleman who stood at the coach door. "Barbara Pomeroy," continued he, "I'm not going to harm you; I give you my word——"

"Villain!" interposed Hugh Wayne, hotly, "you shall never obtain possession of this good girl but over my body!"

In his turn he was interrupted by a blow on the temple from the sledge-hammer fist of Tim Polson, which sent him reeling to the pavement. Barb was torn from him, her frantic cries smothered in the folds of her thick shawl, and feeling herself hustled into the coach, the gentleman receiving her in a vice-like grasp, and the coach dashing off at full speed, an awful panic seized her, and for the first time in her life she fainted.

When Barb recovered her senses she found herself lying on a sofa in a handsomely furnished room, with an old lady, in stiff black silk and handsome furs, bending over her.

Barb sprang from the sofa, uttering a faint cry; then seeing that no one else was in the room, she went back to the lady dizzily, and catching her by the sleeve, exclaimed with intense earnestness:

"If you have any mercy in you—if you have ever had a daughter and loved her—if you hope for mercy yourself when you come to die, let me escape from the man who brought me here!"

The lady regarded her with a stern and stony gaze.

"My commands are to let him know whenever you are recovered; I can listen to nothing you say," replied she, releasing herself. And, in spite of Barb's frantic prayers and endeavors to detain her, she instantly left the room.

Little Barb stood motionless. Where was her help to come from now? Had the hour at last arrived

when she must defend her honor with her life ?   Her
pale face grew paler, her sweet eyes kindled, she
drew a long, shuddering sigh, she glanced at herself
in the tall mirror opposite, with a strange, solemn
smile.

"Good-by, Barb," whispered she, "you may never
see yourself on earth again!"

She passed quickly round the room, looking for
some chance of escape or of summoning help ; then
flew to one of the long windows, and, touching the
spring, threw it wide open.

Far beneath glittered the wide street, sprinkled
with lights of carriages returning from opera and
theatre.   She rested one knee on the sill, holding on
by the rich lace curtain—and waited.

Strange sight for the gentleman who flung open
the door and strode in with black eyes flashing under
his frowning brows !

There she stood, the tiny figure, in its modest gray
gown, with the forgotten crown of the "earth-maiden"
still glittering in her unbound yellow hair, the great,
greenish, glistening stage-jewels still twinkling in her
ears and at her throat, her face blanched death-white,
her great pulsating eyes filled with supernatural light,
and the yawning window and black night behind her !

He stood transfixed, his back against the door, and
a wave of wonder and grief passed over her ghastly

faco. A few moments of dead silence, and she spoke in a hushed voice.

"Mr. Roscoe," said poor little Barb, "is it you who want to do me this great wrong?"

Lionel Roscoe! Yes, it was no other than he who was her abductor.

CHAPTER XV.

"MISERABLE woman!" exclaimed Mr. Roscoe, closing the door; "it comes ill from you to speak of wrong. Come, this folly shall not serve you. Retire from that window instantly."

All his stern scorn of her spoke in his tone and glance. Perplexed, she came out of the niche a step, gazing at him half-affrightedly, half-eagerly.

"Why have you brought me here, if it was you who did so?" asked she.

"To force you to declare the truth to Miss Hendrick before it is too late."

Barb came out of the niche altogether, a flash of joy lighting up her face.

"It is not too late yet, then!" cried she. "Oh, thank God! I feared it was. Miss Hendrick is going to be married to-morrow morning, isn't she?"

Roscoe bowed: he was considerably disconcerted at her eagerness to comply with his wishes.

"You have no objection, apparently," said he, "to

publish your own infamy, and that of Harrison Fairleigh, to the injured lady."

"*My* infamy!" faltered Barb, crimsoning. "What do you mean, sir?"

"You know well," retorted he, disdainfully. "Since the day I saw you with him in Madison Park. I have remembered the name of Barbara Pomeroy, and done my best to bring the shameful history of its owner to light."

She looked at him in stricken silence for a moment, then all the pride of innocence burst forth. She stepped up to him, fearless enough now, and, cresting her little head, said, sternly:

"I am but a poor girl, sir, and I have no one to defend my good name but myself; you are cowardly to traduce it; you are false, too, for my name is all I have, and it is as spotless as any woman's in all America!"

Roscoe received this with a cold, derisive smile.

"This is of course," said he. "Fairleigh's mistress has doubtless been well bribed to attest to her own and Fairleigh's purity!"

"Sir!" cried she, passionately. "Gentleman though you are, I will not be insulted by you. Leave me! Leave me, I say!"

Mr. Roscoe retreated a few steps, amazed at the flashing anger of the little creature before him, and

considerably affected by it, notwithstanding his pre-
conceived opinion concerning her.

"If I wrong you, girl," said he, "I heartily beg
your pardon, though, in that case I confess, I should
hardly deserve it; but appearances are sadly against
you. What was the subject of your conversation with
Mr. Fairleigh when I came upon you in Madison
Square? Were you not threatening him—doubtless
having heard of his approaching marriage—with the
future vengeance of Barbara Pomeroy? For what
purpose did you visit Mrs. Fairleigh's house so frequently during Mr. Fairleigh's illness? Why did
Barbara Pomeroy require Miss Leith to plead her
cause at the masqued ball? And, above all, why
have you suddenly disappeared from your boarding-
house without leaving a single clue by which any
one might trace you, if my worst suspicions are not
correct, and Mr. Fairleigh has not succeeded in buy-
ing your silence?"

Barb listened with growing consternation—appearances were indeed sadly against her. How could she
defend herself? She could think of but the one
way, a very easy and simple way, namely, to put the
shoe on the right foot—to refer him to the other
Barbara Pomeroy. She turned away with a quick
gasp, threw herself into a chair, and covered her face
with her hands.

This looked so like guilt that Lionel Roscoe scowled at her with positive loathing.

" Besides all this," continued he, ruthlessly, " it is enough to shake one's faith in any woman's purity to find her actually for sale as the property of two of the worst characters that ever plied their infamous calling. How is it that with your claims to a good name, I was able to buy you from that woman ? "

Barb flashed up again, quivering with anguish and indignation.

" Are you blind ? " said she, bitterly. " Did I go with you willingly ? Did you not carry me off by violence ? "

" Explained," said he, " by another lover being on the ground before me."

" He was no lover of mine," said she. " I appealed to him to help me to escape from these wretches who have dared to sell me to you, and you would have found, had you really bought me, that I knew how to defend myself as a good woman should ! "

" All this I am willing—I am anxious to believe," said Roscoe, struck once more, in spite of himself, by the mere power of truth. " You have only to explain matters as they really are—surely that is not a difficult thing if you are really guiltless."

To explain matters ! Barb sank down again,

rushed. To say Marah Leith is an impostor and has played a wicked part for vengeance! Tears streamed from her eyes, convulsive sobs rent her innocent breast.

"I can't explain!" gasped she. "Don't ask me to explain! Oh, this is cruel—cruel! I had only my good name, and they have taken that from me!"

"Enough of this!" said Roscoe, harshly, feeling utterly disgusted with her obstinacy. "It grows late; you must come with me at once to Baron Hendrick's house, where I trust we shall find means to induce you to speak the truth."

Barb looked up terror-stricken.

"I am willing to speak to Miss Hendrick," said she, "and I thank Heaven for giving me the chance, but don't ask me to speak before the baron and baroness."

Roscoe shrugged his shoulders slightingly.

"You are scarcely the character whom one would trust in a private interview with one whom you doubtless presume to consider your rival. However, Miss Hendrick shall judge of that for herself, and we shall devise means to protect her from either insolence or violence. I shall now call in Mrs. Archer, the baroness's housekeeper, whom I prevailed upon to accompany me upon this mission in the interests of my own reputation."

9*

He left the room, returning a few minutes afterward with a lady in stiff silk, who, grimly taking possession of Barb by the arm, marched her through the spacious corridor, and down the stairs of the ladies' entrance, to Baron Hendrick's carriage, which awaited Mr. Roscoe's pleasure.

On the way, Barb said to Mrs. Archer—Mr. Roscoe not having deigned to enter the carriage in such company, preferring the driver's seat—

"I must see Miss Hendrick alone; I can't say a word unless I see her alone. Will you plead with Mr. Roscoe for me? And oh! don't tell the baron or the baroness that I am with her; let her tell it herself, if she wishes to do so, after I have told her the thing I have on my mind."

Mrs. Archer answered, with dignity:

"Young woman, I don't know who or what you are, and I don't approve of this expedition—not one step of it. I have other things to attend to on my young lady's wedding-eve than the raking up of old secrets, I think."

When they arrived at Baron Hendrick's door, it was fifteen minutes to twelve o'clock.

Every window was dark except those in the area, behind which the busy cooks still flitted to and fro.

"All abed and asleep, Mrs. Archer," said Mr.

Roscoe, appearing at the carriage door. "Please go up and awake Miss Hendrick. Tell her I must see her. Tell her that I implore her by her future happiness not to deny me."

The disapproving housekeeper conducted the untimely guests into a cold, vacant parlor, lit the gas, and solemnly ascended the stairs.

"I am going to tell the exact truth to Miss Hendrick, as far as it concerns her," said Barb, "but I want to beg you not to arouse her father and mother unless she wishes it. She may decide to let the marriage take place."

"She shall decide everything," replied Mr. Roscoe, haughtily.

Mrs. Archer reappeared.

"Miss Hendrick is not in bed yet," said she; "will you walk up to her parlor?"

Mr. Roscoe, signing Barb to follow, obeyed. They entered Miss Hendrick's beautiful little parlor, where Mrs. Archer had lit the gas, and presently Miss Hendrick's chamber door opened a little way, and she said, sharply:

"What now, Lionel? This is a late visit!"

Nothing was seen of the lady, save her slender white hand holding the door ajar; but there was a nameless expression in her voice which startled Mr. Roscoe, and aroused Barb's curiosity to see the concealed face of the owner. Mr. Roscoe, speaking through the aperture, replied in a low voice, and at some length. She interrupted him fiercely.

"Is it worth while to torture me with your suspicions *now?* Don't you see that you come too late?"

"Never too late, Katherine, till the fatal knot is tied!" exclaimed he, pleadingly. "Oh, don't blind your eyes any longer! Let me save you!"

"Save me, Lionel? O God!" aspirated the bride-elect, and then she laughed a little dreadful laugh.

"The girl may see you, Katherine?" asked he, anxiously.

"What girl? Oh! Your witness against my lover. Well, well, what does it matter now?" muttered she. "Yes, Lionel, send her in."

"I fear for you—she may be desperate—let me wait within call," pleaded Roscoe.

"Tush! She cannot trouble *me*," said the lady. "I am beyond such tiny stings. Come in, girl, I'll hear you."

She opened the door, keeping her person so jea-lously concealed behind it, that Mr. Roscoe could not catch one glimpse of her.

Barb passed in, and the door was instantly shut.

They stood face to face, each pale as death; but while Barb's little heart beat to suffocation, Miss Hendrick seemed cold as ice. She had laid aside her rich evening-dress, and in a flowing white dressing-robe, with her long, deep chestnut hair streaming over her shoulders, and that fixed and fatal look in her face, she struck the young girl with an unutterable dread.

The dressing-room, which Barb could see through the opposite door, which was open, was brightly lighted, and presented glimpses of the bridal-robes laid out for the morrow; the foam-white bridal veil of priceless lace, the glimmering white pearl set, shining in their open casket—everything laid ready, even to the fairy satin shoes buckled with crescents of iridescent pearls.

"What ill news do you bring, girl?" demanded Katherine, seating herself once more beside the gilded tea-poy, and laying her delicate bare arm across an open letter which lay upon it.

"Oh, lady, you know, you know already!" said Barb. "Something dreadful has happened, or you would not look so."

"Something *has* happened," said Katherine, in a faint voice, "and it appears that all the world knew that it was to happen, and no one thought it worth while to warn me in time."

"You have found out that he loves Barbara Pome-roy," faltered Barb, "but that isn't what I wished most to say to you."

The lady lifted her arm and looked at the letter with a strange smile.

"Ah, yes!" sighed she. "He loves her—how he loves her!"

"I wished to put you on your guard," said Barb, weeping. "I've known Barry a long while, and he has sported with her love so cruelly, that I am perfectly sure she means to take some dreadful revenge on you or on him."

Katherine waved her hand impatiently.

"I know all this already," said she, in a hollow voice. "She will take no vengeance upon him, she has wreaked it all upon me."

She thrust her beautiful hands into her hair, and bending over the letter, forgot Barb's presence; and a long, death-like silence ensued.

Barb wept bitterly, but wiped the tears away as fast as they fell, restraining her sobs, lest she should disturb the unhappy bride-elect.

What had Barry done? What was this letter which moved her so?

At last, Mr. Roscoe tapped at the door, calling anxiously:

"Miss Hendrick, what is the matter? I don't hear you speak."

She started, looking about her in a bewildered way, then seeing Barb, and recollecting her surroundings, she rose slowly, moaning to herself: "No peace! no peace!"

She opened the door as before, just enough to speak through.

"Do go away, Lionel!" said she, bitterly. "Why do you haunt me?"

"Has she told you, Kate?" said he, his deep voice shaking.

"Oh, yes; I know all!" answered she, with forced composure. "Shocking! Is it not?"

"Oh! Kate, let me see you, dear!" exclaimed he, impetuously. "This is too much for you. Come out here and let me comfort you."

"No! no!" muttered she, shrinking back. "I can't see anybody. How the world will laugh at me to-morrow, won't it, Lionel?" she added, a peculiarly ghastly smile playing on her bloodless features.

"Don't think of that, Katherine; be thankful that you have escaped him, and that this marriage, which would have doomed you to a life of misery, will never take place."

"Never! Never!" echoed Katherine, wringing her hands.

"Shall I bring your mother?" asked Mr. Roscoe, piteously.

Katherine threw a glance into the radiant dressing-room, and another at the open letter lying where she had laid it, and gasped out:

"No, no! Not to-night! Leave me—leave them all in peace this one night more. It is enough that grief and disgrace should come with the dawn of daylight!"

"The girl need not torture you any longer with her presence, need she?" inquired her cousin.

"No," said Katherine, "you may take her away."

She stopped, for Barb's little hands fell hot and nervous upon her arm.

"Don't send me away!" pleaded she, vehemently. "I'm afraid—afraid to leave you alone. Let me watch by you."

Katherine glanced at her vacantly, but half comprehending her words.

"What does she say?" inquired Roscoe, curiously.

"I don't know," said Katherine. "I think she wants to stay with me."

"Nonsense!" said Roscoe, in a shocked voice. "Send the insolent wretch away immediately."

"No! no! no!" cried Barb, looking up in the lady's large fathomless eyes, in an agony of entreaty. "Let me stay with you to-night. I'm afraid of Barry Pomeroy! Oh, let me stay here to save her from crime and you from danger!"

Katherine's glance grew less distraught; she listened with attention to this.

"Do you expect my rival to murder me to-night?" said she, in measured tones. "You need not; she has taken a vengeance far more cruel upon me. However, since I see that you are really alarmed, and that you would only arouse the house if I sent you away, you shall have your wish. You shall stay with me to-night, upon condition that you sleep on a sofa in the parlor, and don't come near me unless I call you."

"Thank you," murmured Barb, gratefully.

Katherine opened the door again.

"I wish this girl to remain with me to-night," said she. "Make no objections, for I must and will have it so; she has much to tell me before I sleep this night."

"You amaze me!" said Mr. Roscoe, in horror. "Are you sure you can trust yourself with her?"

"I am safer with her than with myself," said Katherine. "Do leave me, please, and madden me no more by your continual objections!"

This she cried with such a sudden frantic outburst of impatience that Roscoe was cowed, and ventured to oppose her no longer.

"I shall, with your permission, stay in your parlor to-night," said he.

"You can't," said she, "she is to sleep there."

"I shall be within hearing somewhere," answered he, doggedly, "if anything happens, call me."

"Nothing shall happen," said she, between her teeth, "that you can prevent."

She then put out her hand through the narrow slit, whispering, with a sob:

"Good-night, Lionel! Good-night!" He pressed it fervently and held it, muttering:

"The wretch!—But he shall pay for this dearly!"·

"Go!" cried she, shrilly. "You only know how to torture me!" And she shut the door in his face. and throwing herself into her chair, leaned her head upon the little table where the open letter lay, and there remained motionless, as if dead.

Barb watched her in awed silence for a long, long while; then her tender pity burst through all barriers; and, kneeling at her side, she wound her arms about the unhappy lady's waist, exclaiming:

"Oh, Miss Hendrick, give him up willingly, cos' Jesus asks ye to, and then He'll help ye to bear yer sorrow, sure!"

The belle of many balls roused herself, shuddering.

"My prayers," muttered she, huskily. "Yes, I must not forget them *to-night.* Great God! has it come to this!"

She rose, scarcely noticing her simple comforter,

and paced up and down her beautiful room, her white lips moving voicelessly.

Suddenly she stopped, with a bitter wintry smile of scorn.

" He does not hear me; bah! prayers are not for the proud, whose pride is blasted," she said. " Heigh ho! my day is done, now for my night. Little one," she exclaimed, turning abruptly to Barb, with a kindness all the more winning, that it came out of her unutterable suffering. " Blighted pride is hard to bear, but blighted love is harder. I thought I had no heart—I gloried that I had no heart. (Take these, child) "—she was undressing, and had handed Barb some laces—" but, to-night, I have learned differently. Alas! alas! I loved him, little one; he was sweet, sweet, to my love-honored soul! I could have parted with my beauty—(put these in yonder casket)—I could have parted with my popularity, my wealth—anything but his love! Oh, fond, blind fool, to build my all upon a mortal! "

" Sweet lady, there is One who never deceives us," sobbed little Barb.

" Too late, He despises my folly—too late! " groaned Katherine.

" Hush, child, you are mistaken, the meek and the simple may make comfort in such thoughts, but not the desperate! Don't weep so. Ah, for tears like hers! Fetch me a string of pearls from the jewel case in that room. His present to his bride! Ha! ha! And she shall wear them, too! Oh, Harrison! Harrison! Harrison!

Blinded with tears, Barb went and fetched the open casket, on which reposed, lapped in blush-rose satin, a magnificent necklace of starry pearls, tied with a gold cord and tassels.

Katherine received it from her with a terrible eagerness which she remembered afterward, with many a vain tear that hers should have been the hand which offered it.

The miserable bride-elect lifted the beautiful thing, and passed it through her long, ivory-like fingers, examining the massive gold setting as each gem in turn, and at last, holding up the shimmering bauble which gleamed like a string of lights, with a frenzied smile of exultation :—

"*His gift!*" whispered she, too utterly absorbed to heed her listener. "He shall know that I loved him, when he hears that I wore them to-night! Precious—precious gift!"

She kissed the gems wildly.

Barb looked on ; a chill sense of inexplicable fear upon her.

"It is late," she ventured; "do let me put you to bed. Sleep will do you good. Oh, that you could have rest—the best kind of rest, dear Miss Hendrick!"

"It *is* time to sleep—to be at rest," answered Katherine, and she finished her toilet, having placed the string of pearls upon the open letter.

"I don't know who you are," said she, turning to Barb, "but I think you have felt for me to-night. I am a proud woman, and I could not accept my parents' pity, or the hard world's condolence—I can accept yours, because you are too humble to feel any superiority while you give it. I thank you for your kindness. You will never regret having shown it to the heart-broken Katherine Hendrick. And now, good-night!"

She drew Barb toward her, kissed her on the forehead, and gently pushed her from the room, closing the door softly behind her.

Barb gathered her shawl around her, lowered the gas, and sitting down on the carpet beside Miss Hendrick's bed-room door, and, laying her head against the rosewood panel, began her night's vigil. She heard the muffled tramp, tramp, of Lionel Roscoe in the passage outside, and the musical tick of the bijou clock on the parlor mantel-piece, but no sound came from the lady's chamber, and gradually she lost consciousness, and slept.

But she dreamed of a mysterious sound, such as

she had never in her life heard, and waking with her hair on end, and her heart throbbing wildly, she found the sounds were a reality.

She rushed into Miss Hendrick's room. She found her lying on her bed; their eyes met, Barb uttered one fearful, piercing shriek, threw herself upon her —there was a short, fierce struggle—then she sank down senseless.

CHAPTER XVI.

BARRY'S REVENGE.

DOES the reader desire his memory to be refreshed upon the movements of Barry Pomeroy in connection with Harrison Fairleigh, which were last recorded? To catch up the thread of her scheme, a reprint of her last letter to him will be necessary. He received it the day before the wedding, on the fourth of February. She wrote:

"HARRISON: Lionel Roscoe is mysterious. He is evidently resolved to bring Barbara Pomeroy and you together, if he can, before it is too late. Tell me once more how you love me, how you honor me; let me read with my eyes what I have so often drunk in with my ears, all you intend to do for me for true love's sake; and if my heart echoes to your words, as I hope it will, you shall find me in Room No. 71, —— Hotel, at midnight of this the fourth of February, ready to go where you will.

"For the last time, I remain,

"Your faithful

"BARBARA POMEROY."

The letter with which Fairleigh answered this crafty appeal, made only, as the reader guesses, to force the deluded fool to commit his perfidy to paper, ran in the following high pressure style :

"My Barbara : For surely Satan himself would be too merciful to snatch you from me now—what can I say to prove the intensity of my passion for you that I have not said a thousand times with more burning fervor—my lips upon your white hand—than I can ever hope to write it ? Oh, Barbara Pomeroy ! you know too well the unutterable power you have over me ; that for love of you I am ready, nay, eager, to throw behind me all that makes men's lives worth the living—honor, the world's approval, social position, even to my sworn faith with Katherine Hendrick. Can man do more for woman than this ? And in the anticipation of the bliss of calling you my *wife*, I glory in the opportunity of thus manifesting the devotion which has so long consumed me. The sneers of the world, the fury of Miss Hendrick, the darkening of all my future prospects seem as a mere breath compared with the ecstacy of the happiness I purchase at their expense. If you will deign to be my wife, sweet Barbara Pomeroy, I shall count myself the most enviable man alive ; and despising all I once held precious, will seek felicity in your dear love, till ruthless death wrests us from each other's arms. Yes, my queen, I meet you at midnight, no more to part. My particular friend, the Rev. Horace Dallas, will accompany me to the hotel, to tie the indissoluble bonds which will make us one forever. Till then, my first, my last, my only beloved, beside whom all others pale into repulsive spectres, farewell, from him whom you have taught to adore you only too well.

" HARRISON."

This missive we have seen Barry place in Katherine Hendrick's hand; this missive we have seen Katherine Hendrick bow over, broken-hearted.

Well, did Barry keep her promise to the man she had lured to this abyss of perfidy ?

Your attention here, if you please; the spectacle will not detain you long.

In a private parlor of one of the fine yet more secluded hotels of the city, a lady, young, gloriously beautiful, and richly dressed, paced slowly up and down the softly carpeted floor, glancing at her jeweled watch from time to time, with eyes which flashed with a weird and eerie light. The dead black silk dress she wore, falling in rich, heavy, unornamented folds to her feet and rustling softly as she walked with velvet tread, seemed to throw the pallor of her countenance into startling relief. Or was it the sump-

10

tuous crimson of her full lips, or the vivid stain of rose on either cheek, that made Barbara Pomeroy look so wildly beautiful, even though so fearfully wan? Sometimes as she passed she caught a glimpse of herself in one of the long mirrors; then she would pause, with a dread smile curling round her roseate mouth, and plunge her glittering eyes into the great fathomless orbs which returned her gaze from the depths of the mirror solemnly; or she would view her magnificent person slowly, from regal head, crowned with its coronet of ebony braids, to her arched bottine of black satin, her breath coming in long, slow gasps the while; or she would dash up the flowing, lace-lined sleeves of her dress, and pass her hands over her delicate, blue-veined arms, and then she would smile a strange smile, and shiver as if an icy wind had struck her to the heart!

Once she lifted her dangling chain and looked at a tiny golden bauble which hung from it, and as the bright gaslight set its facets a-glittering, she dropped it with a single deep sob, and clasped her trembling hands across her eyes, as if its sheen had dazzled her.

"Oh, mother, mother, mother!" groaned Barry Pomeroy. "If you had strangled me at my birth, it would have been better for me!"

A tap at the door.

"He is here," said Barry Pomeroy, and turned to greet her lover with a glorious love-smile.

He took her death-cold hand—his own was burning like his passion-crazed brain, and he presented to her his confidential friend, the Rev. Horace Dallas, a college chum of his, with an eager pride in her and triumph in his approaching possession of her, that seemed nothing more than natural, even to the dispassionate young clergyman the instant he had set his eyes upon her, though only a minute since he had been remonstrating with Fairleigh on his madness.

"You are not regretting?" whispered Harrison, feverishly, as her wonderful eyes rested upon his in a deep, unsmiling gaze.

"No," breathed she; "this night is the culmination of my life. For sake of this night I could consent never to live another."

"God forbid!" aspirated he, hanging over her with looks of delicious adoration. "I have bought you too dearly to lose you, Barbara, and yet the sacrifice was nothing—nothing, compared with the bliss of this moment."

"You have bought me dearly indeed," echoed she, a singular thrill in her cooing tones, "and I have won you as dearly. What I am you have made me; always remember that, Harrison. You know best what I once was."

And this chill truth, falling flat on his hot love, sent a ghastly shudder through all his frame, and blanched his glowing face.

Then it was that Mr. Dallas bade them stand before him, and in a few words bound them together for better, for worse, till death should part them. As he called upon Heaven to bless their union, the husband and wife turned and looked into each other's very souls.

What read Harrison Fairleigh in those mystic depths that froze the fiery kiss upon his bending lips, and wrung from his exulting heart a gasp of nameless terror! Whatever it was, it passed in a moment, and the languorous light of love beamed instead from her eyes.

They were alone at last.

"Never more to part!" breathed he, drunk with his own ecstasy.

" Fold me close, dear," whispered she, yielding her velvet lips in a divine sigh to his, for the first time ; " and oh, love me, love me, love me ! for I have lost my soul for this one hour ! "

* * * * * * *

" Barbara ! "

" My beloved ! "

" You are strangely weary ! "

" Do I seem so, Harrison ? I am not weary of you ! "

"Your dear cheek is pale as a drenched water-lily!"

"Happiness, love! Oh, think of nothing yet but how much we love each other!"

He folded her again to his o'er-fraught heart; his whole soul was permeated with that rapture of felicity which is only to be drunk from the brimming cup of true love; his heart was softened; his nature was ennobled. It was the turning point in Harrison Fairleigh's life; from that hour he might have fared on life's dusty way—a repentant man—a good man.

They were driving in his carriage to the beautiful home he had prepared for Katherine Hendrick; for thither, in Barry's wild lust for vengeance, she had induced him to bear his low-born bride, that his infatuation might blazon itself forth the more shamelessly, and Katherine be yet more brutally humiliated. The whistling wind of that winter night blew sharp-edged through the sumptuous velvets of the richly appointed carriage, and seemed to chill the syren as she lay on his breast, even through all the costly furs which her lover kept carefully round her; even through all the burning kisses which he took from her paling lips, and pressed upon her passionate eyes, and chilling satin cheek.

Was this love-elixir too strong for the woman, now that she had given herself up to the drinking of it, in the perfect abandon of one who, as she had said, had lost her very soul for that one hour?

Or was it that the mighty love this poor creature was cursed with for this, her miserably unheroic lover, turned upon her in its fulfilment, and blasted her with its baleful intensity, annihilating her in its short-lived consummation?

"Barry, surely you are ill?"

"No, love, no! I shall never be better in my life —nor happier!"

"So white, dear! Your very lips—sweet lips that thrill my every vein with rapture!—love, there is a strange lustre in these dear eyes, as if the spirit stood very close behind them, looking out. Barry—Barry —speak to me, my darling, I am afraid!"

"Not of me, Harrison?"

"Heavens! She is too faint to speak aloud! Oh, my angel, love, what have I done?"

"It is nothing; be at peace again. This happiness is sweet, sweet, too deliriously sweet to last forever —let us enjoy every heart-beat of it while we may."

"What should end it, my wife?"

"His wife! O God! am I his wife at last! and —this—hour—is—all."

She burst into a suppressed shriek, and folding her arms round his neck, almost suffocated him with the convulsive strength of her embrace. In startled terror he held her to his breast as she sank down anon, her clasp relaxing, her lips whitening awfully; and pouring forth the most eloquent endearments, besought her to tell him what she felt, or what she meant, or at least to give him some assurance that she loved him truly, and would never remember against him the outrageous insult he had in times past offered her. Presently her glazing eyes opened, she looked up at him with an anguished smile.

"I am faint, my husband," breathed she, in accents almost inaudible. "I would fain be at rest in our new home. Tell them to drive faster—faster, for, oh, the time is passing, and I have much to say!"

So, with the chill of death at his boding heart, he ordered them to speed, and gathering her sinking form close—close to his breast, receiving her fluttering breath on a cheek that was now as white as her own. For oh! he could no longer shut out the grisly presentiment of retribution swift and sure, overwhelming him in the very flush of triumph, crushing him in this, the best, the most joyous moment of his life! He saw in terror and dismay unimaginable the phantom of despair drawing nearer with every muffled heart-beat, stretching out its ruthless hand to part him from her for whose sake he had steeped his name in infamy, his soul in guilt.

They reached the mansion. His confidential ser
vant was ready for them; they were received with
stately honor — servants meeting them with deep
obeisances and well-conned speeches of welcome, lights
blazing, rooms warm and odorous as a Summer morning—all prepared for the bride and bridegroom, just
as it would have been had that wan, dim-eyed shape
that hung on his arms been the queenly daughter of
Baron Hendrick.

He bore her to the bridal-chamber, and laid her on
the sacred couch. She kept her sweet eyes fixed on
his as if they would grow to them. From time to
time a death-like faintness seemed to dim her vision
and drench her lovely face with the fatal dews which
come but once; but even then her glance never faltered, nor did the fixed smile fade from her pale lips.

He untied the magnificent Russian sable which
wrapped her from head to foot, and snatching the
restoratives from the hand of the maid he had summoned to his aid, strove to bring back her vanished
strength, while he prayed her, in heart-rending accents,
to tell him what he could do for her.

"Are we alone?" gasped she.

A motion of his sent the wondering throng of attendants from the room, with the door respectfully
closed.

"Yes, my own sweet wife, you and I are heart to

heart, only God our witness. What have you to say to me, Barry?"

She raised herself from his clinging arms, and passing one shaking hand over her fast benumbing face, uttered a low, shuddering moan.

"Harrison," said she, fixing her gaze once more upon him with terrible intensity, "you would far rather die than lose me now, would you not?"

"God knows I would!" cried he.

"You have ruined yourself to obtain possession of me," she continued. "Henceforth all honorable men will hold you in bitter loathing, all proud women will laugh at you for a deluded fool. If you had simply ruined me, you would have been held blameless; but that you should have ruined yourself to win a wife like me honorably—ah, that is unpardonable. Let me speak, I pray you; I have so little time. Oh, Harrison! why did you not do me this justice at first? Why did you require me to goad you on, through all the shameful dissimulations and cowardices which have blackened your footsteps up to this hour? Had you no eyes to read the fatal truth—that I was luring, luring you on step by step, staining your honor for you, blazoning your folly for you, rendering repentance only ridiculous, and remorse vain, that I might take fitting vengeance upon the man who twice attempted to sacrifice a trusting woman to his lust!"

10*

It was said : the hideous truth was out at last ; and as the monstrous words dropped slowly from her fading lips, the blistering tide of shame spread over her death-stricken face, and at the end she hid it on his stunned heart, and winding her feeble arms about him, wept, poor soul, as if tears could blot out her guilt.

What thought Harrison Fairleigh then ?

For a time earth and heaven reeled before him ; he stood mute as if lightning-struck. This woman, whom he still held mechanically in his arms—this creature who had coiled herself round his heart with such insidious power, in whose mad love he had gloried, whose invincible chastity he had venerated, libertine though he was, giving her only the deeper adoration because of it—this sorceress, for whose sake he had lost the world, counting it but dross to the possession of her—had, oh, unendurable villainy ! but played with him to glut her hellish revenge !

"My God !" groaned he at last, thrusting her from him with such fierce violence that she fell in a heap on the white satin bed, her long black tresses floating about her like a pall ; "my God ! can this be ? Oh, girl, could you not see that you held my very soul in your hand—that for your sake I could be angel or devil, whichever you chose to make me ?"

She answered him nothing ; her eyes were closed,

a frightful convulsion distorted her bloodless countenance, her clasped hands worked spasmodically.

Harrison saw a crimson stain dyeing the glistening purity of the satin coverlet. He bent over it; he saw that it was blood. A piercing cry broke from him once again he snatched her to his breast, and covered her cold mouth with wild kisses.

She opened her sightless eyes for the last time, and gave him her last love-look, her last adoring love-smile.

"And yet," she faltered, in quivering tones, "I loved you all the while, my darling—my darling. So dearly, that rather than live to reap the whirlwind which we two have sown, I've called in death to save us. Kiss me once more, my lover, before my lips grow numb, and my heart ceases to thrill at your touch. Hold me up to your breast, dear; tell me how you love me, poor Barry, whom you have made what she is!"

"Is there no hope, oh! my poor love?" wept Harrison, in frenzied imploration. "Let me save you, sweet. Oh, you cruel girl! can you leave me now?"

"I must!" she shivered out, while the great tears of bitter anguish rolled down her ghastly face. "I did not think it would have been so hard to go. I thought you would have cursed me and taken your love from me, and I dared not live without it!"

"My God! can I not save her yet?" shrieked Harrison; and he would have rushed to summon assistance, but she held him with her feeble clasp, and moaned with agonized tenderness:

"Don't leave me, husband! Give me these few last moments. Death is so near that I scarce can see you now, and I would die with your eyes pouring love and forgiveness into mine. No, beloved, nothing can be done any more for lost Barry—Fairleigh," she uttered the name with a ghost of a smile of pleasure. "As soon as we were married, while I was putting on my wraps, I opened a vein in my arm with my gold penknife, and I have been bleeding to-death ever since."

So, then, these unfortunates clasped each other in a last embrace, and so ebbed her life away.

CHAPTER XVII.

LITTLE BARB BEARS THE BRUNT.

SENSATION of nipping cold, a struggle for breath, as if a mountain lay on her breast, a blurred light growing brighter and brighter, and little Barb Pomeroy came back to consciousness at last, and sprang up with a bewildered cry. She recognized the room—Miss Hendrick's private parlor—and the white, shocked face which bent over her, as Mrs. Archer's, the housekeeper; and, too, the smothered ejaculations, sobs, and confusion which came from the inner chamber as the results of the fearful scene she had taken such dread part in a few minutes ago.

"Oh!" cried Barb, piteously, "is she dead?"

Mrs. Archer recoiled from her with a look of loathing, and, beckoning to some one to approach, gave place, drawing her skirts around her, as one might from some foul contagion.

The next instant Barb's arm was grasped in a strong grip, and, turning in affright, she saw a constable at her side.

At that moment Roscoe entered from the inner room, and seeing the poor girl in the hands of the officer, said, with a visible shudder:

"Take her away! Quick! Don't have her here to blast the eyes of the mother!" and with a gesture of vehement impatience he waved her away as if she was some noxious animal.

Little Barb knew now what all this meant. They suspected her of the murder of Katherine Hendrick.

She stood stupidly staring at Mr. Roscoe, eyes and mouth open, her features rigid, the very personification of apathetic guilt.

"Hush!" said Roscoe, with a look of apprehension, "do I not hear *her* coming?"

They all listened, little Barb taking no meaning out of the sounds of hurried footsteps and breathless ejaculations, and suppressed cries which came from the hall; and anon the door was violently flung open, and the baroness, supported by her female attendant, and closely followed by the baron, burst into their daughter's boudoir.

"What has happened? Where is Katherine?" cried the unfortunate mother, in vehement excitement. "I can understand nothing. What is it, Lionel? The baron won't make himself intelligible."

"For God's sake prepare her, I can't!" said her

husband, hoarsely. "And what's *she* doing here yet?
Has no one the humanity to arrest my daughter's——"
He paused here, Lionel's hand was on his mouth, and
little Barb had uttered a bitter cry, and thrown herself at the baroness's feet.

"His daughter's *what?*" demanded the lady, with
sudden calmness.

No one anwered.

"Stay, I shall see for myself!" cried she, sweeping
across the room with the evident intention of entering Katharine's bed-room forthwith.

Even the accused girl sprang up and attempted to
bar her way, forgetting her own danger for the moment in the horror of the expected revelation which
would meet the unconscious mother's eye.

Every soul in the room participated in her excitement, her captor not excepted, though he could not re-
frain from an internal throe of amazement at the
"cheek" of the young murderess in getting up such
a show of sympathetic sensibility, with her ghastly
work lying a few feet away.

"Who is this?" demanded the baroness, stopping
short.

A motion of Roscoe's sent the constable to the
little creature's side with a touch on her arm.

A wild shriek rang out. It was the mother's cry
of comprehension.

"Something has been done to Katherine—this girl—O Heaven! where is my poor darling?"

"Madam," said Barb Pomeroy, and there was that in her voice, low and tremulous though it was, that forced the lady to listen, and stayed the irritated officer's professional urgency, "your daughter will never know earthly sorrow any more—God pity and forgive her!—but not by my hand, lady—not by my hand has she been thrust out of the world."

The poor woman gazed vacantly at her for a moment or two; then, dead-calm, pushed her aside, and entered her daughter's chamber.

Oh, that fearful cry!

While it yet rang in her ears with a terror never to be forgotten, Barb was hurried from the house. A quarter of an hour afterwards, and the walls of a criminal's prison had closed upon her.

* * * * * * *

What a windfall Katherine Hendrick's death was to the newspapers of the day! It was given to the public with all the graphic power of which their local editors' practised pens were capable.

Strangled by the tiny hand of a jealous rival, twisted in a string of pearls—the bridegroom's wedding gift! A rival picked up by her noble cousin off the boards of a theatre—out of the very ballet corps!

How the eager writers revelled in the piteous details; portrayed the secret interview between the murderess and her victim ; pictured every hideous item of the death-bed scene; the appearance of the dead bride-elect—exquisitely beautiful even in death —with the princely gift of her perfidious lover twined around her slender throat with the horrid tightness of a thug's cord, and held by the child-like hand of her ruthless rival; the bitter vengeance of the illustrious father, growing in fatal intensity every day, the heart-rending grief of the once gay and popular lady mother, who could not be induced to leave the side of her dead, but sat all day long gazing on her face without motion, without apparent fatigue, without the will or the power to tear her eyes away, though the blight of speedy dissolution seemed to be falling upon her own wasting form. With all these fearful details were the greedy public amused, the friends sickened, and the whole city lashed into a fury of impatience for the elucidation of the mysterious circumstances which had led to the murder, and the execution of the murderess.

In the meanwhile, a curious complication had arisen, in the fact, which was at first half incredulously whispered about, but soon came to be proved beyond a doubt, that the bridegroom and his mother's adopted daughter, Marah Leith, was missing.

Little by little those facts, which were known to

this and the other leaked out ; the legal marriage of the pair by his friend, Mr. Dallas, who at once came forward to avow it ; their subsequent appearance at the house on the Hudson ; the fatal indisposition of the young lady, etc ; and, as culmination of the whole monstrous tale, the assertion made by Mr. Fairleigh's servants, that next morning their master and his unexpected bride were nowhere to be found.

Now what was to be thought of this ?

Wild were the opinions hazarded ; but none were half so wild as the reality.

The errant pair were carefully sought by those most competent to the task, and all their ingenuity was in vain—they had left no trace behind.

When the lovely Katherine was carried to her gilded mausoleum, followed by a mile's length of the notables of the city, and the glittering gates were closed upon her dust, Barb's case stood thus :

She had been caught in the very act of murdering Katherine Hendrick.

Several weeks previously she had been seen by Lionel Roscoe speaking to Harrison Fairleigh in Madison Square, and heard to say :

" Beware of Barbara Pomeroy ! "

She was known to have been intimate with Marah Leith, and to have visited her frequently at Mrs Fairleigh's house.

Her antecedents were found to be of the lowest
order. She had been reared by a noted pair of
thieves in a quarter of the city given over to the irre-
claimably vicious; had been easily bought of them
by young Mr. Roscoe, whose motive, as it happened,
was a virtuous one, though no one but himself had
known that; her rescue had been attempted by some
unknown young man who was now, like Mr. Fairleigh and Miss Leith, nowhere to be found; she had
ceased her resistance to the capture whenever she
knew that it was to Miss Hendrick's house that he
intended to bring her; she had ardently wished for
the interview; had worked in some unknown manner
upon Miss Hendrick's mind, so that she, who at first
could scarcely be prevailed upon to see her, presently
begged Mr. Roscoe to leave them alone together for
the night; and then—the murder!

And had she no friends to stand up for her in this
her black hour of terror?

Yes, she had one—He was omniscient—in heaven;
and she had one—she was true as gold—on earth.

Mrs. Fairleigh came to little Barbara the morning
after the tragedy; and, finding her pouring out her
tempest-tossed heart to her other Friend, kneeled
down beside her, put her tender arm around her, and
wept and prayed in eloquent silence with her, and so
comforted the trembling little one and herself in one

bitter-sweet ecstasy of human love and divine trust. Then, lying on her breast, the child told all she had to tell; and this, with many tears of bitter regret, that she had not confided it to the good old lady before, was Barry Pomeroy's story.

The lady heard with grief and amazement unutterable—What? Her Marah capable of imposture, revenge, intrigue, and above all, of betraying this, her too faithful friend, into the foul hands of those worse than fiends, who would have ruined her, body and soul! The sweet soul heard, aghast. It was all but impossible for her to take the monstrous reality in; her ideas of right and wrong were so sharply defined, that but to swerve a step from one was to enter the other; she, who had never been tempted as poor Barry had been, with a nature like a smouldering volcano to begin with, could not now comprehend how that hapless creature could have so deceived her, and not be a hypocrite in the deliberate exercise of her hypocrisy, and capable of anything, even to the leaving of her simple friend Barb, to perish for the crime of which she herself had long been guilty in heart.

In vain the untaught girl of the people strove to rend the vail of the highly nurtured lady's prejudice, and show her the intricate workings of Barbara's misguided heart, which once, pure as Henrietta Fairleigh's own, had passed through all the tragic phases between, till it was what it was to-day.

But, as these two talked of wicked Barry Pomeroy and her impostures, it never once entered into their minds that she might have already passed to the greatest tribunal of all—that Barry might be dead!

Mrs. Fairleigh went from the prison to the office of an eminent counsel, and placed her darling's case in his hands, with the solemn adjuration to save her, or be guilty of innocent blood.

And then the days dragged on; and the papers teemed with fresh items every day: and the lady mothers pined, each in her luxurious abode, while the baron raged and fumed at the tardiness of justice; and the prisoner languished in her lonely cell, and ordered her heart to bear its burden meekly; and the search went on for the missing ones; ah, yes! time passed strangely, and deathly sad till the end came.

CHAPTER XVIII.

THE trial drew on apace; evidence was collected for and against the prisoner quietly and steadily: witnesses were summoned to appear at the coming examination by the lawyers engaged on either side; and oh! how the hearts of the two lady mothers swelled and sickened in anticipation, the baroness's, of her daughter's death being fitly expiated; Mrs. Fairleigh's, of the possible sacrifice of the innocent girl whom she loved!

The latter lady, perhaps, had the heaviest burden of the two to bear.

Her son it was through whom all this misery, crime, and injustice had come to pass; she herself, too, was deeply to blame, inasmuch as she had allowed herself to be duped by a designing woman, who had simply made use of her as a means to her own ends.

Of course the Baron and Baroness Hendrick were incapable of the magnanimity of keeping up the friendship between themselves and Mrs. Fairleigh, and of sharing each other's burdens; in their wrath at the foul play of her son, and in their horror at the girl whom Mrs. Fairleigh so outraged them by befriending, all sympathy with her share of the affliction was forgotten, and they raged and raved against her as if she was as black as the murderess herself.

The morning broke brilliant with spring sunshine —that morning which was to place poor Barb Pomeroy at the bar of the court to plead for her life.

The child sat in her chilly cell, her trembling hands clasped close, close in those of her one earthly friend, Mrs. Fairleigh, and her meek head pillowed upon her breast. The sweet old lady had been with her as constantly as the rules of the prison would permit ever since she had been committed for trial; and to-day she had come at dawn, and devoted herself to the sacred task of encouraging and inspiring the unfortunate little one whose very blood seemed to chill in her veins at the near approach of her dreaded appearance before a public tribunal.

There was a weary change on both the women; these past months of sorrow and suspense had sharpened both the aged and youthful countenances, and blenched them to the same dull parlor; while the dim eyes of Mrs. Fairleigh and the dewy ones of Barb reflected the same haunting look of anxiety. But look beneath these evidences of natural feminine agi-

tation, and you might search far before you would
find a more heroic under-deep of trust in the front of
all the peril than in these pale faces.

The lady's tender kindness had provided many
ameliorations of the rigor of Barb's imprisonment; a
square of soft, bright carpet almost covered the
yellow boards of her floor; several pictures adorned
the whitewashed walls; the bed was draped with
pure white, and flowers bloomed here and there,
shedding their rich perfume—a harrowing reminiscence of meadows and sunshine—for the poor cap-
tive.

"It will indeed be a trying ordeal," said Mrs. Fairleigh, with a weary sigh, "but our sweet little lamb
is not going to be sacrificed unless our Shepherd
wants her for His glorious fold in Heaven, and—no,
no!—He could never desire His dear one to pass to
Him through such a terrible gate!"

Here she buried her face in the girl's soft, yellow
hair, to conceal the throe of agony which this idea
called upon it.

"Has nothing been heard of poor Barry's mother
yet—nothing?" asked Barb, presently; for apart
from the importance to her of such a witness coming
forward to testify to the truth of half her defence,
Barb endured the keenest anxiety concerning the disappearance of the unhappy mother whose daughter

had repudiated her and turned unmoved from her gray hairs.

"Nothing," sighed Mrs. Fairleigh; "nor of your friend, Dr. Wayne, neither. Alas! never was innocence more helpless! Yet fear not, my little Barb, fear not. Ah, the hour has come! Courage—courage!"

A heavy knock sounded at the door; the governor of the prison and his attendants had come to conduct the prisoner to the bar.

With him entered a venerable clergyman, a friend of Mrs. Fairleigh's, who had visited Barb faithfully ever since her arrest. While Mrs. Fairleigh carefully arranged some trifling disorder in the young girl's dress (for she had striven with trembling care to enhance all the natural sweetness of Barb's appearance, knowing well how little often influences a jury), Mr. Ogilvy uttered a few words of such manly cheerfulness and hope that the quailing child nerved herself to what was before her with a sudden rush of confidence in the righteousness of her cause, and presently followed the officials out to the coach, almost with tranquillity.

Her two friends kept by her side, and when at length she was brought into court and placed in the dock, they sat close beside it, ready to receive her first glance, and to smile encouragement upon her.

11

Every nook was crowded to suffocation, the case had been canvassed by the public too long and excitedly not to draw forth a throng unusual even in the annals of murder trials.

As the prisoner entered—a small, blonde, meek, saintly-faced creature, scarce more than a child—a murmur and stir ran through the crowd, and eye sought eye in amazed questioning.

Was this a murderess—this modest, drooping, black-draped girl, with virgin purity upon her downcast countenance, and tender beauty in every shy movement?

Where were the malformed head, the lowering eye, the fugitive side-glance, the cringing attitude, the usual and proper semblance of the blood-shedder?

No wonder the people whispered and jostled to gain a clearer view of the being who so flatly contradicted all the rules of criminal impersonation.

The Baron and Baroness Hendrick, Lionel Roscoe, and many of their friends sat in a conspicuous part of the court, where they could command a full view of the prisoner; and as her shrinking eyes turned round the sea of upraised faces and rested in recognition upon theirs, she grew pale as death, for such bitter animosity and scorn and loathing sure never was poured on helpless mortal before! Seeing her thus overcome, and obliged to lean her swaying form upon the rail in front of the dock, the baron and baroness nodded to each other in bitter significance, and cast looks of eager import toward the gentlemen of the jury, hoping that they, too, had observed and interpreted, as they themselves had, the prisoner's agitation.

But Roscoe bent forward in his seat, gnawing his lip and knitting his brows, and for many minutes did not lift his gaze from Barb's countenance.

The indictment was read amidst profound silence, and the question asked the accused:

"Prisoner at the bar, do you plead guilty or not guilty to the charge?"

Barb knew this was coming, and had nerved herself to answer it calmly. A strange thrill ran through all who heard her low, modest voice exclaiming:

"Not guilty, so help me God!"

In such accents might the purest infant of any parent there have spoken. Hush! how sweet and frail she is! God keep us, gentlemen, from the seductive snares of a siren!

So mused the people; and Lionel Roscoe drew a deep breath, as if his rising heart threatened to choke him with its hard, hot beating.

The case was now duly opened by the counsel for the prosecution.

It may be as well to give in our own words a rehash of the learned gentleman's speech, which held the court in breathless attention for almost an hour; it was in effect a recapitulation of Barb's history, with which we are already acquainted, but so distorted and misapprehended throughout, that it might quite as appropriately have been the history of the blackest wretch ever exposed, as that of our simple girl of the people.

Here is his account, abbreviated:

Eighteen months ago, two young girls came to the Home for the Friendless—a charitable institution in —— Street; their names were Marah Leith and Barbara Pomeroy; they were out of employment, and ready for anything the matron had to offer. She had nothing at the time to offer, but at the end of a week or so, a lady, Mrs. Fairleigh, called in search of a young girl suitable for adoption. She chose Marah Leith, and took her home; and Barbara, partly through her assistance, obtained respectable employment as a dressmaker. All went on with apparent harmony in Mrs. Fairleigh's home, and the dressmaker's humble abode for upward of a year; then Mr. Harrison Fairleigh returned from abroad, saw Marah Leith, and was obviously attracted from the first by her unusual beauty and mental superiority. Witnesses would be summoned to testify to the many attentions he offered her, keeping concealed, both from Miss Leith and his mother, the fact of his engagement to Miss Hendrick, to whom he was to be married in a month. The accused visited Miss Leith more frequently than usual during this period, but there was no testimony to show that she ever met Mr. Fairleigh upon these occasions; though there was to show that she was cognizant of the friendly intimacy between Miss Leith and him, and that she earnestly disapproved of it. In the course of time Mr. Fairleigh made his engagement known, and Mrs. Fairleigh and Miss Leith called upon the Baroness Hendrick and her daughter; it would presently be shown that a spirit of bitter distrust of Miss Leith sprang up in Miss Hendrick's heart from the moment when she first beheld her, and that Miss Leith insolently strove to rouse her jealousy by parading her intimacy with Miss Hendrick's affianced husband. All this might go to prove that Miss Leith was the head in this adventure, and Barbara Pomeroy the hand, and the sequel would bear the speaker out in his opinion, he assured the court. On such and such a date, Mr. Roscoe chanced to observe his friend Mr. Fairleigh stroll into Madison Square, and presently he followed him, expecting to find him smoking his cigar and musing over his approaching happiness. To his surprise, however, he discovered him in close conversation with a young woman, who, as Mr. Roscoe approached, seemed to be taking her leave, and who said, in such a manner as to lend a very sinister significance to the words, that which proved to be the first link of the chain of evidence which fastened the crime of murder upon her to-day.

The next we saw of Barbara Pomeroy in this affair was at the masked ball given by Baroness Hendrick in honor of her daughter's last appearance in society before her marriage. There, it would be shown how the two adventuresses comported themselves; Miss Leith, in audacious defiance of the bride-elect's superior claims on Mr. Fairleigh, and the accused, who had evidently stolen thither from curiosity to see Miss Hendrick and Mr. Fairleigh together, seemingly overawed by the unfortunate lady's exquisite beauty and grace, and slinking away at the first opportunity. From this time it would appear that the prisoner had transferred all her jealousy from her accomplice to Miss Hendrick—that believing such beauty and passion invincible—for on that occasion the bride-elect showed all the fervid passions of a woman in love, whose rights are trampled upon by the base—she ceased to account Miss Leith any longer a rival to be feared in comparison with this fascinating lady; and henceforth, Katherine Hendrick was a doomed woman. Hitherto, probably, Miss Leith had twisted the ignorant girl to her own purposes pretty much as she chose; it was clear that they had started fair with each other in the beginning of their connection with Mrs. Fairleigh; that Mr. Fairleigh's advent upon the scene was the signal for dissension between them, ending in absolute estrangement; there was but one way to account for this state of matters—namely, that the prisoner had had some acquaintance in the course of what would presently be seen was not an irreproach-able pre-history with Mr. Harrison Fairleigh; that she had hoped to recommence it upon his return to New York; that Marah Leith had stepped between, ruining her chances; and that, finally, Miss Hendrick was about to put an end to her nefarious designs on him forever, by uniting herself to him in honorable wedlock. These, the learned gentleman submitted to the gentlemen of the jury as plain and palpable motives for the foul act of which the prisoner at the bar stood accused.

In the meanwhile Marah Leith was playing a game far too deep for Barbara Pomeroy's eye—no less a game than that of seducing Mr. Fairleigh from his fidelity to his bride into a marriage with herself. Unaware of this plot, the prisoner, who had returned some time previously to associates whose reputation smelled foul as any den in Water Street, was captured by Mr. Roscoe on the deceased's wedding-eve, and taken by him to the lady's house, with the hope of wringing from her so much of Mr. Fairleigh's private character as would save his cousin from a miserable marriage, even at this late date.

Mr. Roscoe had been anxiously searching for Barbara Pomeroy ever since the day he saw her in the Square, the capricious conduct of Mr. Fairleigh urging him on to seek some explanation. His agents had at last discovered her living a sort of incognito existence with two old friends of hers, whose characters did not do her much credit. Of these wretches Mr. Fairleigh actually bought the prisoner, who, they assured him, was frequently thus bought and sold by those who were willing to pay their price for her, she being their property.

And here the lawyer paused to give the jury time to take this statement in all its enormity, and the people a chance to relieve their feelings in whispers of horror and disgust. But the prisoner was seen to turn her swimming eyes upon those of the aged lady whose soft old hand grasped hers through the railing, and to straighten her slight figure with a faint, proud smile, such as only the innocent should wear.

Lionel Roscoe, too, half rose from his place with an eager gesture, but was hastily pulled down again by the junior counsel for the prosecution, and pacified by some whispered promise.

The lawyer proceeded.

Mr. Roscoe having effected his purchase, took possession of her when she was making her escape from the theatre, she having apparently some private intrigue of her own choosing on hand which her owners were ignorant of; and having snatched her from the arms of an unknown young man who had never been heard of since, carried her to his hotel, where the baroness's housekeeper waited to assist him in his disagreeable task; and from thence took her to the house of Baron Hendrick. The family had retired, but Miss Hendrick was still up, and when summoned to her door by her cousin, appeared in the agitated frame of mind natural to her interesting circumstances.

At first she refused to be disturbed by the strange visitor, but upon Mr. Roscoe mentioning that the matter was connected with Mr. Fairleigh, she permitted the prisoner to enter her room. In a few minutes she announced to her anxious cousin that she would have the young girl stay that night with her, and, utterly regardless of his horrified entreaties, closed the door upon him.

"Now, gentlemen," said the counsel for the prosecution, impressively, "by what sorcery did the prisoner obtain this extraordinary indulgence? Clearly by working on Miss Hendrick's ever-latent distrust of Marah Leith; most likely by pretending to have something of great moment to communicate concern-

11*

ing her. At all events, she effected her purpose; and with murder in her heart, and the meekness and simplicity of a child in her looks and words—a mere trick of form and expression, gentlemen—she lured her victim into such a feeling of security that she actually fell asleep upon her couch, and then performed the hellish work she long had meditated. At two o'clock in the morning, Mr. Roscoe, who had never ceased to pace before the door of his cousin's parlor, heard piercing screams for help. Before he could break down the door and make his way to Miss Hendrick's chamber, all was over. The lady lay on her bed with the breath choked out of her; her hands were twined in a pearl necklace which was twisted round her throat, in a desperate struggle to loosen it, and the hand of the prisoner was found twisted in it also, but with murderous purpose, she having given way to the horror of her awful deed the moment she saw it was accomplished, and fallen across Miss Hendrick's body insensible."

Again the lawyer paused, not only too much moved himself to proceed, but out of respect to the storm of agitation which swept through the court, and the heart-rending distress of the murdered lady's parents, who both wept unrestrainedly.

Great crystal tears were gushing over the transparent cheeks of the accused also, and she was seen to wring her friend's hand with the most finished expression of grief—a spectacle to which the lawyer presently called the attention of judge and jury in a burst of indignation.

"In the defence you will hear much of the prisoner's gentleness, virtue, magnanimity, and all the other Christian graces. Gentlemen, it is easy for some people to impose upon the charitable and the old. The childish contour of a face, the ever-ready tear, the simulated timidity and helplessness of extreme youth—all are very efficient weapons of defence when their possessor's life depends on their clever use. Hypocrisy, gentlemen, can assume any face that suits its purpose; and what are a few tears in the appropriate place to a practised actress? But to continue. The prisoner is here charged with murder; witnesses are here to prove her guilt, to attest to her motive, and to show that this act came but in natural sequence in a life of vice. If for once I can succeed in unveiling a criminal whose innocent seeming, cunning, simple ways will be apt to mislead the honest-hearted, unless they are forever on their guard against her wiles, I shall feel that justice is not yet dead in America, for all the sneers that are cast at her so-called partiality to the brass-faced evil-doer."

With these words the lawyer sat down.

CHAPTER XIX.

THE first witness called upon the stand by the junior counsel for the prosecution was old Nan.

At sight of her bestial and half-drunken visage, her hair flying about it in ragged elf-locks, and her person filthy and untidy in the extreme (for Mr. Kean, the counsel for the prosecution, understood too well the art of strengthening his case to permit this valuable witness against the accused to appear before the jury in any other than her native rags), a movement of disgust was observed to pass through the court, while the prisoner turned away with a visible shudder, at which Mr. Kean and his junior, Mr. Hawksly, exchanged sarcastic glances, and the people hardened their hearts against her seeming sensibility.

Having been duly sworn, old Nan turned her evil eyes around the court until they fell upon poor shrinking Barb, when she said, loud enough for every one present to hear:

"Oh, ye poor cretur, is this wot ye've come to after all me trouble with ye! I always knew ye wor a bad lot, but I never thought to see the day when ye would disgrace me like this!"

The examination proceeded.

"What is your name?" asked the junior counsel.

"An-toy-net Blaze," answered the lady, with a tipsy leer; "Old Nan for short, and well known an' respected by all me neighbors in Cardinal Court for a honest working woman as has seen no end——"

"Very good, please say nothing but in answer to my questions," said Mr. Hawksly, sternly. "When did you first become acquainted with the prisoner?"

"A matter of eighteen years ago, your honor," replied Nan, overawed for the moment.

"Where?" queried the counsel.

"Five Points," mumbled the witness, with a sinister chuckle. "She wor on'y a babby without ere a cretur to do for her, an' I has such a feel-in' heart, I tuk the little wiper home with me. Little did I think——"

"Never mind what you thought," interrupted Mr. Hawksly, impatiently. "How came the infant to be alone?"

"Her nurse was bringin' her out to some relashuns, but died on the way," muttered Nan, decidedly ill-pleased with the subordinate part she was obliged to play.

"Did you know where these relations were to be found?" continued the lawyer.

"I heard, but forgot right away," said Nan, with a wink. "Sence I wasn't agoin' to give her up, why should I keep their address inter my head?"

"How did you know her name was Barbara Pomeroy?" was the next question.

"'Cos it was marked all over her duds, it wor. No end of expense," said Nan, "them duds wos all the money's worth I ever got of her."

"What was your occupation at that time?" queried Hawksly.

Nan grinned, but made no audible reply.

"I dare say it won't stand scrutiny," said he, shrugging his shoulder. "Well, what did you want with the child?"

"I wanted her for to grow up a blessin' to me!" whined Nan; "but la', I might hev knowed a love-child wouldn't turn out nothin' good."

"Are you sure she was that?"

"In course she were!"

Mr. Hawksly then asked her present occupation.

"Charring," replied the witness.

"Anything else?"

"Am I to make a clean breast right now?"

"You are to remember that you are upon your oath, and to speak the truth accordingly."

" All right: it's so d—d hard to please you law fellows, you tell us to say so and so, and when we do you're down on us like——"

" Hold your tongue, you're drunk!" cried Mr. Hawksly, furiously; while Mr. Kean hitched about in his chair and coughed in an agony of discomfiture. " Take care, or you'll be committed for contempt of court. What do you do for a living besides charring ?"

" Bless my eyes, don't get into such a fluster!" remonstrated the wretch, cringingly. " I'll say or do whatever ye like."

" Stand down !" roared Mr. Kean. " Pardon, Mr. Justice and gentlemen of the jury, but in spite of all our care to produce this witness in a state of decent sobriety, she has contrived to elude our vigilance, and is, as you may see, stupified with drink. Call forward Timothy Polson."

Nobody making any objection to this, Miss Antoynet Blaze was led out of the court, muttering a volley of oaths as she went, and casting a malignant glance toward Barb, whom she had fondly hoped to damage irretrievably by blazoning forth her own shame, and then associating the young girl inextricably with herself. Unfortunately, her natural stupidity had balked her design, for she did not perceive how fatal to her credibility as a witness was the admission she insisted on making, namely, that she had been previously instructed by the counsel for the prosecution what to say.

Some odd glances were interchanged by the other side as she staggered out, and Mr. Bonar, the counsel for the defendant, made a note or two.

Timothy Polson appeared in his associate's place, and the examination proceeded.

This gentleman being far more in fear of the law than Miss Blaze, or not being upheld by her pot-courage, answered all Mr. Hawksly's questions with meekness and a very gratifying directness. From him the assembled throng learned, in unmistakable terms, quite enough of the private affairs of old Nan, connected as they were with his own, to brand them both with a character of blackest infamy; and this having been achieved, Mr. Hawksly continued:

" How long have you known the prisoner ? "

" Ever since I come to Cardinal Court, four or five years ago," replied Tim.

" Was she living by herself ? "

" No; she wor old Nan's gal. Old Nan picked her up somewheres around the Battery or tharabouts, when she wor a brat in long clothes, an' reared her for to be a comfort to her when she got old."

" What was the prisoner's occupation then ? "

"H-m-ahem!   Wal, she wor pretty smart in a crowd; not by no means backward of any of 'em in the court, I rayther believe."

"You mean that she was an accomplished pickpocket?"

"Why, yes, I suppose that's your way of puttin' it."

"What was her age then?"

"Maybe twelve, and the rummest little sly cuss you ever see.   Folks used to stop her in the street to give her pennies, she looked so precious innercent an' harmless, an' she'd take 'em off to old Nan an' me arterwards, fit to make ye bust."

At this monstrous lie the unfortunate young creature turned such a harrowing look of wonder and reproach upon the ruffian that he was fain to snatch his eyes from hers, and take refuge in feeling all his pockets for a quid of tobacco.   More than one of the ladies present catching that eloquent glance grew paler, and tears rushed to their eyes.

But the baron and baroness sat inflexible, passing cruel judgment upon her; the judge and jury, too, received every statement with a matter-of-course air, which boded ill for their leniency.

Mr. Hawksly proceeded:

"As she grew older, what was her mode of life?"

Again Tim cleared his throat with an affectation

of reluctance, and then made a hideous assertion which wrung from the outraged girl a sudden wrathful cry.

"That's false! false"! said little Barb, stretching her slender arms and lifting her crimson, tear-wet face heavenward. "God knows it's false! Your Honor, believe me, I would have starved, or let them beat me to death before I'd have stooped to be what he says!"

"Your Honor," interposed Hawksly, hastily, "we have other witnesses to substantiate what this witness asserts. No doubt the prisoner's counsel will be able to refute them with reliable testimony if they trifle with the truth."

The judge bowed, the throng whispered dubiously, and Hawksly proceeded in a great hurry:

" Under what circumstances did the prisoner leave the shelter of Antoinette Blaze's roof eighteen months ago ? "

The wretch gave a glib account of her flight with Barry, whom he described as one of the " flash customers from Fifth Avenoo," who had lured Barb away to make use of her; and having done everything in his power to blast the prisoner's character, he was about to quit the box in triumph, when Mr. Bonar detained him to put him through a rigid cross-examination, with, however, very little result, thanks to the previous drilling he had received from Messrs. Kean and Hawksly.

After his exit, several disreputable personages appeared in turn on the stand, and swore away the poor remains of little Barb's good name, until there was not a soul there who did not look upon her as an utterly lost and abandoned creature, having come into the world through her parents' shame, her only inheritance their vicious proclivities, and her life a continuation of theirs,—this was accepted by the mass present, with the exception of Mrs. Fairleigh, her friend the good clergyman, and, yes, perhaps Lionel Roscoe, if one might judge by the painful intensity of the gaze he kept fastened upon her, and the impatient gnawing of his nails and frequent writhings in his seat, as if he would fain be on his feet contradicting every word. And yet Lionel Roscoe firmly believed in her guilt as a murderess.

The next to be called upon the stand was Mrs. Fairleigh's groom, who had time and again accompanied Mrs. Harrison Fairleigh and Miss Marah Leith in their drives together, and who testified to the unmistakable affection which was between them, and to the remonstrances which he had more than once overheard Barb making in Miss Leith's room to the intimacy, which she had designated as " dangerous," and " sure to come to no good," etc., etc.

Then Lionel Roscoe was called, and went through the narrative of the interview between Harrison and Barb in Madison Square, with the significant words he had heard her use.

" Beware of Barbara Pomeroy!" quoted Lionel; and a hush fell on the jostling and staring people, and they listened breathlessly to this the first testimony which directly implicated the accused in the crime for which she was being tried. Lionel went through his part with the utmost calmness and moderation, until he came to the period when, having carried Barb off from the theatre in spite of her resistance, he was confronted by her in the hotel.

" Your Honor, and gentlemen of the jury," said the young Englishman, loyal to fair play in the teeth of public opinion, " whatever the faults of the unhappy woman before you may be, I, for one, will never believe her deserving of the tainted character these people have chosen to brand her with. Supposing me to have abducted her for a wicked purpose, she confronted me upon my entering into her presence as any other virtuous woman would have confronted the scoundrel who sought to betray her—she was ready to choose death to dishonor. Had I presumed to touch her she would have thrown herself from the window. Come, whatever she is, she is guiltless of shame ! "

The two lawyers for the prosecution rewarded him with a severe frown, and the judge looked puzzled; but the frail girl at the bar turned her sweet white face upon him with a gentle gratitude that somehow wrung his very heart, and made the next questions which he was called upon to answer seem doubly horrible.

These all pertained to the immediate scenes of the fatal night, from the time when Barb was introduced into the house of the baron to the moment when Lionel rushed into Katherine's bedchamber and discovered her lying dead from strangulation, and Barb lying across her insensible, with her hand still twisted in the rope of pearls which she had used to murder her with.

This portion of his testimony was corroborated by Mrs. Archer, the housekeeper, by the baron, and by a host of servants, who had hurried to the spot upon the first alarm raised by Lionel.

These all having been examined and carefully cross-examined by the counsel for the defendant, Mr. Kean said, solemnly:

"This is the case," and sat down.

"Call forward the witnesses for the defence," said the judge, breaking into the buzz and murmur of excited voices.

The first to enter the box was Mrs. Fairleigh; examined by Mr. Bonar, she gave a beautiful testimony to the worth of little Barb; indeed, so tenderly did she speak of the simplicity, heroism, and pure sincerity of the young girl's character ever since she had known her, that many who heard her wept for sympathy, and looking on the accused through her eyes for the nonce, vowed they saw her lovely spirit shining through, and that such as she seemed could not, for sure, be guilty. She did her best, also, to do away with the unfavorable impression so craftily instilled into the public mind by Hawksly's insinuations regarding her birth, by narrating the conversation which had taken place between Mrs. Pomeroy and Barb on that subject the night the young girl was kidnapped, and though this was scarcely in order, it told decidedly. The jury, too, seemed vastly impressed by the good lady's explanations; in fact, it told on all present, which Messrs. Kean and Hawksly no sooner perceived than they set to work to destroy the effect by holding up Mrs. Fairleigh's well-known charities—of which there were enough to have shamed them into a better spirit—to ridicule, as the one foible of her otherwise well-balanced mind, citing several laughable incidents in which she had been egregiously mistaken. Of course there was but one impression left on people's minds after they were finished with the subject—that little Barb was the latest fraud who had victimized her protectoress. Be sure the name of Marah Leith had not been left out of this discussion; nor Barb's confidential terms with her allowed to redound to her honor. As Mrs. Fairleigh stepped down from the witness-box she had the agony of feeling that she had done all in her power to vindicate the innocent, and that her efforts were already frustrated.

The next witness called up was Hugh Wayne's sister Nettie, whom we last saw at Thunder Peak, sewing on Barry Pomeroy's wedding veil, the night she fled from home.

Mr. Bonar's object in producing her was to prove the existence of another Barbara Pomeroy, and so gradually to build up such a case of circumstantial evidence against this other, that the motive which was ascribed to Barb as actuating the deed, might be explained away. If they could succeed in this, Barb's own story of the manner in which the deceased met her death would have some chance to be received with due weight.

"What is your name?" inquired the counsel for the defence.

"Annette Wayne," replied the pretty young lady, in charming confusion.

"Where do you live?"

"At Rensselaer's Landing."

"Were you ever acquainted with any one of the name of Barbara Pomeroy?"

"Yes, sir," faltered Nettie, looking down.

"Look on the prisoner, if you please. Is she the Barbara Pomeroy you knew?"

"No."

There was a great sensation at this. It was the first inkling the public had that there was another Barbara Pomeroy; it was the first inkling the lawyers on the other side had that there was another Barbara Pomeroy. Astonishment sat on every face. A sudden light gleamed over Lionel Roscoe's. He leaned back with folded arms, almost smiling on little Barb!

"Who was the Barbara Pomeroy you knew?" continued Mr. Bonar, quietly.

"She was the daughter of our late minister, and lived with her mother in her uncle's house at Thunder Peak, some miles from my home."

"Your late minister—was he an American?"

"No, sir, he came from England when he was a young man."

"Do you know anything of his antecedents?"

"Nothing positively. Some said he came of good blood."

"Does the prisoner at all resemble him?"

"Yes, she is as like him as woman can be to man."

"Very good, we shall return to this again. Now about Miss Pomeroy.

"What did you know of her?"

"Nothing but good—nothing but good, poor Barry!" returned the young lady with emotion. "We went to school together, we grew up together. When she became engaged to my brother Hugh, I was as happy as he, for she was the loveliest, the best, the cleverest girl in all the country side; at least, we thought so."

"What is your brother's occupation?"

"He is a doctor."

"How long is it since he became engaged to Barbara Pomeroy?"

"About two years."

"Are they married now?"

"No."

"Are they still engaged to each other?"

"No."

"What broke the match off?"

"Alas! I don't know. Until lately, Hugh himself could not guess."

"When did you last see Barbara Pomeroy?"

"Eighteen months ago."

"Under what circumstances?"

"It was the week before she was to have been married. I and cousin Lizzie Bright were at her uncle's house, helping her with her wedding things; we were to be bridesmaids. She had been in a queer mood all day—sort of nervous and hysterical, we thought; but we supposed it natural enough, and did not trouble about it. However, that evening she seemed so excited that Hugh got alarmed, and went out with her to the garden to find out what was the matter. I believe she put him off with some excuse, promising to tell him what troubled her in the morning. In the morning she was gone!"

"Gone? Where?"

"Nobody could tell. She left a letter for her mother, bidding her good-by, and promising to come back when she was happy again."

"Could no one guess what induced her to act in such an extraordinary manner?"

"Oh, there were many guesses made, but all unjust and without foundation, I am sure."

"Mention some of them."

"I am sorry to do so, sir; I love Barry Pomeroy! They said that she had run off with a lover from the city. I know it was false."

"Can you prove that it was?"

"No."

"What foundation was there for such a rumor?"

"Some of the neighbors said they had seen her in

conversation with a young gentleman, a stranger in our parts. I can't believe it, because she never said anything about any stranger."

"Was it proved that there was a stranger staying at Thunder Peak about that time?"

"No, not at Thunder Peak, but there was at the hotel in Rensellaer's Landing."

"His name?"

"His name was *Harrison Fairleigh!*"

There was another sensation in court at these words. The people swayed to and fro in their excitement; the baron and baroness turned looks of amazed appeal upon their lawyers, who sat glaring helplessly at the witness.

The judge took a few hurried notes, the jurors whispered animatedly together; Lionel Roscoe's countenance cleared yet more radiantly. Even Mrs. Fairleigh glanced around with a more assured air.

But the prisoner's sweet face was hidden in her trembling hands. She was weeping for lost Barry Pomeroy!

"What proofs are there to substantiate this assertion?" demanded Kean, jumping up.

"All in good time," said Bonar, coolly. "Let us finish with one witness before we summon another. Now, Miss Wayne, will you be kind enough to tell the court what you next knew of Barbara Pomeroy?"

"For more than a year we could hear nothing, though my poor brother devoted himself to the search for her, to the ruin of his practice and the breaking of his heart. But one evening last January a young lady came to our house and asked to see my brother on private business. She was a friend of our lost Barry's, and she had come to Hugh with news of her."

"Did you see the lady?"

"Yes, I saw her—I gave her a cup of hot tea, for she was cold and trembling."

"Did you hear her name?"

"I did not.'

"Would you know her if you saw her again?"

"Indeed I would! She came on an angel's errand —I shall never forget her sweet face!"

"Do you see her in court!"

"Yes."

"Where?"

Nettie turned her flushed and smiling face suddenly, and stretching out her arm said, with deep feeling :

"In the prisoner's dock, where I am sure she has no right to be!"

A wave of feeling surged over the court ; a faint hum of applause rose, to be instantly checked, however, by the wily Hawksly springing up with the unsympathetic query :

"Had the doctor's fair visitor come to set him upon her friend's track, that she might spoil her game with Mr. Harrison Fairleigh?"

This, not being a question in form, was suppressed by his Honor with some asperity, but it had served its purpose, and in reminding all present of the allegations under which the prisoner lay, effectually cooled their incipient enthusiasm.

"My brother did not inform me what the young lady had confided to him," said Nettie Wayne, when order was once more restored; "he was in great trouble, and besides, hastening out his carriage to drive the lady up to Thunder Peak to see Barry's mother."

"They went that same night to Thunder Peak, did they?" proceeded Mr. Bonar.

"Yes, in the middle of a snow-storm, through roads drifted in places breast-high, so anxious was the lady to reach Mrs. Pomeroy."

"And what happened then?"

"For three days nothing happened—they were drifted up and could not get away, then they came back with Mrs. Pomeroy, who was very ill; they had found her at the point of starvation beside old Mr. West, who was dying of paralysis. We nursed her until she was able to travel, and then she, the young lady and Hugh, went to the city."

"Were you not informed for what purpose they went?"

"Not in so many words, it was a subject I knew to be frightfully painful to Hugh, and of course I could not discuss it with him; but he let me gather that Barry was in some sort of danger which this young lady was trying to save her from, and that they hoped her mother's presence would be a safeguard for her."

"What excuse did the prisoner give for not revealing her name?"

"She gave none, but Hugh said that the mention of it would only rouse all the gossip in the place. I know now what he meant, though it puzzled me so then—the accident of her name being the same as poor Barry's, not to mention her extraordinary resemblance to our minister, would have been quite enough to set the craziest reports about the country-side, especially as neither the young lady herself nor any one else could account for the coincidence."

"What was the next event that transpired?"

"In three or four days Hugh came back alone, so crushed and despondent, yet trying to look hopeful, that I knew in a minute that whatever had befallen Barry, she had not melted to him. All he told me was, that God had sent one of His angels to look after our poor girl, and that he hoped some day, not too far off, to see her back to her mother's side in safety."

"What next?"

"Alas! nothing but perplexity and mystery for me. A week afterward my brother got a letter written in the most illiterate sort of a hand, evidently by one entirely unaccustomed to writing. Stay, I have it here, he left it on his office-table when he went, for he was in the saddest way!"

She here produced a scrap of paper in a torn envelope, which Mr. Bonar read aloud, and then passed to the judge.

Does our gentle friend who is skimming these pages remember that dreary scene of little Barb in her foul captivity, scratching her appeal to "one-eyed Sal," the organ-grinder, on the backs of a knave of hearts, an ace of diamonds, and a ten of clubs, with the ends of some burnt matches, while her jailor, Tim Polson, smoked in the background and listened enjoyably to the music?

This is the letter of her envoy to Hugh Wayne:

"Sur—Litel Barb of Cardnel Cort says to tel Doktr that she is in trubl cos old nan has her and Bary is wuss, and I nos meself tha tha meens no good by the dere sweet lam that I thot had got clar of them forever. Yu wil find me at my logins at 856 Ave., top floor, hal room, by name one Ide Sal. Very respectfully, Sal."

This humble epistle was addressed in characters and spelling which no one would have been bold enough ever to suppose could reach the person meant, to

> "Doktr Wan
>> Renslrs Landng
>>> Hudsn Rivr."

"This letter you say your brother received a week after his return?" proceeded Mr. Bonar; "he answered it by going to the city, did he?"

"He did. He told me that Barry was worse, he feared worse than dead; indeed, he was in such a frightful state of mind, that he spoke quite wild, and I did nothing but try to soothe my poor fellow. Within an hour after receiving the letter he had gone, and from that day to this, I have neither seen nor heard from him. For—forgive me, but I can say no more now, gentlemen—my—my poor heart is breaking, I think!"

And, bathed in tears, and watched in profound silence with looks of respectful sympathy, the trembling girl was led from the witness-box.

CHAPTER XX.

HOW MAN SMIRCHED THE PAGE THAT GOD COUNTED WHITE.

APROPOS of the last witness's testimony, the next brought forward by the counsel for the defence was One-eyed Sal herself, who, in words uncouth as her own appearance, spoke such things of "little Barb, old Nan's gal," as sent the costliest lace handkerchief in the house to eyes not used to any tears that were not drawn thither by the reigning prima donna's sorrows, melodiously warbled at four thousand dollars a night.

To think of that tiny creature, so wan and sweet, clad in very rags, with the blue marks of brutal abuse on her transparent cheek and shivering, unclothed shoulders, running out barefooted in the snow to give half her scanty meal to Sal's sick boy; or, if she had nothing else to give, to whisper in his wondering ear some loving endearment, and some marvellously pretty verse about "Jesus and the Lamb, and such." To catch glimpses of her here among the desperate women of Cardinal Court, cheering them to "try

12*

again!" yonder among the fierce, drink-maddened brawlers at the tavern doors, begging them in loving tones, by name, every one of them, as if they were her own brothers, to "come away;" to "go home to poor Mollie," or "to cast a thought, for pity's sake, to little Jack tied in his chair in the cold garret, and crying for daddie!"

"Ah!" the rude orator burst out, clasping her skeleton hands together, and looking at the prisoner with eyes as wet and reverent as the best love in her heart could make them; "you knew the way to all our hearts, you did, an' there's a many of us 'ud lay down our lives this day to save ye, an' welcome!"

Thank God for that cheer!

It rang out from bosoms stirred by the divine; it spoke of the presence of the noblest of human emotions; it shivered for a little season that hideous idol —SELF—from his throne in too many hearts there; it thrilled the foes of little Barb with the half hope that, after all, public opinion might cast such a shield around their prey that so-called justice would be balked, and her friends with the full conviction of her innocence being shown out incontestably;—ay, as that cheer rang out from the multitude, it seemed as if the very heavens brightened and glowed in sympathy with the God-like instinct of pure goodness that for one moment magnetized the mass.

When the echoes had died away—and for once no one uttered any protest—Mr. Bonar drew from the woman the most satisfactory corroboration of Miss Wayne's statements in regard to the letter her brother had received, with a characteristic account of the circumstances under which it had been written; Barb's enforced captivity, the current reports of the cruelties practised upon her by her vile jailors; Dr. Wayne's arrival in the city; anxiety about Barb; his letter to her, etc., etc., etc.

Comparing these facts with Kean's dark insinuations concerning the young man who had interfered with Mr. Roscoe's abduction of Barb from the Opera House, how brightly Mr. Bonar flashed forth his client's purity of mind and purpose throughout the whole of the transactions which had been so distorted!

The next witness called was the landlord of the hotel in Rensselaer's Landing, who brought his visitor's book for last year to prove that Harrison Fairleigh, New York, had spent some six weeks at his house during the summer of Barbara Pomeroy's disappearance from her home at Thunder Peak.

After him several residents of the place came forward, who had been eye-witnesses of certain passing meetings between the said gentleman and the young girl. Then the matron of the institution to which Barb had brought Barry the night of that day she had rescued her from the jeering mob in the street. This excellent lady described the young woman whom the prisoner had brought to her so graphically, that the baroness and her husband listened astonished, tracing in every expression a perfect reproduction of Marah Leith, while gentle Mrs. Fairleigh sat pale and downcast, with her teeth buried in her frigid lip, ashamed.

Soon the matron was asked for her impressions of the character of the prisoner; and you should have seen her kindly face light up and her eye moisten as she dwelt on "the child's modesty, industry, and lovely generosity to her friend, the other girl, who seemed of as dark and gloomy a nature as she was open and sweet," as the lady expressed herself. She narrated the incident of Mrs. Fairleigh's visit to the institution in search of a young girl suitable to adopt in place of her own daughter, when, her fancy having been captivated by the gentle graces of the child Barb, she chose her, but was diverted from her choice by little Barb pleading her friend's greater need of such a safe and tender home, and supplicating her to take Marah Leith instead of her.

There was no resisting warm-hearted Mrs. Martyn's story. Again and again a thrill of ungovernable emotion ran through the multitude, and they felt the irresistible power of simple truth as they

could not be made to feel the clever sophistries of
Kean and Hawksly, studied as these were for weeks
ahead. In conclusion, she assured the court that she
had kept loving track of the prisoner ever since, and
had nothing to say of her course but what was admiring; so steadily and nobly had she worked on
alone, keeping her name as pure as the highest lady's
in broad America!

And as she stepped down, again the people cheered
for Barb, till shy roses began to bloom in her thin
cheeks and diamond drops of gratitude to twinkle in
her modest eyes.

After her came Barb's boarding-house mistress, who
testified to her boarder's unassailable character, and
unchangeable goodness of life all the time she had
been in her house; who also attested to the arrival
of an old lady of the name of Pomeroy, whom Miss
Pomeroy had brought from the country with her
some few days before the commission of the murder,
and lodged in her front room, first story; she also
remembered the visits of Dr. Wayne to Mrs. Pomeroy, and wound up with the sudden astonishing disappearance of Barb, succeeded by the no less per-
plexing removal of Mrs. Pomeroy by the strange
young lady at the dead of night. This narration
dovetailed perfectly into one-eyed Sal's account of
Barb's captivity in Cardinal Court, and set the whole

story, neatly linked together, at last before the court.

"This is the last of my witnesses for the defence, your Honor," said Mr. Bonar, somewhat sadly; "none of them, I own, seem to touch the real question at issue; but, surely, in all this heterogeneous mass of testimony to the prisoner's beauty of character, we may hope to catch the glitter of that lost diamond, belief in her innocence. I have now to ask the respectful attention of the court while my client says the few words she has to say in explanation of her entanglement with this most unhappy affair."

With this he sat down, and in deep silence the people waited for little Barb to plead for her life.

So then the child called up all her fortitude, and in low and tremulous accents, which gradually gathered strength as her feelings kindled, she said:

"I ain't got much to say about myself, and what I have ain't going to clear me any, 'cos I have only my word for it, which they say don't go for nothing. What I would like to say, though, is that seems to me things have bore so hard on Barry that she's agoing to be thought worse of than she has any right to be. You see, gentlemen an' ladies," said Barb, warming, "this Barry Pomeroy were born sort of high strung, with a sperrit delicater an' more easy hurt than the like of mine; so that what would ou'y given me a passing sting, hit her mortal. When she were at Thunder Peak, oh, I know she were all that the dear good young lady said—the modestest, the kindest, the dutifulest—oh, my!—to think that a bad man could change her so! · When I fust see her, exclaimed little Barb, looking round with glistening eyes, " she were fresh from her mother; she were that frightened an' innercent, that I felt old, bless you, as Methuselah beside her! an' so pretty an' soft-spoken, though even then she were full of the bitter affront Mr. Harrison Fairleigh had put upon her, by offerin' a love that could on'y disgrace her. It goes agin my heart, God, He knows, to say a word agin the son of my dear lady here, but she has bidden me to speak out and spare nobody, rather than injustice should be done."

And in simple language she told the story which I, far less affectingly and more clumsily, I own, have claimed your attention so long in telling; the story of Barry's wrong and Barry's revenge.

Her narrative necessarily brought in Mrs. Pomeroy and Hugh Wayne, and in such a manner that if they could only have been produced to bear her out, her case would have assumed at once a hopeful color.

But alas! both were mysteriously missing—and who was to prevent the lawyers for the prosecution from insinuating that they purposely kept out of the

way, rather than meddle in a conspiracy which some
trifling folly of the Barbara of Thunder Peak had
laid her open to the suspicion of being mixed up in,
and which they would not expose ?

"If she were here, poor Barry's mother," cried
Barb, eagerly, "she would tell ye all what a comfort
her daughter were to her till *he* came to poison her;
or Dr. Wayne, he would show ye far better than I
can, what a noble nature she had; an' sure, don't the
highest come the lowest of all when they fall? My
poor Barry jest couldn't live peaceable after he'd insulted her, for, d'ye see, she loved him, that girl did,
with all her heart an' soul; an' oh, my ! what a big
heart it were, an' what a proud soul ! an' to think that
any man, with a sweet angel mother to think of, could
go for to make so light of a woman as that ! God have
mercy on Barry Pomeroy, it set her crazy, it did ! no,
no, no ! I'll never b'lieve she were herself the night
she passed her mother by with a laugh in Baron Hendrick's ball-room ; nor when she coaxed me so soft an'
smooth to b'lieve she were a-goin' to give it all up an'
go back to her mother, an' then set old Nan an' Tim
Polson on me—no, God forgive me, I ought ter have
seen she were mad, an' took better care on her."

And then, 'mid death-like silence, she tremblingly
went on to tell her vision of Katherine Hendrick's
death.

"When I heard her speak to Mr. Roscoe, I were struck with the still way she spoke; an' thinks I, 'sure, I never heard a voice so wailin' sad, or is it on'y my own trouble makes me think it so?" An' then she let me in, an' when I saw her face, an awful creep went through me, for it were death-struck, jest as sure as if the pearl rope were round her pretty throat then! An', oh, my! oh, my! to think that I were so blind an' stupid that I couldn't understand!"

And here the prisoner burst into a fit of ungovernable grief, and at sight of her slender figure bowed and shaking with convulsive sobs, the ladies all wept for sympathy and admiration, but Mr. Kean whispered audibly to Mr. Hawksly:

"Bonar knows how to make a point, eh? Very well done, indeed!" and then the ladies dried their tears and felt ashamed of them.

"She had on a white gown, an' her hair were all hangin' down her back wild like, as if she'd been tearin' it," Barb went on; "an' she sat down by a little bit of a table that had a open letter lyin' spread out on it, and she kept a-lookin' at that letter all the time she were a-talkin' with me, as if she couldn't forget it or look at it enough. I can't rightly tell all we said; I'd gone there for to warn her to look out for poor Barry; but when she spoke as if she knew already, an' said, with her eyes on the letter, as if she

were readin' of it there, 'He loves her! How he loves
her!' I saw that Barry had been before me, an'
crushed the poor lady with the truth—maybe written
her the very letter that troubled her so; and I didn't
say much.   But well I mind the shiver in her voice,
an' the white hands of her thrust inter her lovely hair,
as she said, moanin', 'I know all—she'll take no
vengeance on him; she's took it all on me!' an' with
that she turned her to the letter agin, an' forgot me,
till Mr. Roscoe, he called out to her.   After he had
talked to her a bit, she were for sendin' me away, but
I were so frightened that Barry meant her some harm
that night, besides the queer kind of uneasiness I had
about her, seein' her in that state of mind, that I
coaxed her till she let me stay, if I would sleep on
the sofa in her parlor.   Mr. Roscoe, I mind, was very
angry, but she wouldn't hear him, saying that she
was safer with me than with herself, an' he had to
let her have her way.   When we were alone again,
she laid her face down on the letter, an' forgot me;
an' at last I couldn't stand it no longer, an' crept
up to her, an' tried to comfort her with what has
given me the only strength I have for to meet my
troubles with—I mean the love an' pity that's felt for
us up in heaven—but oh! oh! poor lady, she were too
unhappy to heed me!   She said she must not forget
her prayers that night, and had it come to this!   An'

with that up she gets, an' goes about the room distracted. Then she remembered me, an' told me in
her high way that I saw a proud woman whose pride
was blighted: that blighted pride was hard to bear,
but blighted love was harder; that she thought she
had no heart, but that to-night she had found she had.
She said she loved him (Mr. Harrison, she meant), an'
that she could have parted with anything she had, her
beauty, an' money, and popularity—only not his love.
She said she could take no comfort out of what I said
about heaven, she were too desp'rate, an' **envied me**
my tears. An' then she sent me to her dressin'-room
for the string of pearls, sayin' they were his present
to his bride, an' that she would wear them sure that
night. God pity me, I brought them to her—oh,
why was mine the hand!"

There was a pause here, broken by sobs from every
part of the house. It was a pitiful tale, and surely
worth a tear or two, even if not all true.

"I mind now how her eyes seemed to flame up as
she took the thing from me," resumed the prisoner,
"an' how she kissed it over an' over, callin' it a precious gift, an' sayin' that he would know how she'd
loved him when he heard how she wore it that night,
an' then—then she kissed me, an' sent me away. An'
so I sat on the floor by her chamber-door keepin'
watch over her for fear of Barry, till—till the sounds

woke me up from I don't know how long a sleep, and when I ran in she gave me one look, an' twisted her hands in tighter, an' we struggled, an' I got my hands in too, tryin' to break the string, an'—an'—that's all I have to say."

*   *   *   *   *   *

The lawyers rose to argue the case.

Of course the statements made by the prisoner could not materially affect it, as what she said, unsupported by further proof, could not be taken as evidence. Moreover, there was one important discrepancy in her narrative which could not be explained satisfactorily. The letter which played such an important part—where was it? No human eye but her's had ever beheld it. When did it arrive to Miss Hendrick? Not per post; that the footman who brought up the evening delivery from the letter-box could testify. No visitor had been seen to enter or leave Baron Hendrick's house during the evening. No ashes as of consumed paper had been found in Miss Hendrick's grate. In fact the existence of that letter was too important, as furnishing the missing motive for Katherine Hendrick's suicide, to be passed by without keen controversy between the contending counsel: and so acute was their controversy that it came at last to be the one point upon which the whole of the case turned.

If that letter could be produced, Barb's safety was assured ; if not—God have mercy on her !

It could not be produced.

And so, this is how they made the story run.

An ignorant girl, well-meaning, possibly, but bred amid such scenes as would blunt an angel's sensibilities, falls into the hands of a clever young woman, who desires to rise in life by fair means or by foul. When the rich Mr. Fairleigh comes along, the clever adventuress resolves to appropriate him, and makes use of her humbler companion and accomplice to attain her ends. Inflamed with hatred against her rival, Miss Hendrick, she induces her tool to murder her, while she elopes with the prize. The deed is done clumsily, the murderess is caught in the act, therefore :

" Gentlemen of the jury, have you well and truly considered your verdict ? "

" We have."

" What say you, gentlemen of the jury, is the prisoner at the bar Guilty or not Guilty ? "

And they answered :

" GUILTY ! "

CHAPTER XXI.

BUT while all this was happening in New York, some very strange events were happening out of jt; these we will now relate, having once more to retrograde to the night of Katherine Hendrick's death, and Barbara Pomeroy's marriage with her faithless lover, Harrison Fairleigh.

The suicide bride lay stark and stiff in her distracted husband's arms; he uttered a cry that brought the household rushing to the room.

"She's dead!" raved the bridegroom, "oh, will no one rid me of my cursed life too?—Barry—Barry—Barry!" and he poured forth despair like a madman.

Now there chanced to be in the household an old fellow, a worthless, good-hearted, versatile, do-nothing Jack-of-all trades, who had had a probation in every occupation you could name, from a surgeon's apprentice to his present one, an under-butler. He, watching this scene with the moist eyes of sympathetic and spirituous sexagenarianism, felt moved to view the lovely corse yet closer, and ventured near, unrebuked by his frenzied master.

As his wrinkled hand touched the soft and clammy satin of her brow:

"Quick! out with ye, every one; by the Lord, I may bring her back yet!" cried this worthy, and he drove his fellow-servants out with all the impetuosity of the true Bohemian; and struck docile by his decision in the midst of their chaotic panic, they flocked from the room again like sheep.

Then he grasped his master hard by the shoulder, and the painful grip brought him something to himself.

"Where does this blood come from?" queried the man.

"Her arm—she opened a vein, and bled to death," shuddered the master.

"Fool!" muttered the Jack-of-all-trades, with the fearless candor of that character, "why didn't ye bind it up with your handkerchief, and make a tourniquet of yonder essence-bottle, while ye sent for the doctor?"

"Alas! I did try to stop it, and so, sweet soul, did she; but see, the blood would escape, and steal her life away with it!" and in anguish he showed the statuesque arm of his treacherous darling, bound securely enough to all appearance, yet saturated with fresh crimson.

"She helped ye to tie this knot, I'll warrant, grunted the wiseacre. "I can stick my fingers right through it. I see, she was bound to give ye the slip, sir. Ain't that a woman, all over? She'd sell her soul to have her lover from another woman, an' when she got him she'd rather die than put up with the stings of her own silly conscience!"

"Oh, Barry—Barry—Barry!" moaned her lover, subsiding again.

"Mr. Fairleigh," said the man, grimly, and his lithe hands were busy about her exquisite bosom, as he spoke, "Wotever were atween this lady an' you, is none o' my business. Gents has their amoosements an' ladies has their tiffs; wot I've got to say is, do ye want her to live or die, now?"

"Heavens, man, what do you mean? Is she not dead now?" cried Harrison, hoarsely, as he glared with frenzy in his blood-shot eye into the cunning orb of his servant.

"No!" grinned that functionary.

Harrison clutched him—hung on him trembling, sobbing, trying to ask him what he was to do; and his man took in the situation with a practised man's experienced eye, and made his plans with a practised man's promptness.

" Now, sir," said he, pleasantly, " I were once in a surgeon's office in that very city of New York for two years, and saw operations performed that would knock this here one all to sticks. I think I can do it, you've only to say the word, and name your valuation of my services."

" Do what ? " gasped Harrison.

" Why, bring her to life again ! "

" My God ! Can you do it, and you stand there wasting time ! Do it—do it now, I agree to anything ! " cried Harrison, looking frightfully white and eager.

" But if she was to die under my hands ? " suggested the man. " You see, master, I don't want to be brought into this here row, which looks pretty bad for some of us, as it is. There is precious little time, for she's fainted for loss of blood, and will never come to until we do it, but we must risk it, and get her out of this before I'll dare to put a hand on her."

" Anything, only save her ! " groaned poor Harrison, whose hopes were of the slimmest.

" All right—for a thousand dollars I'll undertake it," said the man. Harrison nodded. " You're a gentleman ! " cried the gratified scamp. " If I fail, it won't be my fault. Now, we lock out prying eyes so," suiting the action to the word, " and wrap her up

13

as warm as we can, to keep the life heat in her. No fear of any more hemorrhage, the surface is too cold now. Get your money, sir; prepare for anything, the Lord only knows what's before us to-night."

Harrison obeyed him like a child. Indeed, the horror of that sad night had so perfectly unmanned him, that he was glad to surrender his will to anybody's who seemed cool enough to bring order out of the chaos of his affliction. He ran about at his man's commands; he meanwhile darting out of the room to assure his terror-struck colleagues that the lady had only fainted, and was all right again—and to get a huge jug of hot water, which he decanted into half a dozen bottles, and placed about the body of the bride, securing them in their places by winding them in with the shawls in which he wrapped her up; then, like two robbers, the master and man crept out of the house by the Venetian stairway which led from the bridal-chamber to the river—carrying the motionless form between them—stole the carriage and horses, laid her at full length in the bottom of the carriage, half-buried in downy coverlets—and so, the master inside with his burning cheek to the marble of hers, and the man outside lashing the thoroughbreds, they fled to a solitary house hidden under a cliff, where the man took them in with all the airs of proprietorship.

"It's all right," grinned he, as a buxom woman came forward from a hurried toilet in the inner room, "we've been man and wife for too many a year for to blab each other's secrets now. Poll, look spry, the best bed for the lady."

Too absorbed in his own affairs to notice how much of the comfort of the cottage had flagrantly come from his own mansion, the young gentleman bore his burden into the little guest-chamber, and forthwith Vokes, his ally, commenced operations.

All was now bustle and dispatch.

"Hot water, Poll!" bawled Vokes.

A bucket of it was at his foot anon.

"Are ye willing to shed blood for her, Mr. Fairleigh?" briskly queried the master of the ceremonies.

"Yes, yes, only begin!" cried the impatient and bewildered gentleman.

"Poll, the lancet! Warm this syringe in the bucket. Another candle. Unwind her. Now, sir, your arm. My tools is rather rough, but I guess I kin fix it."

Harrison stripped his arm, and watched in an ecstasy his hot blood being pumped into his darling's cold veins.

"She'll love me forever, now my life-blood mixes with her's!" whispered he, at which the cynic by his side shot a sneer to his spouse, who shook her head and sighed, as saying :

"Ay, youth raves so, but old age finds us colder !"

When he was ready to swoon—and he dissembled his faintness long before he would give in to it, in the fond terror that Vokes would not give his Barry enough of him to live on—they gave him a cordial, and made him lie down and keep quiet beside her ; and so he passed the night brooding over her, and toward the dawn, he and Poll being the watchers, Vokes having driven back with the horses that they might not be traced, Barry opened her beautiful eyes, and slowly came out of the other world with a smile of ineffable love into Harrison's, and then she closed them, and fell at once into a sweet restoring sleep.

This lasted for twenty-four hours, during which master and man lay close, and not a word of the awful events that were going on outside found its way to them in their hiding-place.

Harrison had ample time to cast a retrospective eye over his late proceedings, and having neither the excitement of winning a bride to bedazzle him, nor the anguish of mourning her death to blunt his common sense, he obtained a most prosaic realization of the ass he had made of himself before the world, and felt ready to slink away with his dear-bought prize to the uttermost parts of the earth, where no soul he had ever known should see him.

To think of it! even now—now as he sat by his sleeping Barry's side, watching her bloodless face with the dark hair all drifted about it, his little world was ringing with the news of his elopement with his mother's *protégé*, and his betrayed bride, Katherine Hendrick, was lying crushed under the blow, exciting the honest indignation of all who knew them.

How he was being despised and execrated just now!

How his good mother was suffering!

.Oh, what a fond, blind fool he had been to win the love of his life in this unworthy fashion!

And he groaned so audibly that Poll peeped in, thinking that something was wrong with the patient, and seeing her lying there as calm as ever, said, cheerily:

"Sweet lady! she's just doing the right thing. When she wakes she'll be all the more ready for the beef-tea."

And sure enough when she woke she drank the strengthening nourishment with all the sharp appetite of convalescence, yet, strange to say, seemed not to notice who held the bowl to her mouth, although it was her Harrison.

Vokes, who was standing by, gave a queer start, and turned very purple at this. He also fastened his watery orbs on hers with more than their ordinary quota of speculation in them. Harrison smiled down on her, radiant with present happiness, and waiting for a love-look.

The tea finished, she sank back with a contented murmur, and was for closing her eyes again.

"Darling!" ventured Harrison, disappointed.

She never heeded.

"Barry! my Barry!" cried he.

She held up her ivory-like hand, looking at it curiously. Harrison's wedding-ring shone on the third finger. Harrison put his finger upon the ring, and, bending low, whispered tenderly:

"You remember all, my wife?"

Then she slowly turned her rich black eyes upon his, and gazed for full a minute, unsmilingly, as one might gaze at a picture or a landscape, or anything which had no life to answer back their glance.

And then she drifted off into drowsy unconsciousness.

Harrison fixed his startled eye on Vokes, and caught that wiseacre in the act of telegraphing to his wife something which whitened even her ruddy cheeks.

"Why, man, what's the matter with you?" cried Harrison, seizing him savagely by the shoulder.

"I—I—fear, yet have patience, sir, one can hardly tell all at once," stammered the man.

"Out with it!" gasped the wretched bridegroom—"You think she's—she's——"

"*Mad!* whispered Vokes.

CHAPTER XXII.

THE CRUCIBLE.

SHE fell into another fathomless depth of slumber, from which not all the babel of sounds which followed this awful announcement had the power to bring her back to consciousness.

They thought Mr. Fairleigh would go mad himself next. He tore his hair; he called on Heaven to take his miserable life at once, and spare him this too dreadful punishment of his folly; he cast himself on his knees by her couch, imploring her in language fit to break your heart, to give him one little look of recognition; and then, turning like a tiger on his ally Vokes, he cursed him for bringing the sweet soul back to a life bereft of reason—and, trembling with fury, ordered him from his sight if he valued his own life.

Vokes bore all meekly; in truth, he was too much shocked by the result of his surgical experiment to say a word, he could only gape at the poor lady and bite his nails.

Ordered out, he obeyed, and sat with Poll in the

woodshed faltering his consternation, and wondering what would be done next.

An hour or two afterward, Harrison answered that question himself.

He came to them as they shivered together, pale and haggard, but quite calm.

"Vokes," said he, "go, get me some sort of a carrage in which I can convey Mrs. Fairleigh to the railway-station. Your wife can get her ready while you are gone."

"But—but—where?" shivered Vokes, struck stupid.

"We go South to my plantation," said Harrison, then added to himself, "ay, there I can hide my misery and ruin as long as I like; no one will dream of looking for us there."

"To-night?" gasped Vokes.

"To-night," answered Harrison, "you and your wife accompany us."

Reassured by this command, the rascal departed on his errand with alacrity, and his sentimental and docile wife devoted herself to the mournful task of dressing the unconscious lady, and preparing everything for the tedious journey.

And so, in the dead of night they locked up the lonely cottage under the cliff, and carried the mad bride away to hide her in the solitude of the long deserted plantation in Virginia, which had once been the family homestead of the Fairleighs.

Not a whisper had reached them of the events which were happening in New York, even Vokes, usually so wide-awake, failed this time to gather his budget of news, partly because of his enforced seclusion, partly that he was so painfully interested in the situation of affairs at the cottage, that the outside world had shrunk for the time into small bulk in his estimation.

Yet, absorbed in his own affliction, the weak and erring man who had waded through such sullied waters to gain possession of that prize which could only harrow him with intolerable woe when won, now fled from the scene of his dishonor just when he should have stood firm and prevented the sacrifice of her who had ever been angel-kind to his unhappy Barry! Ignorant of Katherine's suicide and of Barb's danger, he hastened into a seclusion which, as he guessed, would never be broken by the friends he had left, as he supposed, too disgusted with his frailty to seek him out.

Lakelawn, the Fairleigh plantation, had once been a noble property, but the mansion had been burned down during the late war, the slaves scattered, and much of the wealth accruing therefrom lost in the general devastation. Its wide tobacco fields were now worked by hired hands, under a grim Scotch manager, and the family lived North, never having revisited the place since that woeful day when tho venerable lady was supported from the smoking ruins of her home by her son, then a youth of fifteen.

The spot where the plantation was situated was one of those wild regions common in Virginia, where the eye lifts itself to towering mountains whose sunny summits are lost in the pure ether, or plunges itself into fathomless pools, whose bottoms are covered by strange thickets of petrified trees and fantastic vegetation.

The valley where Lakelawn lay, spreading its rich acres to the genial sun, was one of those rock-encircled nests of verdure. Oaks and spicy walnuts had once wreathed their friendly arms around the mansion, but now they stood black and shivered, pictures of desolation fitly surrounding the great, ghastly ruin which was once the home of the proudest family in the State ; and behind, no longer vailed by the graceful tracery of vine and arbor creeper, stretched a solemn sheet of water, black and lifeless, and overhung by two savage, beetling crags, which flung midway a natural bridge overhead—a single arch of fairy stone-work, so delicate and brittle that no human foot had ever been known to cross the dizzy pathway.

The pond went by the name of "Lost Lake," and from it the plantation had received its title " of Lake-lawn."

The old mansion house, built in the ancient baronial days when the cavaliers of Virginia were trained in the court of England, and came fresh from its splendor to emulate it in their principalities across the ocean, had been burned down during the late Southern war. Here a crumbling martello tower, and there a fragment of a mighty archway, were all that remained to indicate the grand proportions of the ruin, with the exception of part of the western wing, which, for more than a century, had been given over to the rats and the antiquarian. The conflagration had swept over these naked walls without finding food enough to stay it as long as to consume them. A few of the outbuildings around also stood untouched ; they were now occupied by Mr. Cargill, the manager, and his men ; and a surly set they were in their solitude, unbroken by anything more exciting than the weekly day of rest, or the occasional visit of some talkative pedler, for the nearest city was quite far enough distant to isolate them practically from their kind during the busy season.

Upon this forlorn community there came, one morning, a gloomy young gentleman, riding superbly a fine " bit of blood," as old Cargill expressed it ; and what does this apparition want but lodging for his invalid .wife, his servants and himself!

"An' whar ye think I can pit ye is what I wud like to ken ?" grumbled the Scotchman, furtively eyeing the visitor.

"There is room there," said he, waving his hand toward the western wing. "I shall have the interior repaired and furnished, and take possession before the end of the week."

"An' wha' the deil are you that has the assurance to come here, takin' possession o' the auld hoose o' the Fairleighs? An' wha think ye, am I, to let ye in till I write the young maister?" growled Scotia.

The stranger thrust his hand into his pocket, and brought it out full of gold.

"I am in trouble," said he, looking the old fellow eye to eye. "My wife has gone mad, and my only hope for her is to hide her away from all disturbing causes for a time. Help me in this; let me rent that ruin there, which is of no earthly value as it is; keep well the secret of my residence here—even from your master, until after I am gone—and, see here, you shall have a double-handful of these every week!"

The old gentleman's sharp eyes softened, his long upper lip relaxed its grim compression, a beam of sympathy lit up his lean visage :

" Hoot, man !" cried he, heartily, " that alters the

question.   If ye're in affliction, an' in want o' a quiet hame, an' maybe a no unsympatheesing freend, this is the very spot for ye, an' fiend tak' me if I mak' or meddle in your family matters.   An' noo jist please to pit up your siller ; what's richt an' fair I'm willin' to tak', an' we'll settle that when we've gane over the place thegither."

And the stout old fellow was as good as his word ; went cannily over the ruined wing, helped to calculate what the probable cost of the proposed repairs would be ; fixed upon a rental, not generous, but just ; asked no inquisitive questions, and parted from the unhappy young man—in whom he never for a moment dreamed he beheld the proprietor of the plantation— on the best of terms.

He set his men to work upon the ruined building at once ; and what with their industry, and the young gentleman's constant presence, urging them on with his impatient and miserable looks, and the inexhausti- ble activity of the servant Vokes, two apartments were actually ready for their occupants by the end of the week—lathed, plastered, furnished, and tho- roughly aired, all in the space of six days; showing that where there's a will there's a way.

The dusk was falling that summer evening when Mr. Clifford, the new tenant, brought home his afflicted wife.   They came in a close carriage ; their servants, Vokes and his wife, were there to receive them at the broken portal; and, as the prudent Scotchman—who stood with a gang of curious negroes by the carriage-step—observed the gentle solicitude with which the young gentleman carried the lady in his arms from the carriage to the house, not suffering her foot to touch the ground, and the pitiful glances of the two servants, if he had harbored any suspicions as to the cause of the secrecy which Mr. Clifford insisted upon, they were all dispelled.

So they hid them away from the world in which they had cut such a poor figure; and which was most pitiable I knew not: Harrison, with his remorse, his passion, and his blasted hopes of happiness; or Barry, with her frail and sinking body and distracted mind.

Alas, if poor Barry had suffered much at this man's hands, she was inflicting anguish enough upon him now to atone for even a darker wrong than that he had put upon her!

Imagine a hot-hearted man whom love at its strongest has taken full possession of, condemned to this sort of thing.

Scene, a quaint triangular chamber in the ruined wing, its broad window overlooking the glassy waters of Lost Lake; sumptuous upholstery, delicate decorations fit for a lady's bower, flowers, pictures, pretty conceits scattered everywhere, in the forlorn hope

that they will catch her attention and please her wan
dering fancy.

Barry reclines on the azure sofa, her white face
and jet-black hair, and gleaming orbs in startling
contrast to her brilliant crimson dress—for it is one
of her insane fancies to wear blood-color, and nothing
else will she endure.

Harrison bends over her with a piteous smile of
love into those restless, fire-filled eyes of hers; she
heeds him not—she weaves her slender hands together
and twines them in her superb tresses with feverish
persistency ; and her lips of burning red move continually in incoherent whispers.

"Sweet Barry!" wooes the unhappy husband for.
the millionth time, "don't you know me, your Harrison ? Look at me, my girl, my poor, poor girl!
Barry—Barry—sweetheart! O God, this is death!"

And he flings himself on the carpet beside her sofa,
convulsed with sobs.

A bobolink perches on the open window-sill, and
sends a shower of thrills into the hushed chamber.
Barry turns her too brilliant eye upon the tiny song-
ster, and her blank face lights up with a flicker of
comprehension. She listens ; she raises herself weakly
on her elbow—she tears her hair no longer.

Suddenly, a wild note pierces through the bobolink's song and shivers it into dissonance—the mad

girl has snatched the song out of his throat, she is singing herself.

And what is the strain which wells from her in tones sweet as silver, but distraught and out of tune as the babblings of earliest infancy?

Ah, once she sang it nobly; it was a favorite of Barry Pomeroy's in her home at Thunder Peak, long ago!

> "An empty sky, a world of heather,
>   Purple of foxglove, yellow of broom,
> We two among them wading together,
>   Shaking out honey, treading perfume.
>
> "He prays, 'Come over,' I may not follow;
>   I cry, 'Return,' but he cannot come.
> We speak, we laugh, but with voices hollow;
>   Our hands are hanging, our hearts are dumb.
>
> "Glitters the dew and shines the river;
>   Up comes the lily and dries her bell;
> But two are walking apart forever,
>   And wave their hands for a mute farewell."

Harrison Fairleigh listens with haggard eyes fixed on her's, and every note stabbing him with fond reminiscence. She used to sing it to him in those her innocent and credulous days, before she knew him for a villain. Is her memory coming back to her, that . she can recall it thus correctly?

"O Heaven! if she would but remember me!" he groans.

He takes her in his arms, for once she seems to notice; she starts violently, places her two hands on his shoulders, and throwing back her head, scans his countenance with terrible intensity. He calls a gentle smile to his paling lip—he looks at her as of old, with his soul in his eyes—he draws her softly toward him —nearer—nearer—his heart swells to bursting—oh, Barry, have you come back to him again ? Ah !

A wild shriek cleaves the tingling air; with flaming eyes and glittering teeth buried in her foam-flecked lip, and lovely visage horribly distorted, she hurls him from her with a supernatural strength, which sends him reeling across the wide room as if he were a mere feather-weight, and then she dashes herself against the window, from which the bobolink flies in terror of the awful advancing vision.

In dumb desperation her miserable husband darts after her, and catches her flowing skirts just in time to prevent her from throwing herself headlong into the still pool which lies under the window; she struggles frantically with him, as if she felt the red-hot arms of the " Maiden " of the Inquisition around her, and her fearful cries ring far over the quiet spring scene, so wild and unearthly that the laborers half a mile off turn pale and drop their implements;

and Vokes and Polly rush in, ready for the worst, and find it as much as they can do with all their united strength to pinion the arms of the panic-stricken maniac.

And when they have by the mercy of God succeeded in drawing down the window—out of which they found the husband and wife hanging, she writhing and tearing in his desperate grasp—and are looking at their young master in shocked silence, his face torn and bleeding, his coat in ribbons, and his whole frame trembling and panting, she utters a last quivering moan, like some wild animal spent in the chase, and down she goes among them in strong convulsions.

And that is how she remembers her Harrison.

Alas, poor souls!

A terrible punishment, is it not?

CHAPTER XXIII.

Y, ay! a bitter punishment indeed!

She who was willing to lose her soul for one little hour's purchase of the bliss of being his wife, can now only shriek and hide her eyes and go into convulsions at his approach.

And yet he loves this wreck of his darling so dearly, ah! so dearly, that he will sit by her all the time she sleeps, poring over her wan loveliness in speechless sorrow and helplessness, and hurrying away with anxiously averted face on her awakening, to linger unweariedly in the little ante-chamber adjoining, where they have cut a slit in the velvet curtain which hangs over the door, to let him see her unobserved; he seems to have no interest in life out of her presence; sunshine, human society, books—all are unheeded in the terrible fascination of mad Barry!

As time wore on he devised a plan by which he could stay at her side without danger of another scene such as the last. She appeared indifferent to the presence of any one else who chose to enter her chamber—she even grew attached to Polly, who, it must be confessed, was sentimental enough—or the scamp, Vokes, called it so—to fall hopelessly in love with the afflicted lady, and who tried all her little feminine, petting arts to win her confidence; this indifference to strangers Harrison took advantage of, by disguising himself with a false wig, whiskers, and loose Western costume, and then presenting himself with prudent care to Barry.

At the first glance she seemed satisfied enough, but presently the poor fellow followed the dictates of his yearning heart, came and sat on a stool at her feet, and began to sing a tender little air which he had wooed her with long ago.

She stopped that dreary endless wringing of her hands, and listened with wondering face;—he went on, encouraged, and venturing to look up, met her great fire-filled pulsating orbs fastened wildly upon his. Struck dumb, he lowered his, when she seemed to breathe freer, and after a moment's pause, she laid her thin fingers on his mouth and hummed a bar of his song, signing him to go on with it as you have seen babies do.

So then he sang again, but kept his eyes to himself, and gradually her slight excitement was allayed, and she listened to him, and looked at him quite re-assured.

So, little by little he taught this poor distracted heart to lean on him, and to find pleasure in his coming; and the day when she tottered to meet him at the door, flowers in her hands, which kind Polly had brought her, and kissing these first in her old gracious way, laid them softly in the bosom of his vest, his tried heart swelled so big that it forced tears of happiness into his eyes, and he gasped out a heart-felt " Thank God!"

And after that, bitter as his life was, he began to take courage and look forward almost with hope.

The months slipped by, and strength came slowly back to Barry's frame, but her mind still remained a blank. She seldom spoke, and then only in broken murmurs, her hand to her poor confused forehead, and her wistful eyes fixed perplexedly on one or other of those around her. She walked out every day lean-ing on her disguised husband's arm ; and all the sweet sights and sounds of the full summer time passed her by in glorious pageantry, and she looked on with only half-comprehending interest, whispering her pleasure in her sadly inconsequent way, yet lis-tened to with rapture by Harrison.

TRUE LOVE!

Thank God—thank God—for creating such a God-like thing!

What else, oh, selfish world, would have chained this man, black with fashionable sins as we know him to be, to this woman, whose utmost reward for his most sublime devotion could only be a wistful glance or a half-demented murmur of joy?

Ay, True Love is a full cup which runneth o'er upon the dry, parched path of life, and where its precious drops do fall, sweet flowers of the soul spring up, and so is life made beautiful.

But it would have to be a brimming cup; for, oh, the way is sometimes long and dreary, and woe betide him who attempts that lonely road with little in the magic chalice!

Not a whisper came from the outside world to warn Harrison Fairleigh of the terrible march of events in New York.

Mr. Cargill, with a delicacy one would never dream of expecting from one of his grim exterior, who lost thereby the current gossip of what was going on, without these ruined walls; and being Scotch, with that sturdy nation's strong nationality, he despised the newspapers of his adopted country too sincerely to subscribe for any of them, or even to read them when they were offered him; consequently, the whole of the murder-case in which Katherine Hendrick and

Barb Pomeroy played such tragic parts, draged its slow length through the New York papers, and was copied more or less faithfully into the Richmond sheets; and so insolated were the denizens of Lake Lawn, and so wilfully ignorant, that, as we have said, not a whisper of the dreadful truth had reached Harrison when the event transpired which we are about to narrate.

One midsummer night, Harrison, whose bedroom adjoined Barry's, and indeed was the only mode of egress from hers, awoke with that instant consciousness of all around him, and mental excitation which are the frequent experiences of mesmerist, clairvoyant—what you will, at all events, have been felt by many and many a staunch skeptic in the supernatural, and will continue to be as long as the mind lives in the body.

Having thus been waked from a dreamless sleep, with all its faculties on the alert, and by no apparent cause, the immediate idea that darted into Harrison's brain was of necessity connected with the grand source of his anxiety—his helpless wife.

"Something wrong with Barry!" thought he, flinging himself off the bed into his dressing-gown, and thence to her chamber.

The dainty white couch was tumbled and empty; Polly, usually a faithful guardian, lay on her bed on the floor, dead drowsy; the taper which always burned on the dressing-table was gone.

The young man's shout brought Polly to her senses; she bounced up, saw the empty bed, uttered an answering howl, and ran to the window.

"Locked, master, locked!" panted she. "Oh, my heart! I thought she'd got out o' the window."

"She must have gone through my room, that's what woke me!" said Harrison, rushing back thither; and, snatching up a few clothes, he hurried them on, while Polly filled the house with her screams.

Anon, Vokes appeared from his quarters, cursing and swearing at his wife for her unfaithfulness, till the poor creature, who adored her young mistress, was ready to cut her own throat in her remorse.

Harrison escaped the mingled execrations and lamentations by rushing out of the house, flinging back at his ally an impatient command to set Polly to search every cranny of it, while they searched the grounds.

The moon shone bright as day, not a sound was to be heard but the faint rustle of the dewy leaves, and the tinkle of some distant thread of water trickling into the lake.

"The lake!" gasped Harrison.

"Lord, help us now!" faltered Vokes; "what should she go for to go there for? she ain't melancholy, she's as happy as a babby, bless her sweet face!

"Rouse the men!" said poor Harrison, distractedly. "Fly! we must lose no time." Then he darted off on the pathway which meandered round the lake, calling in a voice that rang far and near, "Barry! Barry! Barry!" and the cliffs that overhung the lifeless pool echoed back his desolate cry with a lonely wail, but nothing else responded.

The path had once been completely overshadowed by handsome cedar-trees, but these had been ruthlessly felled to furnish the fires of the bivouac in 1864, and now their mutilated trunks stood up in weirdly irregular file, some mantled by the riotous creepers of the South, some grim and stark-like skeletons of themselves, with a gnarled and leafless arm stretched out, or a bleached rootling protruding, like a half-buried bone. The path itself, once so daintily smooth and gravelled, was choked with running vines, briers, and tall rank couch-grass; and so sunken, that the still, moveless lip of the lake covered it in many places, so that the unwary passenger had much ado sometimes to tell land from water in the eerie light.

On fled Harrison shouting her name, stopping ever and anon to gaze into the silvery margin of the pool with dreading eyes; suddenly he stopped short.

Across the lake, nearly opposite to him, he saw a tiny light flickering.

"Her candle!" thought he, and burst into a laugh of joy; his idol was safe thus far!

"She has taken the opposite direction; if I run on I will meet her soon," thought he, and keeping his eyes fixed upon the light, he redoubled his speed. He ran, he tore, he stumbled on through the weed-grown wilderness, he often waded up to the thighs where the path had fallen in, and often was forced to scramble up a fragment of the cliff which thrust its jagged columns into the water here and there, but as long as he could see that tiny speck flitting to meet him across the lake, he sped on with good heart. Presently he stopped again, and this time no joyful shout escaped him, but a tremor ran through all his frame, and he turned sick.

The light had begun to mount the cliff.

Does the reader recall the description of Lake Lawn which prefaces this portion of the history, where a natural bridge is mentioned which spanned the pool from two points of the overhanging cliff, a slender thread of stone so high and narrow that it turned one dizzy to look up? Toward this fearful bridge the little yellow light was climbing—up the broken wall of rock which rose in rude steps from the edge of the pool a hundred feet in height—now lost behind a projecting buttress-like mass, now flashing into view again farther up the rugged pass—climbing, climbing upward like a star the bare blue pinnacle which no human foot had ever scaled before.

Nothing but madness could have retained a footing there : nothing but madness could return to earth again !

Harrison, struck to stone, watched the light.

He stood on his side of the pool almost under the arch, and the rock-wall rose above his head smooth and inaccessible as the side of a castle, stretching away before and behind in vast irregular heaps.

Climb these!

He groaned in despair.

Fly round the pool and catch her!

Ha, ha! Look at her, floating up, up, up—already half way to the apex of the pinnacle, from which was flung the airy web of weather-rotted stone.

"Barry! Barry! Barry!—for God's sake stop!"

Ah ! a silver voice comes pealing back in a sudden thrill of melody—the very words come strangely distinct, like dropping water !

Hush !

> "The pearly gates are open wide,
>   I see the bright array ;
> On either side the angels glide
>   To keep the shining way !"

God have mercy ! The first time Harrison Fairleigh ever set his fatal eyes upon Barbara Pomeroy she was singing these words in the Sunday school at Rensselaer's Landing, into which he had strayed one sultry Sunday in search of a new sensation! So fresh, so joyous, so pure-sweet were her notes that day that they sent a shiver of emotion through him then—but sweet tones never wrung human heart as these to-night, broken, as they were, and dropping ever and anon out of tune.

The first sounds he had heard her utter—were they to be the last?

"Barry—Barry—Barry—oh, come back!"

And still the taper floats up, up, up, and the silver voice rings on:

> "When storms arise, and darkness clouds
> The faithful pilgrim's way,
> The angels glide on either side
> To drive the clouds away!"

Harrison falls on his knees, imploring the heavens to perform a miracle for him.

The heavens gleam wide and purple, and the little light sails nearer them.

He staggers to his feet, panting, and wet with the sweat of agony.

Heaven helps those who help themselves. Here's at it then, and God have mercy on his soul!

He springs up the slippery face of the cliff—he will mount it on his side as she has done on hers, and,

God willing, meet her on the bridge; or, if that is impossible, why, then, the death that is good enough for his Barry, his victim, is far, far too good for him, poor, miserable coward, who, for the sake of gratifying the basest passion in man's nature, has brought her to this!

And so, God's angels whispering repentance in his ear all the way, he scrambles, he leaps, he claws his way up with bleeding hands and grasping feet, from which he has kicked his shoes. The miracle for which he prayed is—oh, wonderful!—being wrought quick upon the prayer; for, let me tell you, God's ear is so near, and His heart so kind, that when we cry to Him, straight He sends us strength to do ourselves that which we thought nothing short of Omnipotence could do; and thus He works His miracles nowadays.

And, all the while, the little light on the opposite side is flickering higher and higher, and the silver voice is ringing on :

> " And brighter gleams the morning light
>   Behind the gentle rod;
> For Christ's redeemed more clearly see
>   The shining way of God ! "

Harrison Fairleigh has reached the top of the cliff; and, balancing himself on hands and knees on the slippery, knife-like ridge, looks for his guiding star.

And he sees his mad wife standing in her pure white night-dress on the spider-thread which spans

the abyss, her sweet face so radiant with more than
mortal happiness as she raises it skyward, that at the
wonderful sight his heart stands still, and a great calm
falls upon his spirit.   Her long rich hair streams back
from her slender form, and, with her filmy robes,
waves softly in the passing breeze ; an unearthly light
illumines her upraised eyes, and the moon bathes her
whole figure with a soft and glistening brightness.

How have her delicate feet succeeded in bearing her
there over the sharp rocks ? In the pale light they
shine white and bare, just as she stole out of her bed.
Harrison's are red with blood ; how has she escaped ?
Have the angels indeed walked beside her on either
side, bearing her softly over the cruel path ?

She is singing still.   Oh, Sweet ? is it your death-
song ?

> "And soon they walk the golden streets,
>   Not slighted and alone ;
>   On either side the angels glide,
>   To lead them to the throne."

A hoarse cry comes up from below. Harrison,
glancing down, sees in the pathways on either side
the pool, the dim figures of his servants and of the
men they have roused, looking small as the toy-men
in a child's play-house. They are waving their arms
and gesticulating wildly at the perilous position of
the unfortunate lady. As yet they have not seen
Harrison, who, to preserve his equilibrium, is com-

pelled to lie flat on the ridge, grasping it with arms and knees.

That discordant shout seems to startle the rapt singer. She stands mute, one hand to her poor, bewildered forehead, and the taper hanging unheeded in the other, in terrible proximity to her floating dress. Her dark eyes turn from the calm heavens and wander slowly around the moon-bathed scene, down, down to the shadowy earth and steel-bright pool, lying so far beneath.

There is a moment's awful pause; Harrison hears her breath coming hard and fast, sees her eyes dilating in horror, feels the heart of her beating faster and faster as she realizes where she is; knows that her safeguard, insanity, has for the time dropped from her, as sleep drops from the somnambulist, leaving him face to face with death;—tells himself, in tragic resignation:

"That ends all!" And, with the words on his rigid lips, springs upright on the sharp and jagged ridge, extends his arms like the balancing-pole of a rope-dancer, and runs lightly, surely, safely out to her!

Transfixed, she heeds him not till his arms close round her like a steel-trap; then a cry bursts from her; she looks at him wildly, she sees a face she never saw in her days of sanity. Alas! Harrison is too well disguised.   And, comprehending nothing but that she is standing on a strip not half a foot in width, in the grasp of a stranger, with a sheet of water gleaming a hundred feet beneath, she makes an involuntary spring backward, and over they go!

14*

CHAPTER XXIV.

YES, over they go backward, she clasped in a convulsive grip to his breast, and a fearful shriek comes up to meet them from the spectators below. Over? Ay, but not down yet!

He grasps at the narrow spar of stone with his leg as he falls, and, like any other gymnast, having caught it, he holds on for dear life, shifts his burden—a dead weight now—into one arm, works his body to and fro until, weighted as it is, it acquires spring enough to swing up level with his knees, and then he snatches hold with his other arm of the rough spar, and clings there for a moment to rest and get a better clasp of Barry; and the people burst into frantic hurrahs of delight, yell up a dozen strong, " Hold on, we'll get ye off! " and run about like ants when a foot has stirred their hill.

This all passes in three seconds, but so much horror and suspense have been crowded into them that now, when Harrison has time to look downward to

the sinister pool shining serenely beneath, he is im-
measurably astonished to observe his hat still in mid-
air, spinning down to disappear anon like a stone
under the gleaming surface.   Three seconds more
drag by, and he feels his arm that holds Barry begin
to tremble and turn nerveless; he casts a wistful
glance after his allies; two of them are running as
hard as they can go back to the house for a rope;
they have not gone twenty paces yet, and his strength
is giving out!

He clenches his teeth, braces his nerves, and shifts
his position to a better one; in so doing he all but
drops his inert burden, and that sickens him; so that,
for a few minutes afterward he leans across the rock
panting and blind, with the sweat oozing from every
pore.   Meantime they bawl up to him again, " Hold
on, we're coming as fast as we can!" and their
voices sound so indistinct up there, with all these
pulses beating in his ears and his quick breath choking him so, that he fears he is going in a swoon, and
gnaws his lip till the blood trickles from it.

All this time she lies with her pure white face up-
turned to the saintly moonlight, her head thrown back
on his shoulder, and one lovely arm where he has
contrived to place it—round his neck;—her beautiful long hair streams far down and gently sways to
and fro in the soft midsummer's zephyrs, sometimes

drifting round them both like a black vail, sometimes floating wide and into his eyes. She lies such a dead weight that he feels her continually slipping, slipping down, as if some fiend in the air was pulling her out of his grasp; and when he dares to unclasp his arm to jerk her back to her place, it is so paralyzed with the convulsive pressure of its grip that he is quite sure its strength will not be enough to uphold her till the tardy help arrives.

Moment by moment slips past, making minutes eternities long to his anxious computation, and now a dreadful groan falters from his sinking heart.

"Are ye coming?" cries he, in fainting tones. "I can't hold out much longer."

His voice is so weak that they never hear a word, and seeing this, the poor fellow believes he really is going to faint, and makes one bold though desperate effort for safety.

He edges the unconscious burden which is dragging him down, on to the narrow bridge, gets its weight to lie across the stone, and, relieved of this, clinches hold again with arm and legs, and works his way slowly along the spar, stopping every couple of inches to drag his companion after him; his success inspires him with hope and strength, and so busy is he that he is at the main cliff anon, and the messengers are back with the ropes, shouting good cheer to him and swarming up the crags, and safety seems at his fingers' ends.

All at once Harrison stops his toil, and hangs oscillating between heaven and earth.

Why ?

Something has cracked.

Hush ! Again—again—great heavens, the bridge is parting from the main cliff !

Yes, the treacherous stone, perforated by the raindrops and rotted by the sunshine of ages, is crumbling away bit by bit—pieces as big as a hen's egg dropping sheer down into the water, and Harrison hangs at its junction with the bare bald rock, one hand on the main and one on Barry as she lies on the sinking bridge !

He grows cold as death, a minute since and he was dripping as if he had just scrambled out of the water; then his mind becomes all of a sudden inconceivably clear, so that he is able to see the situation with all its possibilities in a flash of supernatural comprehension.

He runs his eye down the furrowed scar, and sees a jutting spur some ten feet beneath—already the treacherous bridge is slipping toward it—he gathers Barry up in his one arm, and crushing her face against his breast, guides his course toward the ledge.

And just as Vokes and a couple of the men arrive at the top of the cliff, having contrived to scale the slippery wall by the aid of grappling-hooks, snatched out of the little boat-house on the bank of the lake—down goes the bridge with a crash and an involuntary cry from Harrison, and the next thing they see, he is crouching on his knees on the shelf of rock, with Barry held to him in a death-grip.

This all passes in such short space that the shouts of triumph at their safe ascent are still on their lips when they see him fall—and their roar of horror is again interrupted by the joyful cry that he is there safe yet; next instant a rope dangles over the face of the cliff, and he catches it.

He is knotting it around his wife to send her up first, when she stirs and looks up with a great sigh.

Now it happens that the roughness of his recent adventure has torn off Harrison's disguise of hair and beard, and it is his own countenance which meets her gaze.

Her dark eyes open wide and wild, she half rises in his arms—a sudden light illumines her whole face, and she curls round his neck with the single gasping cry: "Harrison!"

The man shakes with awful joy.

She knows him—her reason is restored!

Never a word he speaks, but holds her close, trembling.

The men above shout.

"Ready?"

He does not hear them—he is trying to collect his courage to speak to her.

She raises her face again, all shining with a solemn smile.

She scans his features narrowly, puts up her hand and feels his cheek, catches him by both shoulders in a fierce little clutch, and draws him toward her, and their lips meet in a breathless kiss.

And when she feels his tears dropping upon her face, and his arms trembling around her, she falters, in tones rich with rapture:

"Oh, love, you've come back to me at last—at last!"

"Barry!" whispers he, his deep tones shaken, "we shall never part again, shall we?"

"No, no, no!" cries she, affrightedly. "Oh, what a fearful time I have had searching for you! Where were you, my own dear?"

But the men on the cliff here shout again, alarmed at the long delay; and she hearing, for the first time looks about her, and sinks down speechless with horror.

"Fear nothing, my darling—my darling!" cries

Harrison, almost beside himself with joy. "You had a dream, and came out here in your sleep; but you are quite safe now, only shut your eyes and let them pull you up; and oh, love—love—don't drift away from me again!"

She looks in his face, and gathers courage from it.

"I don't understand," falters she, plaintively. "But I will do whatever you say, Harrison."

He passionately kisses her, and then calls out:

"All right, Vokes," and they gently pull her up from the ledge.

He has wrapped his coat around her to prevent the ropes from hurting her, and deep is the astonishment of the men, when having received her on the perilous apex of the cliff and unloosed the rope, she unties the coat from her waist, and in a collected manner, says:

"Send this down also, Mr. Fairleigh will require it."

They glare at her. She returns their gaze curiously, then all at once becoming aware of her dress, throws herself on her knees and covers her burning face with her hands.

"By——! she's herself!" mutters Vokes to his companions, in wildest excitement.

For the moment they forget the other unfortunate on his ticklish perch, and gather round her.

She looks up again, crying, sharply:

" Why do you stay ? Go, help Mr. Fairleigh ! "

Vokes drags them away; they, meanwhile, muttering in bewilderment:

" She says ' Fairleigh !' Now, wot's that for ? "

" Never you mind," quoth the prudent Vokes, recovering his presence of mind. " The poor lady's wanderin' a bit yet, though her wits is comin' back wonderful."

So then they drag Harrison up, and there is an affecting meeting between the rescued husband and wife; and they manage to get the lady safely down the cliff, sometimes in her husband's arms, sometimes supported between him and Vokes; but though the path is not more steep and cragged than that which she had mounted on the other side, without so much as a scratch on her delicate feet, or a rent in her filmy robe, now that her senses have returned to her, her talisman of safety seems to have deserted her, for her feet stream with blood, her dress catches on the toothed points of the rocks—by the time she reaches the lake-path she is exhausted, shivering with cold, and faint with excitement.

But for all that, when at last Harrison and Barry were alone in her pretty chamber, with the red dawn struggling in through the curtains, and the silvery songs of the bobolinks bubbling in, and the cheerful bustle of Vokes and Polly stealing to their ears from the kitchen, I can't believe that there are two people in the Union so full of gratitude to God and love to each other, as they!

CHAPTER XXV.

REPENTANCE AND EXPIATION.

HOW can we account for this wonderful restoration?

It is simply impossible.

All that can be said is that, as the shock of her conflicting emotions had unseated Barry's reason, the shock of realizing her fearful personal danger had, as it were, sobered her heated brain and restored reason to its throne.

Perhaps the very fact of her stealing out of her bed to walk at night proved that a new phase of her malady had appeared, and that it needed but some powerful agitation to rend the vail which obscured her intellect, and bring back the past to her.

And here, while Harrison hangs over his idol in unutterable happiness, let me gladly do justice to the quality of his love for her.

We have seen how base a character his so-called love bore when first we beheld it—mere passion, having its central spring in self—not worthy of the name of love! We have seen how, in the very climax of this selfish passion, he lost in his bride all that he had hoped to enjoy—and ever since, how gradually his passion became purged of all its unworthy characteristics—no longer evolved from self, —how to succor her pitiable need he lived, her well-being his only aim; how patiently he bore the curse which had fallen upon them; pouring the best of his heart out at her unconscious feet; how faithfully he devoted himself to her, with no expectation of her recovery to sustain him,—could human frailty offer nobler love than this?

Ah, no—what refined gold is to the rough ore, Harrison's present love for his wife was to the love he had offered her before marriage!

*   *   *   *   *   *   *

" What ! tears, Barry ? "

" Forgive me, love ! but do I indeed recall everything ? "

" Surely you do, my poor wife. We two have walked through very dark paths, God forgive us ! "

" Amen ! But—but—surely there is something else yet—something which has followed me through all my mental wanderings with awful persistency. What was it, Harrison, that I did, that made me feel that I was fit to live no longer ?—something that made me think the eyes of all the world were looking at me in horror, ay, and God's eye, too—in mercy try to recall that for me, my husband!"

"Oh, Barry, why torture yourself? We repent of all the past; there let it rest!"

"If you love me, my dear, recall this thing for me? I have been chased by it so long—so long—it seems like centuries since it first began to haunt me—and now, when I can grapple with the horror and perhaps lay it at rest forever, it eludes me! Think, Harrison, think——"

"My poor girl, how can I tell what distressed you most?"

"It was not little Barb, though I did her such monstrous wrong—(how can you endure me, Harrison?)—and it was not my cruelty to Katherine, though that was bitter enough; what could it be? It was the one idea which was always revolving in my poor brain—why, I remember when I went out that night with the taper, it was to look for something or somebody. Did I say nothing, dearest? not one word that might serve as a clue?"

"Sweet, pray don't agitate yourself so. I will try to recollect all that happened. When you began to climb the cliff you sang something, a hymn, I suppose."

"Did I? What were the words?"

"I can't repeat them. Something about, ' *The angels glide on every side!* ' "

"' *The angels glide on every side!* ' O-h! My mother!"

A piteous wail burst from her very soul; she sat pale and gasping.

Harrison, heart-sore, tried to compose her. She laid her head on his breast and wept in rending agitation.

"My poor old mother!" moaned she. "Yes, yes, it was the memory of my monstrous conduct to her that followed me like an avenging spirit. My sweet old mother, who loved her Barry, believed in her—came to take her back to her own pure bosom!"

In anguish she sank lower and lower, till she was on her knees, her face buried in her lap, humbly praying Heaven's pardon; and Harrison mingled his tears with hers.

Suddenly she started to her feet with a cry that struck terror to the heart of her companion.

"This is it—God help us! It has just occurred to me!" gasped she; "I hid my mother away so that she would not be able to interfere with my plans. I put her in a quiet boarding-house with a German lady, leaving money for her support, a mere trifle, but it was all I had; I had expected that upon my death you would return to New York and find a letter among your papers where I had put it, commending her to your care; but, instead of that, you remained with me. My mother was too ill to arrange her own affairs—the money I left must have been exhausted long ago, and what has become of her? Oh, Harrison, is my mother's blood upon my head along with all my other sins?"

"No, no, dear love; God forbid!" exclaimed he, fearfully shocked. "Hope for the best. Who would turn an aged woman out on the street? No one with a human heart, I am sure!"

"Can you still trust in human goodness, knowing me?" cried she, in bitter self-loathing. "Ah, no, hearts are hard where the grace of God does not dwell. My mother has starved to death."

"No, Barry!" said her husband, firmly. "Have you so little faith in God as that? Would He let her white hairs fall so miserably for no sin of hers?"

"He might!" shivered she. "She would go to the angels; on me would fall the anguish. Do I not deserve it?"

He calmed her by-and-by; and then asked her where she had put her mother.

With a confused look she sat thinking; then she turned a glance of piteous helplessness upon him.

"I fear I can't recall where just now!" stammered she.

He begged her to compose herself, and think calmly. She put her trembling hands to her forehead, closed her eyes, and tried to recollect. She looked up again with a forlorn attempt at a smile.

".Just because I am trying to recall it I can't," said she. "Let us talk of something else, it will come to me."

Her husband began to make arrangements for returning to New York immediately.

Half abstractedly she assented to all he said; but she was growing frightfully pale.

At last she seized his hands with a wildly-excited air, crying:

"I can't remember, Harrison: do you hear? I can't remember! Do you see what my punishment is to be? I am never to be able to remember where I hid my mother!"

Again he anxiously strove to soothe the afflicted girl. For his sake she made an effort to calm herself, but her words were too true. Do what she might, she could not recall the secret place where she had hidden her aged mother!

"We return to New York at once," said Harrison, the chill of death at his heart. "Our lives must henceforth be dedicated to expiation."

*   *   *   *   *   *

"Five o'clock *Telegrame*, Ee-evenin'; *Sun*, extra; *Telegrame*, sir. Here you are!"

" *Tribune! Times!* special sheet—cable dispatch —Prince of Whales in the desert."

" Boss Tweed on the grand tower—end of the Katherine Hendrick murder—Barbara Pomeroy guilty!—sentenced to—hilloa, Mister!"

The bawling news-boy stopped in the middle of the train through which he was elbowing his way after his comrades and rivals in the trade, for a gentleman had jumped up beside him as if a pistol had gone off at his ear, and had seized him unceremoniously by the ragged collar.

"What did you say? Barbara Pomeroy?" The gentleman's voice sank into an incoherent murmur, and he glanced a side-glance of vivid apprehension towards the lady who occupied the seat with him.

" Or right, here y' are," said the juvenile, dexterously selecting the sheet from his miscellaneous stock. " News pipin' hot; court ain't broke up yet; four— or right—*T-i-m-e-s*, *Tri-bune*," and off he shot to supply another customer.

Harrison Fairleigh sank back in his seat beside his wife, with a scared face. They were just arriving in New York after their six months' absence, and this was the first whisper from their old life which had reached them.

They had proposed going to some secluded hotel until they could set as much of their past errors right as was in their power, beginning, you may be sure with the search for Mrs. Pomeroy; for, somehow, so omnipotent had been the power of little Barb's simple goodness over the straying Barry, that she had felt scarcely a pang of anxiety concerning her fate, believing, with all her heart, that the Heavenly Friend who had made Barb what she was, would sustain her safely through the perils of that life into which she had so wickedly thrust her back.

As Harrison surreptitiously refolded the paper to get at the column which was headed

"THE KATHERINE HENDRICK MURDER,"

Barry lifted her head and leaned towards him.

He had thought her asleep—he trembled as he met her great pulsating eyes now.

"Husband," said she, her whole stricken soul so poured into that word that it seemed fraught with a fulness of meaning never heard before, " what is this that we two have done?   Katherine—Barb—my mother!   Oh, Harrison, what a union is ours—cemented with blood!"

"Hush!" faltered he, shrinking as if her words were poniards. "Surely there is some hope of redeeming the past!"

"Bound to each other by a curse!" said she, in tones the more terrible from their silvery softness and

. evenness; " we two have loved so impiously, my husband, that our love is all that is to be left us, and· in
it we must walk—we two alone—bound by our mutual
sin, and accursed by the world, till death severs us.
Henceforward you and I dare not part, no, not for a
moment, lest we be swallowed up in the deadly chill
that waits us in solitude. Our guilty past wreathes
itself in inextricable folds around our two souls, and
merges them into one which shall never be disassoci-
ated. Bound by a curse, my husband; bound by a
curse!"

These fearful words poured from her lips with
such intensity and conviction that Harrison shuddered.

It was as if she had prophesied!

CHAPTER XXVI.

MPRISONMENT for life!

That was the sentence passed upon little Barb Pomeroy, the reputed murderess of Katherine Hendrick.

As she was led away, she cast one pathetic glance of wondering reproach around the sea of excited faces, few, few of which gave back a look of sympathy. Then her head dropped, she folded her pale hands on her meek heart, and followed her jailers.

Half suffocated with grief, Mrs. Fairleigh rose to accompany her to the condemned cell, but would have sunk helplessly to the floor had not a strong arm slid round her and a deep voice spoken in her ear:

"Madam, let me support you—let me accompany you. Good God, madam! I believe the child is innocent!"

She faced round in astonishment. Yes, it was Lionel Roscoe who spoke.

"I thank you for that," said the aged lady, with proud dignity. "The child is one of God's little ones. Woe to him who shall offend the least of these!"

She threw an eloquent glance at the baron and baroness, who stood together watching the departure of the prisoner with cruel exultation. They caught her eye, and made her two freezing bows, scornful pity in their faces.

When Mrs. Fairleigh and Mr. Roscoe arrived at the prison to which Barb had been conveyed for the night, they found her seated calmly on her bedside, thinking.

The lady went in first, and took her in her arms with a heartbroken cry.

"No, no, don't fret your heart over me," said Barb, tenderly. " I've always been took such good care of. Oh, He's been so wonderful kind to me right along, that, somehow, I darn't think this here hard. We can't go for to expect to understand the pattern, 'cos we see such a teeny bit at a time, but He knows what He's workin' into it, an' some day we'll see too; an' oh, just won't we think it beautiful!" And the sweet soul's simple features shone as if a light from heaven illumined them.

Lionel Roscoe, standing out of sight at the door, heard, and came in. His head was bowed, his eyes sought the prison floor humbly; he entered as one might enter a consecrated cathedral.

"Miss Pomeroy, may I speak to you from my heart?" said he.

She gently bade him speak on. Through his testimony, principally, she had been brought to this dire pass, but she felt no bitterness against him; she gave him credit for believing what he had said.

"I have studied you, Miss Pomeroy, throughout this unhappy case," he exclaimed, with much feeling. "I began by believing you capable of anything; I end by believing you spotless in heart and life as one of the angels in heaven. I have no words in which to express my admiration of your generosity, truthfulness, and purity of soul. I thank God that I have seen what the Christian religion can do for human character. Your conduct throughout has been worthy of God himself, who dictated it. By the greatness of your noble heart, by your unselfishness, by your steadfast faith, I venerate you as my superior; and while I entreat your forgiveness for the calamity I have brought upon you, I vow to dedicate all my wealth and influence henceforth to the task of revealing to the world your innocence. I have come here to say this before God and my friend Mrs. Fairleigh. Now, farewell, and may Heaven continue to uphold you!"

The two women listened to this outburst in speechless amazement.

Barb was the first to recover herself; she rose

from the bed, and, her dove eyes beaming with seraphic fire, put her two hands in his, crying out:

"There! you've healed every wound you gave me, with your generous tongue. You believe me; after that—well, it doesn't matter much. Thank you, sir, for lifting the ban off me—for your offer to clear me before the world. Only God can reward you as you deserve." And with that she broke down, and flinging herself into Mrs. Fairleigh's arms, wept a little wildly.

The elder lady gave him her hand, pressed his convulsively, and smiled him out of the cell as if he had been the angel Gabriel; and so, even mid storm, the inky cloud turned out a silver edge, and

> "Behind a frowning Providence
> God hid a smiling face."

*   *   *   *   *   *

"A lady to see you, ma'am," said the jailer, through the grating of Barb's cell-door, next morning.

Barb awoke from a celestial dream, and sat up in her poor, straw pallet to see the dim dawn struggling through the window-bars, and a white face gleaming behind the jailor's.

"Come in, dear Mrs. Fairleigh," she called, in her gentle, sweet way.

But oh! who is this?

Who is it comes swooping in like a rushing wind, and snatches the astonished little one out of her couch to a bosom that swells and pants with a passion of speechless emotion ?

" Barry ! " sighs Barb, half swooning.

And the repentant one, having expended the first gust of her excitement in. wild tears and kisses, gradually recalls her grievous fault, and sinks to her knees to little Barb, moaning and praying for pardon, pardon, pardon !

And the little one's loving-kindness enfolds her like a royal garment, hiding all the ugliness of her sin, and shedding over her the softer sheen of pity and forgiveness; so that by-and-by Barry draws Barb to her erring yet noble heart, and pours forth such rich streams of contrition that not only the angel on earth who listens to them glows with admiring rapture, but the angels in heaven rejoice over the sinner repentant !

" I've come to set you free, my little sister ! " cries Barry, a strange light flitting over her haggard face, as if her soul, devoted to expiation, had peeped out for a moment; " I will not rest until you are outside these walls and your innocence established before all the world."

And little Barb can only cry for joy, and whisper her admiration at God's goodness to her and Barry.

Then they tell each other all the strange things which have happened each; and at last, when Harrison and Roscoe come, Harrison leaning somewhat weakly on his companion's arm—for they also have had a trying interview—they find the two sitting hand-in-hand, happy tears glistening in their eyes; and anon, what a hand-shaking, what thrilling words are spoken—what throes of bitter-sweet emotion stir all hearts!

Presently, in comes Mrs. Fairleigh, faint yet from the shock of the reünion, but whitely smiling; and seeing Barry and Harrison clinging together, and watching in silent satisfaction Lionel hanging over Barb with adoration pouring unconsciously from his great black orbs, she blesses each pair with her eyes, and quietly weeps for joy.

*   *   *   *   *   *   *

When Barbara Fairleigh had told the true story of her revenge upon Katherine Hendrick; when she had confessed all her machinations to get rid of little Barb, her mother and Hugh Wayne; when she had repeated word for word the letter she had caused Harrison Fairleigh to write to her, which she had given to Miss Hendrick; when she had thus clearly proved Barb's motives for interfering to have been pure, and Katherine's cause for despair to have been sufficient to drive her to suicide—then little Barb was taken out of the prison with such rejoicings that all the city rang with them—all the louder that it was already whispered that the noble Englishman had lost his heart to the lovely character of the American waif, and was minded to take her home to rule in his castle, Combe-Roscoe.

And presently the patrician, having no doubt a natural desire to obtain the best possible excuse for indulging his inclinations towards a romantic marriage, set to work to trace the long unknown origin of his little Barb, and with such success that soon all the world had the proofs of that very parentage which Mrs. Pomeroy had suspected.

The Rev. Arthur Pomeroy's younger brother Henry and his wife had both died about the same time, (although separated through their domestic disagreements), eighteen years ago; their only child, a girl, had been despatched in the care of a faithful nurse out to America to be placed in the hands of the clergyman if he could be discovered; but she dying during the passage, the poor child had been brought ashore by a family of emigrants, who were soon glad to get rid of the helpless burden, to Nan Polson, who in her turn, was glad to take her for the sake of her expensive clothes, with the view of training her up to support her by-and-by, in a life of infamy.

Doubtless the haughty Roscoe took much comfort out of this establishment of the patrician birth of his little untaught Barb, and, prizing pedigree as no republican mind can quite comprehend—though those who know the value of " blood " in horse-flesh, should get pretty near the idea,—calmly undertook the education of his future bride with a conviction that her blue blood would enable her to make a creditable appearance anon among the noble circles to which she was eventually to be introduced ; deeming that the graces of the soul which had first subjugated his heart, were most fitly embodied in one whose family name was inscribed in that sacred volume " the Peerage of Great Britain."

And 'twas said that the little one showed as lovely a spirit in the hour of her triumph as in the hour of her adversity, so that many who had flung shallow sneers all their lives at religion, seeing what it had done for her, the city-waif who had been taught of God alone—took a second thought on the vexed question, and owned that there was more in heaven and earth than they had dreamed of in their philosophy.

. Meanwhile, the missing ones were diligently sought for.

Hugh Wayne was traced first : Tim Polson having been arrested for one of the daily thefts by which he was enabled to support himself in modest comfort, and having been exposed to the ruthless anatomy of a lawyer skilled in such work—confessed that the sledge-hammer blow with which he had felled the young doctor on his interfering with the abductors of little Barb at the stage-entrance of the Opera House, had so seriously injured him that he and his " pals " were fain to carry him to the first hospital at hand. There he lay between life and death for a month; then getting convalescent and evincing a desire to meddle in the affairs of his betters—to wit, the parents of the murdered lady who had made it worth Polson's while to prevent all such complications—he had smuggled him on board an outward bound vessel, and so got rid of him as long as it took him to sail to India and back. Instantly on his return he had been obliging enough to fall desperately ill of a fever brought on by constant wearing anxiety, and was now battling for his life in Tim's own salubrious abode.

So then they brought him to Mrs. Fairleigh's home, and the first blessed sight his eyes had seen for many a weary month dawned on him the third day, when he awoke from a profound sleep, to see the two Barbaras bending over him—one on either side —and both softly weeping.

Dear, humble, faithful Hugh

On such as thee earth places not her crown of triumph, but, dear simple heart, thou knowest there is a crown more beautiful by far laid up for thee in that sweet haven where

> ."Angels glide on either side,
>   To lead thee to the Throne."

* * * * * * * *

In vain they searched for Mrs. Pomeroy.

They advertised, they set detectives to work, they consulted clairvoyants—they spent money like water and they could not find her.

This fatal cloud lowered so blackly over Barry's life-sky that I do believe it would have again obscured the light of reason had she not taken little Barb's advice and "prayed without ceasing."

And in God's good time, when He saw that His poor straying lamb was quite ready to be taken back into the fold of His full favor, He showed that He is mightier than all the human intellect and supernatural agencies in or out of the world.

One morning Barry rose from her knees, and slipping, in her pure white robes and flowing hair—like a holy nun—to Harrison, who still slumbered, she awoke him and said quietly:

" *Husband, I have remembered!* "

And he sprang up with a shout, and folded her to his breast with a rapture of joy he had never known in her before.

Hand-in-hand these much tried souls went straight to the house where Barry had conveyed her mother nore than nine months previously. The German woman met them in the parlor; Barry was so changed that she did not recognize her till Harrison, who spoke German, recalled the circumstances of her former visit.

Then her kindly eyes glistened, and she would have hurried out of the room, but that Barry flew to her, detaining her by a convulsive clasp, while Harrison asked:

"Is the English lady with you still?"

"Ja, ja!" cried she, nodding her head joyously, and got away; but Barry kept at her heels, and hid in the shadow of the door through which she darted.

And the erring daughter beheld her long-deserted mother leaning back peacefully in a great soft chintz elbow chair, and her big Bible lay open on her lap, her spectacles on her nose, and her beautiful hair, white as the driven snow, was combed, oh, so neatly, upon her tranquil brow; her soft, gray shawl folded, oh, so tenderly, around her bent shoulders; and, as her feeble finger travelled slowly along the line, she lifted her eyes, dewy with the light beyond the grave, to the German woman who had taken her in when her own forsook her, and murmured:

"'The Lord is my shepherd, therefore I can lack

nothing.' 'Yea, though I walk through the valley of the shadow of death, I will fear no evil, for Thou art with me; Thy rod and thy staff they comfort me.'"

A single deep sob—some one at her feet clasping her hands, kissing her garments, wetting her trembling hands with tears.

"Dear Jesus, my Barry at last!"

Ay, hold her close, poor daughter—come too late! for the pearly gates are wide—for the golden street is thronged with welcoming hosts—for another soul has gone up thither; well beloved, long expected.

Ay, ay, poor Barry, all the tears that ever were shed will not bring her back from yonder bliss. In that supreme instant of earthly happiness her heart burst, and her spirit winged its way to that shining land where happiness is the native air, and cannot kill!

*　　*　　*　　*　　*　　*

And so my Barbara sinned and repented, and I dare swear lived a nobler, because a more pitiful and lenient woman ever after.

She will never gather her unsmirched robes about her with bitter look askance at those her sisters who have lost their way, poor souls, and cannot find it until a tender hand like hers is stretched out to drag them back to it.

She will not spend her life in the small gratifications of infinitesimal whims according to the usual *rôle* of ladies of fashion, "God forbid!" my Barry is fond of saying, "that I, a brand plucked from the burning, should ever flaunt my scorched and blackened self in Vanity Fair! No, no, there is work to be done for my sisters out there in the world, let me do what I can!"

And Harrison helps thankfully; for, trust me, sisters, walk boldly into some path of Christian benevolence, exercising what common sense you have been endowed with, and your men will not be a step behind, only tell them that you need them.

But though they have repented truly, and now venture to love each other purely, and to take comfort out of their love, Barry will never hold a child of their love to her empty heart.

And Barb!

God bless her!

She is a great little lady now, and has her servants, carriages, society, appears at court, and shows herself at the opera; but with all, she retains the sweet simplicity and crystalline purity of soul which won our love the first day we saw her in Cardinal Court.

Hugh Wayne and his sister Nettie keep house together; it is the regular rendezvous for all the young couples in Thunder Peak, and Hugh beams on their happy loves as if the sight awoke no moaning voice within; and Nettie, watching, brushes her eyes, and firmly refuses every swain in turn, saying, quietly.

"I will never leave Hugh."

Mrs. Fairleigh still lives in the town house, but not alone. She has devoted herself to one of those delicate charities which only women of high culture and inherent delicacy can successfully conduct; she is blessed and happy in her labor of love, and often remarks to Barry, who sees her every day, living only a square or so distant:

"I am all the better, ay, and more useful, from having known, and suffered by, and loved 'The Two Barbaras!'"

And so, sweet friends, farewell!

THE END.

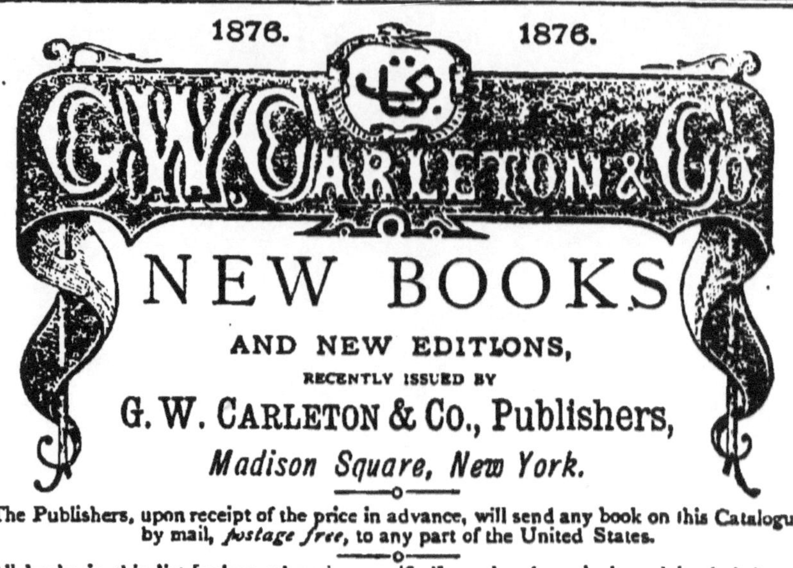

NEW BOOKS

AND NEW EDITIONS,

RECENTLY ISSUED BY

G. W. CARLETON & Co., Publishers,

Madison Square, New York.

———o———

The Publishers, upon receipt of the price in advance, will send any book on this Catalogue by mail, *postage free*, to any part of the United States.

———o———

All books in this list [unless otherwise specified] are handsomely bound in cloth board binding, with gilt backs, suitable for libraries.

———o———

Mrs. Mary J. Holmes' Works.

Tempest and Sunshine	$1 50	Darkness and Daylight	$1 50
English Orphans	1 50	Hugh Worthington	1 50
Homestead on the Hillside	1 50	Cameron Pride	1 50
'Lena Rivers	1 50	Rose Mather	1 50
Meadow Brook	1 50	Ethelyn's Mistake	1 50
Dora Deane	1 50	Millbank	1 50
Cousin Maude	1 50	Edna Browning	1 50
Marian Grey	1 50	West Lawn........(New)	1 50
Edith Lyle........(New)	1 50		

Marion Harland's Works.

Alone	$1 50	Sunnybank	$1 50
Hidden Path	1 50	Husbands and Homes	1 50
Moss Side	1 50	Ruby's Husband	1 50
Nemesis	1 50	Phemie's Temptation	1 50
Miriam	1 50	The Empty Heart	1 50
At Last	1 50	Jessamine	1 50
Helen Gardner	1 50	From My Youth Up	1 50
True as Steel......(New)	1 50	My Little Love. ....(New)	1 50

Charles Dickens—15 Vols.—"Carleton's Edition."

Pickwick, and Catalogue	$1 50	David Copperfield	$1 50
Dombey and Son	1 50	Nicholas Nickleby	1 50
Bleak House	50	Little Dorrit	1 50
Martin Chuzzlewit	1 50	Our Mutual Friend	1 50
Barnaby Rudge—Edwin Drood	1 50	Curiosity Shop—Miscellaneous	1 50
Child's England—Miscellaneous	1 50	Sketches by Boz—Hard Times	1 50

Oliver Twist—and—The Uncommercial Traveler ... 1 50
Great Expectations—and—Pictures of Italy and America ... 1 50
Christmas Books—and—A Tale of Two Cities ... 1 50
Sets of Dickens' Complete Works, in 15 vols.—[elegant half calf bindings]. 60 00

Augusta J. Evans' Novels.

Beulah	$1 75	St. Elmo	$2 00
Macaria	1 75	Vashti	2 00
Inez	1 75	Infelice........ ....(New)	2 00

Miriam Coles Harris.

Rutledge	$1 50	The Sutherlands	$1 50
Frank Warrington	1 50	St. Philip's	1 50
Louie's Last Term, etc	1 50	Round Hearts, for Children	1 50
Richard Vandermarck	1 50	A Perfect Adonis. (New)	1 50

May Agnes Fleming's Novels.

Guy Earlscourt's Wife	$1 75	A Wonderful Woman	$1 75
A Terrible Secret	1 75	A Mad Marriage	1 75
Norine's Revenge	1 75	One Night's Mystery. (New)	1 75
A New Book	1 75		

Grace Mortimer.

The Two Barbaras.—A novel	$1 50	Bosom Foes. (In press)	$1 50

Julie P. Smith's Novels.

Widow Goldsmith's Daughter	$1 75	The Widower	$1 75
Chris and Otho	1 75	The Married Belle	1 75
Ten Old Maids	1 75	Courting and Farming	1 75
His Young Wife. (New)	1 75		

Captain Mayne Reid—Illustrated.

The Scalp Hunters	$1 50	The White Chief	$1 50
The Rifle Rangers	1 50	The Tiger Hunter	1 50
The War Trail	1 50	The Hunter's Feast	1 50
The Wood Rangers	1 50	Wild Life	1 50
The Wild Huntress	1 50	Osceola, the Seminole	1 50

A. S. Roe's Select Stories.

True to the Last	$1 50	A Long Look Ahead	$1 50
The Star and the Cloud	1 50	I've Been Thinking	1 50
How Could He Help It?	1 50	To Love and to be Loved	1 50

Charles Dickens.

Child's History of England.—Carleton's New "*School Edition.*" Illustrated.. $1 25

Hand-Books of Society.

Habits of Good Society.—The nice points of taste and good manners.. .... $1 50
Art of Conversation.—For those who wish to be agreeable talkers or listeners.... 1 50
Arts of Writing, Reading, and Speaking.—For self-improvement............ 1 50
New Diamond Edition.—Small size, elegantly bound, 3 volumes in a box...... 3 00

Mrs. Hill's Cook Book.

Mrs. A. P. Hill's New Cookery Book, and family domestic receipts......... $2 00

Famous Books—"Carleton's Edition."

Robinson Crusoe.—New 12mo edition, with illustrations by ERNEST GRISET.... $1 50
Swiss Family Robinson.—New 12mo edition, with illustrations by MARCKL.... 1 50
The Arabian Nights.—New 12mo edition, with illustrations by DEMORAINE..... 1 50
Don Quixote.—New 12mo edition, with illustrations by GUSTAVE DORÉ.......... 1 50

Victor Hugo.

Les Miserables.—An English translation from the original French. Octavo..... $2 50
Les Miserables.—In the Spanish Language. Two volumes, cloth bound....... 5 00

Popular Italian Novels.

Doctor Antonio.—A love story of Italy. By Ruffini ....;............. $1 75
Beatrice Cenci.—By Guerrazzi. With a steel engraving from Guido's Picture.... 1 75

M. Michelet's Remarkable Works.

Love (L'amour).—English translation from the original French...... .... $1 50
Woman (La Femme).—.....Do........Do........Do...................... 1 50

Joaquin Miller.

The One Fair Woman.—A new novel, the scene laid chiefly in Italy. $2 00

Joseph Rodman Drake.

The Culprit Fay.—The well-known fairy poem, with 100 illustrations.... .... $2 00

Artemus Ward's Comic Works.

A New Stereotype Edition.—Embracing the whole of his writings, with a Biography of the author, and profusely illustrated by various artists $2 00

Josh Billings.
A New Stereotype Edition of the complete writings of Josh Billings. Four vols. in one, with Biography, steel portrait, and 100 comic illustrations.........$2 00

Bessie Turner.
A Woman in the Case.—A new novel, with photographic portrait of author. . $1 50

Wm. P. Talboys.
West India Pickles.—Journal of a Winter Yacht Cruise, with illustrations $1 50

Dr. A. K. Gardner.
Our Children.—A Hand-book for the Instruction of Parents and Guardians......$2 00

C. H. Webb (John Paul).
Parodies and Poems.......... ..$1 50 | My Vacation.—Sea and Shore.....$1 50

Livingston Hopkins.
Comic Centennial History of the United States.—Profusely illustrated.....$1 50

Allan Pinkerton.
The Model Town, etc......... . $1 50 | A New Book. (In press)........$1 50

Mrs. M. V. Victor.
Passing the Portal.—A new story.$1 50 | A New Book. (In press)... ....$1 50

Ernest Renan's French Works.
The Life of Jesus.................$1 75 | The Life of St. Paul... ....$1 75
Lives of the Apostles...... ..... 1 75 | The Bible in India.—By Jacolliot..2 00

Geo. W. Carleton.
Our Artist in Cuba.—Pictures.....$1 50 | Our Artist in Africa. (In press). $1 50
Our Artist in Peru.　Do. ..... 1 50 | Our Artist in Mexico.　Do.　.. 1 50

Verdant Green.
A racy English college story—with numerous original comic illustrations......$1 50

Algernon Charles Swinburne.
Laus Veneris, and Other Poems.—An elegant new edition, on tinted paper...$1 50
French Love-Songs —Selected from the best French authors.................. 1 50

Robert Dale Owen.
The Debatable Land Between this World and the Next................$2 00
Threading My Way.—Twenty-five years of Autobiography..... .... 1 50

The Game of Whist.
Pole on Whist.—The late English standard work.　New enlarged edition.......$1 00

Mother Goose Set to Music.
Mother Goose Melodies.—With music for singing, and many illustrations... ..$1 50

M. M. Pomeroy ("Brick.")
Sense—(a serious book).............$1 50 | Nonsense—(a comic book).........$1 50
Gold-Dust　Do. .... 1 50 | Brick-Dust　Do　..... .... 1 50
Our Saturday Nights............ 1 50 | Home Harmonies. (In press).... 1 50

Celia E. Gardner's Novels.
Stolen Waters—(in verse).........$1 50 | Tested..... ....(in prose).$1 75
Broken Dreams　Do. .... 1 50 | Rich Medway's Two Loves. Do.. 1 75
A New Novel. (In press)........ 1 50 |

Mrs. N. S. Emerson.
Betsey and I are Out.—Poems...$1 50 | Little Folks' Letters.—Prose.....$1 50

Louisa M. Alcott.
Morning Glories—A beautiful child's book, by the author of "Little Women.".....$1 50

Geo. A. Crofutt.
Trans-Continental Tourist from New York to San Francisco.—Illustrated..$1 50

Miscellaneous Works.

Johnny Ludlow.—A collection of entertaining English stories.................... $1 50
Glimpses of the Supernatural.—Facts, Records, and Traditions............ ... 2 00
Fanny Fern Memorials.—With a Biography by James Parton.................... 2 00
How to Make Money; and How to Keep It.—By Thomas A. Davies........ .... 1 50
Tales From the Operas.—A collection of Stories based upon the opera plots.... 1 50
New Nonsense Rhymes.—By W. H. Beckett, with illustrations by C. G. Bush.. 1 00
Wood's Guide to the City of New York.—Beautifully illustrated............ 1 00
The Art of Amusing.—A book of home amusements, with illustrations.......... 1 50
A Book About Lawyers.—A curious and interesting volume. By Jeaffreson.... 2 00
A Book About Doctors.   Do.   Do.   Do. 2 00
The Birth and Triumph of Love.—Full of exquisite tinted illustrations...... 1 00
Progressive Petticoats.—A satirical tale by Robert B. Roosevelt.............. 1 50
Ecce Femina; or, the Woman Zoe.—Cuyler Pine, author "Mary Brandegee." 1 50
Souvenirs of Travel.—By Madame Octavia Walton Le Vert 2 00
Woman, Love and Marriage.—A spicy little work by Fred Saunders.......... 1 50
Shiftless Folks.—A brilliant new novel by Fannie Smith...................... 1 75
A Woman in Armor.—A powerful new novel by Mary Hartwell................ 1 50
The Fall of Man.—A Darwinian satire. Author of "New Gospel of Peace.".... 50
The Chronicles of Gotham.—A modern satire. Do.   Do.   25
The Story of a Summer.—Journal Leaves by Cecelia Cleveland.......... ..... 1 50
Phemie Frost's Experiences.—By Mrs Ann S. Stephens..... .... 1 75
Bill Arp's Peace Papers.—Full of comic illustrations....................... 1 50
A Book of Epitaphs.—Amusing, quaint, and curious....(New)... .... 1 50
Ballad of Lord Bateman.—With illustrations by Cruikshank, (paper).......... 25
The Yachtman's Primer.—For amateur sailors. T. R. Warren, (paper)....... 50
Rural Architecture.—By M. Field. With plans and illustrations.............. 2 00
What I Know of Farming.—By Horace Greeley................................ 1 50
Transformation Scenes in the United States.—By Hiram Fuller......... 1 50
Marguerite's Journal.—Story for girls. Introduction by author "Rutledge."... 1 50
Kingsbury Sketches.—Pine Grove doings, by John H. Kingsbury. Illustrated.. 1 50

Miscellaneous Novels.

Led Astray —By Octave Feuillet..$1 75
She Loved Him Madly.—Borys.. 1 75
Through Thick and Thin.—Mery. 1 75
So Fair Yet False.—Chavette..... 1 75
A Fatal Passion.—Bomard........ 1 75
Manfred.—F. D. Guerazzi.......... 1 75
Seen and Unseen...... .... 1 50
Purple and Fine Linen.—Fawcett., 1 75
Asses' Ears.............. Do.   1 75
A Charming Widow.—Macquoid. 1 75
True to Him Ever.—By F. W. R.. 1 50
The Forgiving Kiss.—By M. Loth. 1 75
Loyal Unto Death................. 1 75
Kenneth, My King.—S. A. Brock.. 1 75
Heart Hungry.-M. J. Westmoreland 1 75
Clifford Troupe.   Do.   1 75
Silcott Mill.—Mrs. Deslonde...... 1 75
Ebon and Gold.—C. L. McIlvain.. 1 50
Robert Greathouse.—J. F. Swift.. 2 00
Charette............................ 1 50

Saint Leger.—Richard B. Kimball.$1 75
Was He Successful? ....Do. 1 75
Undercurrents of Wall St.   Do. 1 75
Romance of Student Life....Do. 1 75
Life in San Domingo.........Do. 1 50
Henry Powers, Banker ......Do. 1 75
To-Day...... ....Do. 1 75
Bessie Wilmerton.—Westcott..... 1 75
Cachet.—Mrs. M. J. R. Hamilton... 1 75
Romance of Railroad.—Smith.. .. 1 50
Fairfax.—John Esten Cooke........ 1 50
Hilt to Hilt.   Do. 1 50
Out of the Foam.   Do. 1 50
Hammer and Rapier. Do. 1 50
Warwick.—By M. T. Walworth.... 1 75
Lulu.   Do. 1 75
Hotspur.   Do. 1 75
Stormcliff.   Do. 1 75
Delaplaine.   Do. 1 75
Beverly,   Do. 1 75

Miscellaneous Works.

Baldazzle's Bachelor Studies....$1 00
Little Wanderers.—Illustrated.... 1 50
Genesis Disclosed.—T. A. Davies.. 1 50
Commodore Rollingpin's Log... 1 50
Brazen Gates.—A juvenile......... 1 50
Antidote to Gates Ajar........... 25
The Suoblace Ball................. 25

Northern Ballads.—Anderson......$1 00
O. C. Kerr Papers.—4 vols. in 1.... 2 00
Victor Hugo.—His life............:... 2 00
Beauty is Power............ ..... 1 50
Sandwiches.—Artemus Ward...... 25
Widow Spriggins.—Widow Bedott. 1 75
Squibob Papers.—John Phœnix.... 1 50

CHARLES DICKENS' WORKS.

A New Edition.

Among the many editions of the works of this greatest of English Novelists, there has not been until now *one* that entirely satisfies the public demand.—Without exception, they each have some strong distinctive objection,—either the form and dimensions of the volumes are unhandy—or, the type is small and indistinct—or, the illustrations are unsatisfactory—or, the binding is poor—or, the price is too high.

An entirely new edition is *now*, however, published by G. W. Carleton & Co. of New York, which, it is believed, will, in every respect, completely satisfy the popular demand.—It is known as

"Carleton's New Illustrated Edition."
COMPLETE IN 15 VOLUMES.

The size and form is most convenient for holding,—the type is entirely new, and of a clear and open character that has received the approval of the reading community in other popular works.

The illustrations are by the original artists chosen by Charles Dickens himself—and the paper, printing, and binding are of an attractive and substantial character.

This beautiful new edition is complete in 15 volumes—at the extremely reasonable price of $1.50 per volume, as follows:—

1.—PICKWICK PAPERS AND CATALOGUE.
2.—OLIVER TWIST.—UNCOMMERCIAL TRAVELLER.
3.—DAVID COPPERFIELD.
4.—GREAT EXPECTATIONS.—ITALY AND AMERICA.
5.—DOMBEY AND SON.
6.—BARNABY RUDGE AND EDWIN DROOD.
7.—NICHOLAS NICKLEBY.
8.—CURIOSITY SHOP AND MISCELLANEOUS.
9.—BLEAK HOUSE.
10.—LITTLE DORRIT.
11.—MARTIN CHUZZLEWIT.
12.—OUR MUTUAL FRIEND.
13.—CHRISTMAS BOOKS.—TALE OF TWO CITIES.
14.—SKETCHES BY BOZ AND HARD TIMES.
15.—CHILD'S ENGLAND AND MISCELLANEOUS.

The first volume—Pickwick Papers—contains an alphabetical catalogue of all of Charles Dickens' writings, with their positions in the volumes.

This edition is sold by Booksellers, everywhere—and single specimen copies will be forwarded by mail, *postage free*, on receipt of price, $1.50, by

G. W. CARLETON & CO., Publishers,

Madison Square, New York.

MARY J. HOLMES' WORKS.

1.—TEMPEST AND SUNSHINE.

2.—ENGLISH ORPHANS.

3.—HOMESTEAD ON HILLSIDE.

4.—'LENA RIVERS.

5.—MEADOW BROOK.

6.—DORA DEANE.

7.—COUSIN MAUDE.

16.—WEST LAWN.

8.—MARIAN GRAY.

9.—DARKNESS AND DAYLIGHT.

10.—HUGH WORTHINGTON.

11.—CAMERON PRIDE.

12.—ROSE MATHER.

13.—ETHELYN'S MISTAKE.

14.—MILLBANK.

15.—EDNA BROWNING.

17.—EDITH LYLE.

OPINIONS OF THE PRESS.

"Mrs. Holmes' stories are universally read. Her admirers are numberless. She is in many respects without a rival in the world of fiction. Her characters are always life-like, and she makes them talk and act like human beings, subject to the same emotions, swayed by the same passions, and actuated by the same motives which are common among men and women of every day existence. Mrs. Holmes is very happy in portraying domestic life. Old and young peruse her stories with great delight, for she writes in a style that all can comprehend."— *New York Weekly.*

"Mrs. Holmes' stories are all of a domestic character, and their interest, therefore, is not so intense as if they were more highly seasoned with sensationalism, but it is of a healthy and abiding character. Almost any new book which her publisher might choose to announce from her pen would get an immediate and general reading. The interest in her tales begins at once, and is maintained to the close. Her sentiments are so sound, her sympathies so warm and ready, and her knowledge of manners, character, and the varied incidents of ordinary life is so thorough, that she would find it difficult to write any other than an excellent tale if she were to try it."—*Boston Banner.*

"Mrs. Holmes is very amusing; has a quick and true sense of humor, a sympathetic tone, a perception of character, and a familiar, attractive style, pleasantly adapted to the comprehension and the taste of that large class of American readers for whom fashionable novels and ideal fantasies have no charm."—*Henry T. Tuckerman.*

☞ The volumes are all handsomely printed and bound in cloth,—sold everywhere, and sent by mail, *postage free*, on receipt of price [$1.50 each], by

G. W. CARLETON & CO., Publishers,

Madison Square, New York